I LOVE
YOU SO
MOCHI

I LOVE YOU SO MOCHI

SARAH KUHN

Scholastic Press / New York

Library of Congress Cataloging-in-Publication Data available

ISBN 978-1-338-30288-2

10 9 8 7 6 5 4 3 2 1   19 20 21 22 23

Printed in the U.S.A.   23

First edition, June 2019

Book design by Shivana Sookdeo

For Jeff Chen—I love you so . . .
well, you know the rest

PROLOGUE

I'm supposed to be embarking on a quest of self-discovery, but I keep getting lost. I don't mean that in the super intro-spective, "let's talk about my feelings" kind of way. I mean I literally don't know where I am.

It's my first day as a spring break tourist in Japan (on a Super Important Quest of Self-Discovery) and I've taken the train from my grandparents' tiny town to Kyoto, hoping to walk something called Philosopher's Path. That sounded peaceful and contemplative and like just the thing to do when you need to figure out your life. Instead I ended up wandering in the wrong direction because I saw a girl wear-ing a tiered skirt made out of two different kinds of material—wispy tulle contrasting with heavy wool—and she looked so incredibly cool, I just had to know where she was going. Then I got caught up studying the cherry blossoms overhead, a glorious canopy of pink and white fluff that seemed to go on forever. Now my distracted wanderings have led me to an outdoor market with food stands frying, steaming, and boil-ing everything from delectably salty squid to buttery sweet taiyaki.

There are tons of people jostling around these stands,

and the burble of their excited chatter mingles with the hiss and sizzle of food cooking. The smells crash into each other, a mishmash of clashing scents that assaults my nostrils. I feel overwhelmed by the sights and sounds and the sheer mass of humanity.

"Irasshaimase!" a man bellows to people approaching the food stall I'm standing next to, and I let out a pathetic-sounding "Meep!" then shuffle awkwardly out of the way. But there's not much room to shuffle and I bump into an elderly, stoop-shouldered lady in a giant sun hat.

"Sorry!" I blurt out. "I mean, um . . . pardon? I mean . . ." I realize that I have no idea how to apologize in Japanese. She gives me a classic Disapproving Auntie Stare and moves on to the next food stall.

I take a deep breath and stand still, trying to reorient myself. I don't want to bust out my map; I'll look like a tourist. (Okay, okay: *even more* like a tourist.) I could use my phone, but I'm still not entirely sure how the international data plan works, since Dad had to add it on last minute and all. I don't want to run up a huge bill my first day here just because I accidentally wandered off.

You mean: Because you allowed yourself to get distracted by frivolous things instead of focusing on what you're supposed to be doing, my mother says in my head. *Get your head out of the clouds, Kimi-chan: You have important things to figure out.*

I know, Mom.

I find a bench on the very edge of the market and plop myself down. I had high hopes for today when I got dressed this morning. I'd donned one of my favorite dresses—a midnight blue concoction of asymmetric layers and sparkly buttons that I'd constructed out of the bones of an old prom gown. Wearing it always gives me that extra shot of confidence when I'm feeling low. But right now, surrounded by the overwhelming bustle of the market, I just feel . . . well, lost.

I suppose I could try sketching. Sketching always soothes me. Sketching is what I meant to do on Philosopher's Path, figuring all those peaceful drawings of nature would somehow spark major life revelations.

I reach into my messenger bag, pull out my sketchbook and pencils, and flip to a blank page. I spy the girl I saw before, the one in the tiered skirt. She's met up with a whole group of friends and they're all wearing awesomely creative street fashion: dramatic layers and unexpected materials and fun little accessories. They look like fashion superheroes, and if I were feeling braver and less out of place, I'd—well. Actually, I probably wouldn't go talk to them.

Because, as my best friend Atsuko is fond of pointing out, it's always easier for me to live in this space where I haven't made something real yet. It's easier for me to sit here and think about talking to those girls because that way it remains a perfect fantasy, where we laugh and exchange cool fashion ideas and I magically know perfect Japanese. The minute I make it a reality by actually talking to them . . . I'll ruin it.

I take a deep breath and try to refocus on my quest of self-discovery. I came to Japan hoping to find answers to big, important questions. Like:

Who am I?

What am I supposed to do with my life?

What do I really *want out of my future?*

I thought arriving here would spark major revelations, but instead I'm sitting on some random bench, staring at a blank page. I press my pencil to paper, willing the revelations to come.

They don't.

Crap. Did I really just travel halfway around the world on a whim to a place I know nothing about?

I may have just ruined *everything*.

Chapter One

One Week Earlier

I have to be honest—there was a moment when I regretted trying to make a dress out of candy wrappers.

It wasn't because I'd spent a solid month collecting them: scouring the recycling bins in the cafeteria, squirreling away the remnants of Dad's secret Twix stash, and (in a fit of impatience once I realized how long it actually takes to amass a whole bunch of candy wrappers) buying an economy-sized bag of Starburst and gnawing my way through endless fruit-flavored goodness during the more boring parts of Calculus. And it wasn't because the process of making legitimately sewable fabric out of candy wrappers was more complicated than I'd originally thought, requiring hours of ironing the wrappers between sheets of newspaper, Mod Podging them onto muslin, and hand-stitching the ones that refused to stay put.

No, it came down to this: When I presented my best friend Bex with her custom candy wrapper dress—a rainbow delight that I'd fashioned in a simple skater cut with tiny ruffle flourishes at the sleeves and the bottom of the skirt—one of her eyebrows twitched upward and the smallest of crinkles creased her brow. But no smile. No grin stretching from ear to ear, no exclamation of "Wow, Kimi!" or other discernable signs of pleasure, happiness, and/or excitement.

Now we're standing in front of the big mirror in the Drama Club room and she's wearing the dress and twisting this way and that, the wrappers crinkling softly as she examines every facet of her appearance.

I can't tell if she likes it and it makes me feel like a rabid animal is chomping my insides.

I thought the bright colors and quirky material choice were perfect for Bex's unicorn-and-sparkles-loving personality, that they would complement the flaming magenta she's dyed her hair. That this dress would give her the confidence of the superheroines who star in her beloved comic books, finally allowing her to ask out her crush, Shelby Perkiss.

"Just leave it to me," I'd said last month, waving a hand. I was wearing rings made out of tiny rocks twisted up in wild threads of metal and they gave my hand-wave an extra touch of drama. "I'll make something for you, Bex. The *perfect* thing."

"No makeovers, Kimi!" screeched our other best friend, Atsuko. We were sprawled all over our usual lunch "table," a patch of grass hidden behind the library, just out of the way enough that no one ever bothered us. Atsuko was tapping away on her phone, composing her latest advice column. "I hate that movies never show the part *after* the makeover," she continued. "You know, when that new look that'll help land you a new honey—and the new personality you've suddenly gained along with it—becomes a pain in the butt to maintain and you go back to wearing sweats and flip-flops."

"Bex doesn't wear sweats in the first place," I said, rolling my eyes and gesturing to Bex's cute dress. It had a Peter Pan collar and a whimsical mermaid print. We'd all been especially excited when we found it because some of the mermaids actually look like us. There's a tall Atsuko mermaid with long black hair and broad shoulders and a smattering of freckles; a curvy Bex mermaid with dark brown skin and a dreamy look on her face; and a shrimpy pipsqueak Kimi mermaid with messy bangs and intense dark eyes that look like they are always thinking just a little too hard about something. Or maybe we sort of projected some of those qualities onto them, since, as Atsuko noted, "most mermaid-fairy-elf-whatever prints are one hundred percent white, blonde girls and *no percent* everyone else, so you know, go this dress for being like ten percent Asian and Black and giving us some twee role models to call our own."

"Anyway, I don't believe in makeovers," I added, poking Atsuko in the arm. She elbow-nudged me halfheartedly and kept thumb-typing her advice column. I turned to Bex, who was regarding me with a mixture of hope and trepidation. "I want to arm you with a dress that enhances your natural charm and style and gives you the confidence to finally ask out Shelby Perkiss. I want you to feel like, like . . . Ultimate Bex."

"Ultimate Bex," Bex said, her eyes lighting up. "*Yes.* I love that. It sounds like a superhero name. Like I'm Kamala Khan and you're going to help me become Ms. Marvel. And Ultimate Bex will *not* get all flushed and weird and tongue-tied around Shelby Perkiss."

"Exactly," I said, grinning at her. "I'm gonna make you a Kimi Nakamura Original. Something that will make you feel like the best *you.*"

"You've really bumped up your Kimi Originals game this year," Bex said. "Your outfit output is on point."

I smiled back and tried not to think about the fact that my "output" increase had nothing to do with better productivity or a desire to make my senior year the best ever. It had *everything* to do with the fact that I dropped out of Advanced Fine Art after slamming my head against complete and total lack of inspiration when it came to painting anything new. Every time I picked up my brush, all I saw was endless blank canvas, mocking me. All I felt was the pressure that came with being accepted early admission to the Liu Fine Arts Academy, one of the best in the country. And all I heard was my mother's voice, taking on that tone she likes to imagine is "soothing," but is weighted with way too many expectations about me becoming a Great Asian American Artist to be anywhere near the "soothing" ballpark. "You should work on a new set of paintings before college starts, Kimi-chan," she'd say. "Go in with a theme, a voice, a point of view. Every great artist needs a point of view."

My current point of view is that I can't paint to save my life, so I've spent senior year pouring my energy into things like designing costumes for the school play, adding to my overflowing wardrobe of thrift store finds and my own creations, and now . . . creating a Kimi Original for Bex. You know, fun things. But also—as my mother would be the first to remind me—goofing off–type things. Things that have nothing to do with the important art career I'm about to embark on.

"Atsy, are you down with this plan?" I said, nudging Atsuko. She was still glued to her phone. "Because we need your approval as Culver City High's resident advice columnist to the love-challenged."

"I approve," Atsuko said. "But only if you both acknowledge that Shelby Perkiss could still say no, because when it comes to any romantic endeavors, it's very important to prepare for all possible outcomes, to not build up your expectations, and—"

"Yes, yes, we get it," Bex said, flashing me a conspiratorial grin. "And I fully accept that I may still be heading down the path of loser-dom, Madam Therapist."

"That is *not* what I meant," Atsuko huffed. "I just want to make sure you're taking care of *you* first, because what most people don't realize—"

This was the point where I tuned them out. My brain was already buzzing, fantasizing about color palettes and sweetheart necklines and a dreamy full skirt that would swish beautifully around Bex, making her into her wildest daydream of a superheroine.

But now that we're standing in front of the mirror, now that the skirt is actually swishing beautifully around her . . . I can't help but wonder if I miscalculated. Maybe the candy wrappers are too outrageous, too weird. Maybe Bex feels self-conscious, like the dress is overwhelming. Like the dress is wearing *her*.

"Bex," I whisper, unable to contain myself any longer.

She's swinging her hips side to side now, allowing the skirt to really swish. The effect of all those bright colors, shiny with Mod Podge, is beautiful to me. Like a kaleidoscope brought to life.

"So?" Atsuko sidles up next to us, munching on a handful of trail mix. She's wearing baggy yoga pants, layered tank tops, and sneakers with satin ribbons for laces. Atsuko loves the athleisure trend because it allows her to basically wear pajamas in public. Bex is always teasing her because she doesn't actually play any sports. "We ready to do this thing or what?"

"Bex?" I repeat, keeping my voice soft. She still hasn't said a word. Not one single word. "Do you like it?"

Bex's brow crinkles again as she regards her colorful form in the mirror, swishes the skirt around again. She's silent and my heart sinks like a stone. Did I get it all wrong? Am I even failing at my goofing-off, having-fun attempts now?

Bex turns to face me, clasps my hands in hers, and meets my eyes. Her face is deathly serious. I'm already preparing my apology speech. Then she breaks into a giant grin.

"I. *Love*. It!" she yelps, her voice escalating with each word.

And just like that, my heart bounces back up again, a buoyant beam of light shooting through my chest. The dress is doing just what I hoped it would: Bex is standing up straighter, smiling brighter, and cocking her head in that way that indicates she's feeling good about life in general. She looks ready to take on the world. Or at least to ask out the girl she's been crushing on almost all of senior year.

"I'm ready," she says, giving a determined nod.

Linking arms with Bex and Atsuko, I beam at my two best friends. "Let's go ask out Shelby Perkiss."

10

"So, have you talked to your mom yet?" Atsuko shoves another handful of trail mix in her mouth and kicks my foot. We're camped out in one of the far corners of the quad, where most of the student body eats lunch, watching Bex swish her way over to Shelby Perkiss. There's a concrete planter thing containing three teeny sprouts trying valiantly to become real plants and we've sprawled ourselves on the edge of that, sitting end to end so that our feet are touching.

"Excuse me, but why are we talking about this right now?" I say, inching my foot out of kicking reach. "Let's focus on the mega-couple forming on the other side of the quad. Ooh, what should their 'ship name be? Shex? Belby?"

"We're talking about this because your state of denial has reached epic levels of epicness," Atsuko says, stretching her leg to kick me again. Damn her tallness. "Like, it's a *continent* of freaking denial at this point. You dropped Advanced Fine Art a mere month into the spring semester. It's freaking *March*. Spring break is in a week. Then we have finals. Then school is basically *over*. The longer it takes to tell your mom you dropped that class, the more she's gonna blow like a full-on rage volcano. It's Asian Mom Math, and you know I'm right about this."

"Bleah," I say, swinging my legs around so my feet are on the ground, no longer touching hers. I cross my arms over my chest and hunch, a pose that always makes Mom fret about my posture. "Don't therapize me, Atsy. You've got plenty of our peers asking you for advice. Romantic advice, specifically. Meanwhile, I'm over here minding my own business, not asking for *any* kind of advice."

"Actually, the romantic advice I'd give you is in the same general area," Atsuko says, wriggling closer and poking my hip with her foot. She needs to stop with the foot. "What happened with that theater guy, Justin, again?"

"He enjoyed wearing the costumes I designed, said they really helped him get into character," I say, my face getting hot. "Then he gave me a rock at the wrap party, which was a super strange thing to give someone, and then we never spoke again because we don't have any classes together."

My face has gotten increasingly hot as I talk. This is why Atsuko is such a good advice columnist: She always cuts straight to the heart of the matter. Her fans love it. I . . . only love it sometimes. Like when it's directed at someone else.

"It was a rock like the ones on those weird rings you're always wearing, therefore not a strange gift at all," Atsuko says, unable to let it go. "Actually a very thoughtful gift. Some might even say sweet. Beyond the realm of 'let's be friends' and edging into 'let's go on dates and make out and stuff.'"

"Well. I don't know about that," I say.

The truth is, it *was* a really thoughtful gift. And yes, I might have spent a night or two crafting elaborate fantasies about Justin's and my first date, which would somehow involve a scavenger hunt where we searched for different kinds of rocks to turn into all sorts of whimsical jewelry. But then he started texting me and trying to make plans and I just couldn't do it. Couldn't move beyond the perfect fantasy I'd made up in my head.

I focus on Bex across the quad. She's made it all the way over to Shelby Perkiss and they appear to be chatting. Shelby laughs at something Bex says and brushes her long swoop of platinum blonde hair out of her eyes, revealing her multi-pierced ears with their dangly feather earrings. All of this looks flirty, at least from far away. I cross my fingers, hoping it's going well.

Bex turns and heads back toward us and she looks happy, but I can't tell if it's happy like she's trying to keep from bursting with joy or happy like she's trying to put on a brave face and not cry after being rejected.

"De-ni-al," Atsuko says, sounding out each syllable. "Man. What's the weather like on your lovely continent this time of year?"

"Shut it," I say.

"What are you so afraid of, Kimi?" she murmurs.

I don't have the chance to respond, because suddenly Bex is there and her smile is spreading over her face and we can tell she's happy like the ready-to-burst-with-joy kind.

"She said yeeeessssssss!" Bex sings out, sweeping us into a big group hug. "Ohmygod, you guys, she said *yes*. We're going to the movies tonight!"

The candy wrapper dress crinkles against us and then we're all screaming and I feel like my heart is going to explode. Bex is getting this big, awesome thing she's wanted for so long and the sheer triumph of that sweeps aside the weird conversation I was just having with Atsuko, over-whelming me with joy.

"Kimi!" Bex pulls out of the hug and grasps me by the shoulders, beaming. "Thankyouthankyouthankyou! The dress did it. It really does make me feel like Ultimate Bex."

I smile back at her. The sheer force of her happiness is so fully encompassing, like she's projecting some of her superheroine-ness onto me. Like I helped her get this big, awesome thing she's wanted for so long. And just for a moment, I feel like Ultimate Kimi.

CHAPTER TWO

I practically float home after school. Well, technically I sit in the passenger seat of Atsuko's old beat-up Mustang and we put the top down and drive through McDonald's to get french fries and sing along when one of our favorite songs comes on the radio. I feel light as a cloud, nourished by So-Cal sunshine and greasy, salty goodness. And Atsuko, thankfully, doesn't try to give me advice about anything.

I'm still humming the chorus of the song as I shimmy through the doorway of my house. Which is maybe why I don't notice Mom until she's right in front of me.

"Kimi!" she cries, at approximately the same time as I go, "Aggghhh!"

"Sorry, Mom, you startled me," I say, slipping off my shoes and dumping my messenger bag next to the couch.

"Oh, Kimi-chan, I have incredible news." Her short, angular bob swings as she gestures. She's wearing her "outside clothes"—an emerald green silk blouse paired with a black pencil skirt and chunky gold jewelry. Mom's a freelance graphic designer with an impressive roster of regular clients, so she mostly works from home and keeps to a wardrobe of baggy tunics and patterned leggings. Outside clothes mean she must have had official in-person business today. "I had a meeting at the Eckford Gallery," Mom says. "The one over on Washington? And . . ." She clasps her hands together and smiles at me. "I am—what's the word? In. I have a spot in their Voices of Asian America gallery show next month, which is spotlighting the best and brightest up-and-coming Asian and Asian American artists in the greater Los Angeles area."

She says it like she's memorized the promotional catalog blurb—and she probably has.

"Oh, that's awesome, Mom!" I say, happy for her. My mom is a total artistic badass. Her paintings are wild and bold, splashes of gorgeous abstract color forming all kinds of impossible shapes. Sometimes she'll stay up all night painting in her studio—a converted garage attached to our house— and bustle into the kitchen the next morning chanting, "Coffee, coffee, coffee," just waiting for my dad to smile indulgently and hand her a cup. But it's taken her a while to get to this point.

Mom always wanted to be an artist—going back to when she was a kid growing up in a small town just outside of Kyoto in Japan. But she's had to put that dream on hold so many times over the years. When her parents disapproved of some of her life choices, for example. And when she had me—all her time and energy had to go into making sure I had food and clothes and could eventually be whatever I wanted in life.

And yes, sometimes I feel guilty about it. More than sometimes.

But recently she's gotten back to it and started to win spots in gallery shows and I couldn't be more proud.

"It is a big honor," my mom is saying. "And . . ." She takes my hand in hers, squeezing tight. Then she pulls me over to the couch, sitting down and taking me with her. "It's made me even more excited for your future, Kimi-chan. You will have so many opportunities like this one." She squeezes my hand again. Her eyes have gotten all bright and shiny and— oh, crap. My mom, who never cries, is *tearing up*. I find myself getting a little misty in response. "Especially with Liu Academy to your name," Mom continues. "You're so young— your whole life is in front of you and you don't have to put your dreams on hold. You can just go for it. You're going to *do* so much."

My eyes are suddenly very dry and I feel all the triumphs of the day melting away in an instant. Because it doesn't matter that I made a beautiful outfit for my friend or that it helped her get a date or that Atsuko and I got the freshest, crispiest fries straight out of the fryer after school. No, what matters is that I haven't completed a single painting this entire semester, I have nothing to show when I start Liu Academy in the fall, and I'm about to be the biggest disappointment ever to my mother, who sacrificed her dreams so I can have mine.

I am awash in guilt—a heavy, oppressive force that wipes the smile from my lips and makes my shoulders slump, settling over me like an unwanted blanket on a hot day.

"What have you been working on?" Mom says, jiggling my hand. "Can you show me yet?"

"N-no," I say quickly, snatching my hand away and bolting to my feet. "I'm still—um—working on things. Finding my unique point of view and voice and all that. And also, my room's a total mess right now. No one should have to witness the chaos except me."

"Chaos can be part of the process," my mother says. "You know, if you got rid of some of your clothes—"

"I'd have more space and less clutter. I know," I say, plastering on a smile. "But for now, I'm gonna go paint for a bit before dinner."

"All right," Mom says with an approving nod. She reaches over to the side table, grabs a small white box, and hands it to me. "Here, take this with you for a snack—new mochi samples from your father. I stopped by the restaurant while I was out and he wanted you to try these when you got home from school."

"Okaythanksbye!" I say, my voice high-pitched like a cartoon chipmunk.

I grab the box and my bag and zip down the hall and into my room before she can ask any more questions. My room *is* a mess—sketches and clothes and bits of fabric everywhere, candy wrapper remnants from Bex's dress project. But what I really don't want my mom to see is the thing that's haunted me the last few months, the thing that's remained exactly the same even as the chaos around it has changed: the blank canvas propped up on my easel in the corner. White, pristine. My brushes and paints are stacked neatly next to it, the only bit of order in the whole room. Because I haven't touched them in months.

But surely now is the time to start, right? Surely the

fresh guilt I'm feeling over seeing my mom's excited smile and teary eyes will be enough to get me going. To make inspiration strike. I make myself toss aside the remnants of crimson velvet dotting the chair in front of my easel. I acquired these scraps from the local fabric store, which I haunt regularly for the stuff they'd throw out otherwise. Then I take a deep breath and sit down.

Okay. This isn't so bad. I'm sitting. I'm comfortable. Inspiration is just moments away, obviously. I stare at the canvas, willing it to talk to me. It's not saying much, so I open the box of mochi samples from my dad, take one out, and take a bite.

"Holy crap!" I say out loud, my eyes widening. Dang. That is *good*. Different kinds of homemade mochi are a dessert staple at my dad's restaurant and he's always experimenting with different flavors. He usually whips up at least two new variations for my parents' big Oshogatsu party at New Year's. This one is filled with a smooth combination of peanut butter and chocolate, which is delectable. But of course the real treat is the mochi surrounding it, the wonderful rice cake that is somehow smooth and soft and chewy and ever so slightly gelatinous at the same time. My dad knows how to make it so it has just the right texture, practically melting in your mouth.

The longer I stare at the blank canvas, the more an all-too-familiar feeling builds in my gut. It's like a weight, pulling me downward into the pit of total . . . *unspiration*. Is that even a word? It's the opposite of inspiration. It's like a combination of guilt and the pressure I feel whenever I think about the future. Mom's voice keeps floating through my head: *You're going to* do *so much*.

How can that be true if I can't even get started?

It didn't used to be this hard. As a kid, I would doodle all the time. On pieces of scrap paper, in the margins of coloring books (because, Mom likes to claim, my toddler artistic vision was simply *too vast* to be contained in restrictive lines). And, during one infamous afternoon, all over the bathroom wall of the tiny one-bedroom apartment where we lived before Dad's restaurant took off. I can still remember my mom practically hyperventilating when she realized I'd created this astounding mural using permanent marker and she was going to have to explain it to the landlord. Luckily, Atsuko's mom had some handy solution involving vinegar, milk, and lemon juice, and the crisis had been narrowly averted.

I can't explain the utter dread I've felt since getting the acceptance letter from Liu Academy. Painting instantly morphed from something I generally enjoyed doing to something that means *everything*, something that signifies *my entire future.*

That's all I can think about when I face the canvas.

Whatever you paint next has to be absolutely perfect.

You can't be a great Asian American artist unless it's perfect.

You're going to mess it up.

I stand up from my chair in a huff, glaring at the stupid blank canvas. It feels like a battlefield. And I, intrepid warrior Kimi, cannot seem to traverse it. Or even start traversing it. Or . . . or . . . do whatever the step before that is. The Ultimate Kimi who helped Bex is nowhere to be found. I fling myself onto my bed and grab my trusty sketchbook and a pencil. Sketching always feels more freeing to me. Sketching is less permanent than paint on a canvas. Soft pencil lines that look like they could evaporate into nothing. They don't have to be perfect. They can just be.

I drum my pencil on the sketchbook and gnaw on my lip.

Inspiration . . . inspiration . . . where are you? Where's that amazing "voice" and "point of view" I'm supposed to have?

My own work is abstract, like my mother's. I like playing with exaggerated shapes and contrasting textures—sharp angles against soft swirls. And I *love* experimenting with bold colors, pairing bright hues that some might consider "clashing." I think fire engine red and flaming orange look absolutely beautiful together, for example. I try to think about all that, but I find my mind drifting back to the blank canvas, to the idea of it being a battlefield. I sketch a loose figure, giving her my shoulder-length, choppy cut black hair and bangs. I give her a fierce scowl.

She's a version of Ultimate Kimi. Battle Kimi, maybe?

She will not be defeated by the canvas! She will triumph over artist's block! She will . . . she will . . . um, make lots of brilliant paintings and stuff! Rawr!

My brain clicks into a nice groove as I sketch, the lines flowing from my pencil, from my hand. I start imagining what Battle Kimi would wear. Full set of armor for the actual battlefield, of course, but what about her everyday look, like when she has to take a Comparative Lit pop quiz before going to vanquish a bunch of dragons after school or whatever? I love thinking about the things we put on our bodies for different situations, how we use clothes to express ourselves.

21

Even Atsuko, with her slouchy athleisure wear, is saying something.

My brow furrows as I draw a crimson dress with a full skirt that tears away to reveal practical-but-stylish trousers, a high neckline, and a dramatic armor breastplate that fits over it. I get stuck wondering about the exact mechanics of Battle Kimi's skirt/pants combo, and before I know it, I'm roughing out a pattern that fits my measurements, and then I'm at my sewing machine, stitching those crimson velvet remnants together.

When I finally have something semi-complete, I hold it up in front of me, scrutinizing it. It's not bad—but the skirt isn't falling exactly how I'd like and the whole thing is a little too bulky, especially if the pants are supposed to fit under actual armor. Maybe if I change the way the waist-band is gathered, I can—

"Kimi!" Mom's voice shatters my train of thought. "Dinner!"

I blink at the garment in front of me, still startled, then glance at the clock. Holy crap. Four hours have passed, and I barely noticed. But all the sketching and sewing and battle-field flights of fancy have made me feel calmer inside. Soothed. Even though I haven't actually solved any of my problems.

"Kimi!" Mom calls again, her voice more insistent.

I hang the crimson velvet garment over my canvas, enjoying the bright splash of color against all that whiteness. At least for the moment, my dark pit of unspiration has been pushed to the very back recesses of my mind, fought off by Battle Kimi and her not-quite-perfect skirt/pants combo.

"Kimi, guess what came in the mail?" My dad waggles his eyebrows in that goofy way he has and takes a big bite of dinner. He's brought home chicken katsu sandwiches and potato salad with carrots, cucumbers, Kewpie mayonnaise, and a dash of hot mustard. Both specialties at Dad's restaurant, Yonsei, which he always says features "the best of Japanese, American, and Japanese American comfort food." And it *is* comforting—there's nothing like the crunch of panko bread crumbs surrounding a juicy chicken cutlet, and when the whole thing is pressed between the soft sweetness of a Hawaiian roll? Heaven.

I don't even know where to begin with the guessing, but this is one of Dad's favorite games. He likes to give the most minimal of hints and then see how outrageous your guess can get. Mom *hates* this game because she doesn't see the point in "dwelling on made-up possibilities" when Dad could just, you know, tell us what the answer is. But it makes his face light up so much, I can never resist.

"Hmm," I say, pretending to think about it as I wipe excess panko from my lips. "Is it a dragon? Like, my own pet dragon?" My brain is still on the adventures of Battle Kimi, I guess.

"No way," my dad says. "I'd never get you a mail-order dragon. Only the best for my daughter."

My mom groans but doesn't say anything. She's humoring my dad, I can tell. She must still be in a good mood from her art show news.

"Is it . . . a bag of rocks?" I say.

"Are you kidding? That would cost zillions of dollars in postage," my dad says. "You need a rock, just go outside and get one. Plenty of decent, home-grown Culver City rocks round these parts."

I can't help but giggle. "Clothes?" I say, running out of creative guessing juice. "Aw, Daddy, did you order me Anna Sui's new collection? Because she has some lace detail work this season that is just *beyond*."

"I don't know what any of those words mean," Dad says.

"You don't need more clothes," Mom interjects. "And you know, Kimi-chan, you might want to consider editing your wardrobe in a more polished direction. For when you start at Liu Academy."

"Says the woman who mostly lives in 'inside clothes,'" my dad says, raising a playful eyebrow at my mom and her wild patterned leggings.

"Well," Mom says, clearly trying to save face, "that's different. I mostly live inside. You know, with my paintings. It's a happy inside life."

Then they exchange one of those gentle, knowing smiles that only two people who have been together for twenty years and are still disgustingly mushy can share. Atsuko always says that given my parents' relationship, I shouldn't have a problem imagining that level of gross in-love-ness for myself one day. It's harder for someone like her, whose parents are divorced and still have loud, shouty fights on speakerphone about who's supposed to pick her and her sister up from where on what day and if she should get a "proper" after-school job to build character. Atsuko says she gives love advice because she wants to save people from themselves . . . but she doesn't understand why I need any since I have such a perfect example of love sitting right in front of me.

The thing is, the perfection of my parents' relationship, the fact that they've been through so much together and can still look at each other like that, makes me feel like I have to get love exactly right on the first try. Like they did. I know they want something like what they have for me, just like my mom wants me to be able to achieve all my dreams as an artist.

What are you so afraid of, Kimi? Atsuko's voice says in my head.

I brush the thought away and refocus on my parents.

"So, what actually came in the mail?" I say. "Apparently my guessing game is off today."

My dad grins at me, but I sense a note of something underneath—a hint of nerves, maybe? At the same time, my mom clears her throat and looks down at her food. Before I have time to fully parse their reactions, my dad slides an envelope across the table to me. It's delicate, tissue-thin stationery and my name is carefully printed on the front in small, precise handwriting. I recognize the handwriting, I realize—this is from my grandfather. Mom's dad. Who still lives in Japan.

Now I understand my parents' weird reactions. Mom's relationship with her parents is still basically nonexistent, even after all this time—they haven't spoken in years. In addition to not loving the fact that Mom and Dad were super young when they got married, Mom's parents also disapproved of her marrying a fourth-generation Japanese American dude rather than a more traditional Japanese man. (Mom pointed out she could have gone for a white guy, like Atsuko's mom did, but they didn't see her choice as being much better.)

Mom has never quite forgiven them—every phone conversation I've ever heard her have with my grandmother has mostly involved a lot of yelling. And, for their part, I think my grandparents still don't understand her life choices—they had always hoped she'd return to them and their farm just outside of Kyoto. I get birthday cards from them every year but have never met them. They're like fairy-tale characters to me—the evil king and queen from a far-off land who tried to forbid their princess from marrying her true love. Only, you know, not totally evil because they still send me the birthday cards.

"Well, open it," Mom says, her voice a bit tight. "See what they want."

I slit the envelope open and take out the letter inside—more of my grandfather's small, neat writing.

"They . . . they want me to visit," I say, my eyebrows quirking upward. "They want me to come stay with them in Kyoto. For spring break."

"Spring break is in a week," my mother huffs. "That's not nearly enough time to plan travel, not to mention—"

"They included a ticket," I say, still not quite processing what's happening. "Um, sorry for interrupting, Mom. But yeah, they included a ticket, and it's refundable if I decide not to go."

"I still don't think you need to be going anywhere for spring break," Mom says, stabbing at her potato salad, determined not to let her parents get the best of her. "You should be spending that time working on your paintings, getting ready for the Academy. An international trip is a big distraction you don't need right now."

"I don't know," my dad says.

Mom's head and my head swivel in near unison to look at him. Because part of my parents' perfect love involves Dad pretty much never disagreeing with Mom—at least not in front of me. "I can never say no to your mother," he'll say, smiling fondly as she goes on about why I need extra art lessons or why we simply must go see the Magritte exhibit at LACMA.

But now he's saying something different. "It might be good for Kimi to have an adventure on her spring break—it *is* her last one before we release her into the wilds of college," he says. He's being very careful with his words, very mild with his tone. Even so, my mom is frowning, a crater-sized crinkle appearing between her eyebrows. "And . . ." He hesitates, giving both of us a soft, wistful smile. "You might enjoy the chance to meet your grandparents, explore your Japanese heritage. I wish I'd done more of that when I was younger."

"Meh. You are as Japanese as I am," Mom says to Dad, waving a dismissive hand. "Just—"

"—in a different way. I know," he says, giving her that smile again and covering his hand with hers. I know this line is something Mom said to her parents repeatedly when they kept telling her not to marry my dad. "But I think this should be Kimi's decision. Yes?"

"Yes, yes, I suppose," Mom says, still huffy. "But I'm sure

she doesn't want to go, either. She's dedicated to her painting. Right, Kimi-chan?"

"Of course, Mom," I say, smiling at her.

With that settled, we all go back to our food and Dad tries to make Mom laugh by telling her about some of the more colorful customers who came into the restaurant today, like the guy who asked if he could have his chicken katsu sandwich served "skinless and without the bread."

"'Like, Paleo-friendly, my dude,'" Dad says, imitating the customer's flat surfer drawl.

I tune in and out, scraping up the last, precious few bits of panko with my fork and mixing them into my potato salad. As we finish up the main course and my dad brings out a plate of his peanut butter–chocolate–filled mochi for dessert, my gaze can't help but drift back to the letter. I can't go—I mean, Bex and Atsuko and I have been planning our spring break for *months*. We're going to ride the Santa Monica Ferris wheel and climb the Temescal Canyon hiking trail and explore the Hollywood Forever Cemetery. Bex even made us a color-coded chart detailing each day's plans and maybe now she'll invite Shelby along and Atsuko and I will get to tease them for being all flirty and cute. Plus, I'm scheduled to work extra shifts at the thrift store where I have a part-time job and they always have an amazing spring break sale. Plus-plus, my mom will be mad if I go— even though she'll say she's not. (Moms being mad when they keep insisting they're not is definitely an equation in Atsuko's Asian Mom Math. Truly one of the most complex and terrifying equations.)

But even as I remind myself of all this, my ever-helpful

brain reminds me of something else: After every day of spring break fun time, I'll have to come back home to that stupid blank canvas. I'll have to be reminded of all the ways I'm failing. My dark pit of unspiration will be right there waiting to pull me back in. I pop a whole piece of mochi into my mouth and chew, trying to get the magical combo of flavors and textures to soothe me. It's delicious, but it can't distract me.

The idea of escaping to a whole other country fills me with a strange feeling of lightness. Of relief.

De-ni-al, Atsuko says in my head.

I brush the thought away.

I'm not going. I mean, it's tempting, but I *can't*.

But, for the rest of dessert, as my dad teases my mom and my mom tries not to laugh and they exist in the bubble of their perfect love, I fantasize about escaping to a corner of the world where none of my uncertainties about life, the future, and everything else exist. Where I'm not thinking constantly about how I'll ruin everything if I don't get it perfect on the first try.

I imagine myself in my Battle Kimi getup, charging my way across the ocean, sword in hand, gleeful expression overtaking my face. Traveling to a place where the dragons can't get me.

CHAPTER THREE

"So, she brought me a candy bouquet. Like, instead of flowers, it was a bunch of lollipops and candy bars tied together with a ribbon. Because of the candy wrapper dress. Isn't that the cutest?" Bex twirls around like a tornado on our little patch of grass behind the library. Her arms are outstretched and she's holding her water bottle in one hand and I'm kind of worried she's going to drop it and spill everywhere, but she's so happy, I don't want to say anything. Apparently, her date with Shelby last night went extremely, extremely well.

"And she pulled all of that together in an afternoon?" Atsuko looks up from her phone, where she's composing yet another advice column, and nods approvingly. "That means she's already putting a lot of thought into your needs. Into making you feel like a priority."

"Annnnnnd . . . it's just freaking romantic," Bex says, flopping down next to us and rolling her eyes. "Feel the swoon! *Feel it*, Atsy!" She grabs Atsuko by the shoulder and shakes her pseudo-dramatically.

"Hey!" Atsuko starts laughing and bats at Bex's hand, nearly dropping her phone in the process. "Okay, okay, I'm swooning up a storm over here. Kimi, are you swooning?"

"Totally swooning," I say, giving them a game smile. But my heart's not quite in it. It's not that I'm not happy for Bex—I am. I just can't seem to muster the level of outward enthusiasm I'd normally have because my brain feels like it's caught in a never-ending hamster wheel loop and I can't make it stop. The loop kept me up all night, spinning and spinning and spinning, and when my alarm went off this morning, I felt like I'd only just fallen asleep.

Japan. Escape from the battlefield of the blank canvas. No more pretending you've got it all together around Mom. All your worries about the future an entire ocean away . . .

But! You don't even know your grandparents! They might be mean to you. Or just weird. Not to mention the fact that you've never been to another country before, except Canada and that barely counts. And you'll miss out on spring break fun times with Bex and Atsuko. And . . . And . . .

"Kimi?" Bex's voice jolts me from my mental hamster wheel. I picture myself as a tiny, hapless hamster, falling off its wheel and stumbling around its cage.

"Sorry," I say. I force a bright smile. "That all sounds great, Bex! Especially the candy bouquet. Maybe that will become a thing with you guys, like a different candy bouquet for every anniversary or something. And I could totally make you more dresses out of the wrappers and then you'd have, like, a whole candy wrapper wardrobe and you can dye your hair to match and it will be *so cute*, so . . . so . . ."

I'm babbling and my voice is too loud and my words are too fast. My friends are looking at me strangely, heads cocked to the side, brows furrowed.

"Um," Bex says. "That's awesome, Kimi, but I was actually

31

just asking if it's cool if Shelby joins us for our spring break plans? I mean, not all of them, I know some of it is stuff the three of us have wanted to do forever, but she really loves hiking and old Hollywood lore, so I was thinking—"

"Of course!" I say, my voice still way too loud. "Shelby should definitely come with us. This spring break is going to be the best ever."

Even though you were just thinking of flaking on all your plans with your two best friends to flit off halfway around the world . . .

"Hey, Kimi," Atsuko says, poking me in the arm. "Your phone's buzzing."

My head swivels to find my phone, lying in the grass. It is, in fact, buzzing. I've been babbling and hamster wheeling too much to notice. I snatch it up and scrutinize the screen. A long series of texts from my mother stares back at me, every single one punctuated by an emoji.

Where are you? Confused, thinking face emoji.

I'm at your art class. Girl shrugging emoji.

The teacher says you dropped out?! Surprised emoji.

What is going on? Angry cat emoji.

Get over here right now. Three running girl emojis. And an eggplant. (Atsuko and I might have lied a little and told my mom using the eggplant "is like adding an extra exclamation point.")

"Oh, shit," Atsuko says, peering over my shoulder.

"She can't be too mad, she's using emojis," Bex says, trying to sound reassuring.

"Please," Atsuko says. "In Asian Mom speak, emojis mean *death*."

I swallow hard, trying to rein in the roller coaster of emotions crashing through me. Mom *knows*. She knows everything. The lie I've been telling her the last few months has finally unraveled and come back to bite me on the ass. A weird sense of relief mixes in with the panic coursing through my blood, like at least *I* don't have to tell her now . . .

"Her next emoji will show how she's gonna kill you," Atsuko says, and then the panic takes over fully, smothering any relief.

"I . . . I guess I should go over there. To art class," I say, my voice high and thin.

"We'll come with you," Bex says, squeezing my shoulder. I barely hear her, but manage a small nod.

I get to my feet and start walking. I feel like I'm on a weird kind of autopilot, like my feet are carrying me to my doom and I can't do anything to stop them. I hear Bex and Atsuko behind me, gathering the stuff I've left behind on the grass and following me into the school, down the hall, and to the art room.

It's the tail end of lunch hour—Advanced Fine Art starts right after, so there are a few early birds milling around, along with the teacher, Ms. Koch. And my mom.

She's standing at the front of the art room, hands on her hips. And even though she's a full head shorter than Ms. Koch, my former art teacher looks *terrified*.

Well. She should be.

Mom's got her glower on and as I enter the room, she turns the full force of it away from Ms. Koch and onto me.

"Kimiko," my mom says, her tone like ice.

33

"Oh nooooo," Atsuko breathes at the sound of my full name.

"I came here with exciting news," Mom says. "It was so exciting, I couldn't wait, and I had to share it with you immediately. I spoke to the organizers of the Voices of Asian America show and they agreed that you should have a spot in it. Alongside me."

"Oh, that's . . . that's really cool," I manage, my voice barely a whisper.

"But Ms. Koch says you dropped out of class—how can this be?" Mom barrels on. "I told her she must be mistaken." Some hopefulness mixes in with her glower. Like I'm going to clear all of this up and, surprise, I've been in art class the whole time after all and now everything can go back to normal. But as I stand there in front of her and the growing number of students filtering into class, I have the sinking sensation that nothing will ever be normal again.

"No, she's right, Mom—I dropped the class," I say. For a brief, shining moment, it feels good to say the truth out loud. That feeling is quickly dashed by the look on my mother's face—now, confusion and hurt are lacing their way through the glower.

"Did you feel you needed to work more independently?" my mother says, grasping for an explanation. "That the formal nature of the class was stifling your creativity?"

"No," I say. She's giving me an opening to lie my way out of this, but now that I've started telling the truth, I just can't stop. "I haven't painted in months. I . . . I can't."

"Can't?" My mother shakes her head, as if this is an impossibility. To her, it probably is. She's had to overcome too much in her life for there to be any "can't" getting in her way. So how could it get in mine? "Well, what have you been doing with all your time, then?"

"Other things, Mom," I say. "I made costumes for the school play. I've been designing a bunch of my own outfits. And I made Bex a candy wrapper dress."

"It's really beautiful," Bex murmurs.

"So you've just been goofing around?" My mother shakes her head again. All of this is too much for her to comprehend. "Kimi-chan. These are distractions. And senior year is not the time for distractions. You're supposed to be preparing for your future, for your time at the academy. Finding your voice, finding—"

"—my artistic point of view, I know," I blurt out. My voice is getting louder and my face is getting hotter and I feel the weight of everyone looking at my mother and me, facing off in the middle of the art room. But the words are just spilling out now and I can't stop them. "But . . . but I don't even know what that means, Mom. Every time I stare at my blank canvas, I just freeze up, I can't figure out what to do next. I . . . I don't think I love painting anymore." And as I say that, a funny little thought worms its way through my brain: did I ever love—like, really *love*—painting? Or did I just think I loved it because I'd been doing it so long, it seemed like the thing I was supposed to keep doing forever? Because it made my mom so proud, so happy? Because she wants so badly for me to achieve a dream she had to leave behind?

"Why didn't you ask me for help with this block?" Mom says. "I could have talked to you about it—"

35

"Because I didn't want to disappoint you!" I exclaim. Now my face feels like it's on fire and my voice is getting dangerously shaky, a sure sign that I'm about to cry. I swallow hard, trying to tamp down on the frustration exploding in my chest. How can I get her to understand? Especially when I feel like I'm having all these realizations now, in this moment?

"I . . . I think painting . . . no, not just painting, all of it: painting and the academy and the art shows and . . . and being the next great Asian American artist is what *you* want for me. Not what I want."

"Well, what do you want?" Mom crosses her arms and frowns at me. That canyon-sized crease has appeared between her eyebrows again. "Because all these years, you've painted. And you always had that same joy about it that I did. Were you pretending the whole time?"

"N-no, Mom," I say. "Of course not. I just . . . I liked it. But lately I haven't felt the same way and I didn't know how to admit that to you . . . or . . . or even to myself."

"Art is not always fun," my mother says. "Creating is hard work, too. You have to be prepared for that, be ready to work through the blocks—and I thought you were. You've always put in so much extra time, taken so many extra classes . . ."

"But I don't know if painting is what . . . what *fuels* me. Drives me. Lights me up inside, the way it does with you."

That canyon between her eyebrows just keeps getting deeper.

"Then what does?" she says, her voice urgent—like maybe she really does want to understand.

"I . . . I don't know," I say. Now the tears are in my eyes and I can't stop them. My voice cracks and I feel like such a baby. And of course, the entire Advanced Fine Art class is witnessing this. I feel the weight of their combined gaze boring into me, burning through my skin. The thing is, I really don't know. I wish I did. But in all my tunnel-visioned pursuit of painting, I've never stopped to think about what else *could* fuel me. I mean, I like all the goofing off–type stuff I've been doing this semester. I like the little spark I get when I'm dreaming up a new outfit or the way the world melts away when I'm trying to solve problems like stitching a bunch of candy wrappers together. But all of that feels silly and inconsequential and I don't even know how to begin to express it.

"I like . . . clothes," I finally say.

"Clothes?" my mother repeats, sounding a bit incredulous. "Well, that's fine, you can like clothes. But that's a hobby, Kimi, not a career. Not a passion. Not something that will take you through life in a meaningful way or set you up for a good future." Her frown deepens, and her voice is laced with disappointment. "I don't understand you. You have so much talent and so many opportunities."

The *opportunities I would have killed for* part goes unsaid, which somehow makes it even worse.

"So many chances to do so much. And you're throwing it all away," she continues. "Lying to me and spending time on, what? Frivolous things like obsessing over clothes?"

"I was just . . . having fun," I say, blinking like mad so the tears won't fall. One of them rebels and slides down my cheek. I barely register a hand on my shoulder—Bex or Atsuko, trying to comfort me.

There's a silence, one of those heavy silences that goes on way too long. One of those silences that somehow contains

37

every bad thing about this moment, rolls it all up into a great big ball of terrible feelings.

"Well," my mother finally says, her shoulders slumping, "I hope it was worth it."

She turns to Ms. Koch and gives her a slight nod. "I apologize for causing a scene in your classroom. And for my daughter."

"N-no problem," Ms. Koch says, still looking a little scared.

My mother holds her head high and strides out, barely looking at me as she passes. I follow her like a sad puppy dog, stumbling out of the art room with Bex and Atsuko trailing after me. I hear scandalized murmurs running through the class, but I don't even care.

"Mom," I say, even though I'm not sure what I want to say after that. Tears are falling freely down my face now and I can't stop them. She's so disappointed in me. The daughter she was so proud of for getting into the academy has disappeared. It's like I've shrunk to pea-sized Kimi right before her eyes. Like I'm an actual hamster, I guess.

"I will see you at home, Kimi," she says, not stopping as she heads for the school's exit.

Atsuko and Bex wrap me into a pretzel of a group hug, making soothing little noises. And Atsuko tactfully refrains from noting that anyone who knows Asian Mom Math knows that silent, disappointed anger is way worse than the screaming and yelling kind.

Everything is quiet when I get home. Mom is out in her studio and Dad isn't back from the restaurant yet. I flop on my bed and stare at my unfinished Battle Kimi outfit from yesterday. I think about tinkering with it, but I can't seem to focus. Instead, my gaze keeps wandering back to the letter from my grandfather. To the plane ticket. If getting away from all my problems seemed like a tempting fantasy before, it has now morphed into a full-blown siren song of a fantasy, calling to me like fresh mochi or a perfectly cut pleated circle skirt or a half-off sale at an expensive vintage boutique.

Why does it have to be a fantasy, anyway?

I mean . . . I'll have to explain it to Atsuko and Bex. They'll be disappointed I'm flaking on the plans we've had forever. Actually, *how* am I going to explain this to them?

Hey, guys, so you know I had that huge fight with my mom, but also I need to go on this international journey of self-discovery in order to finally figure out what my passion is. Since it's apparently not painting.

I'll have to figure that part out later.

I finger the tissue-thin stationery, considering.

When Dad comes in hours later to tell me dinner's ready, I'm rereading the letter for what must be the millionth time.

"I really messed up, huh," I say, not looking up from the letter.

"You did," he says, but his voice is gentle. "Kimi, you can't lie to us like that. Your mother and I are discussing your punishment, but I'm not going to yell at you. I get the feeling your mother's done plenty of that already."

"She actually didn't yell," I say. "She was more . . . quiet about it. Disappointed."

39

He winces. He knows that's even worse.

I hold up the letter. "Maybe putting a whole freakin' ocean between Mom and me is a good idea right about now?"

"Oh, sweetheart." I finally meet his eyes and his expression makes me want to cry again. He looks like he's trying so hard to understand me but can't quite get there. "I think if you want to go, you should go. It's a wonderful opportunity. But do it because *you* want to. Not because of what you think someone else wants."

I nod slowly, even though I don't know how to figure out what I want anymore. Did I ever?

I get up and follow him to the dining room, where Mom is sitting at the table, her face blank as she studies her food. Tonight's dinner is a spin on Japanese curry, involving bits of ground beef in a delicious spicy gravy over rice. And I know there will be mochi for dessert, but even that doesn't make me feel better.

My dad and I sit. Everyone is silent. It's only then that I realize I'm still clutching my grandfather's letter like some sort of talisman.

"I've decided that I'm going to take Grandpa up on his offer," I say, trying to ignore the way my palms are sweating and my face is getting hot. "I'm going to Japan for spring break."

There's a long silence, punctuated only by the soft click of chopsticks against bowls. When my mother finally speaks, her voice is measured and quiet. And she still won't look at me.

"Perhaps that would be best," she says. She frowns at her curry, mixing it around with her chopsticks. "Kimiko, I'm not sure what to say. I feel like you are suddenly a stranger. Like I don't know you at all."

I don't know how to respond, so we eat the rest of the meal in silence. As we do, a tiny thought circles around in my head—like the hamster wheel's back and as unrelenting as ever.

I don't know who I am, either. But maybe, just maybe, this trip will give me the chance to figure it out.

CHAPTER FOUR

How do you tell if you're having an existential crisis or you're just terrible at making decisions?

Because ever since I made the incredibly impulsive decision to catapult myself halfway around the world, the sentiment that keeps running through my head is: *I don't know what I'm doing.*

Not with this trip, not with my future, and not with my life.

I wish I could make that statement with gusto. I can totally see Atsuko doing that—in fact, I *have* seen Atsuko doing that, back when we were sophomores and snuck into senior prom, where we most definitely did not belong. I wasn't quite in the zone with my Kimi Originals game yet and our plan had been sort of last-minute and haphazard anyway, so we'd "borrowed" these ridiculous long slips from Atsuko's mom's closet and strung piles of fake pearls around our necks and kept saying "We are such gla-mooooo-rous ladies" to each other in what we imagined to be high society–type voices. Of course as soon as we'd gotten there, I'd felt silly and childish and out of place. A kid playing dress-up among the throngs of actually gla-mooooo-rous seniors. I'd wanted to leave immediately. Atsuko, on the other hand, had plunged herself into the middle of the dance floor, flailing her arms with wild abandon. Her pearls whipped around her, clacking in time with the beat. Atsuko is *not* a good dancer. But she so obviously didn't care what anyone thought about her, it kind of didn't matter. She was mesmerizing.

"Kimi!" she'd cried out, throwing her head back and raising her hands in the air. "Come on, dance with me! I don't know what I'm doing!"

She'd said it in a way that seemed to imply this was a *good* thing—breathless, enthusiastic, lost in the moment. Like there was so much fun to be had in the process of figuring out what she was doing. I'd danced awkwardly alongside her for the rest of the song, then convinced her to leave.

In the few days between deciding to go to Japan and leaving for Japan, I tried to convince myself that going on this journey of self-discovery and figuring out who I *really* am and where my passion *really* lies could be fun in that "Atsuko figuring stuff out on the dance floor" kind of way. I decided I needed to embrace this state of not knowing what I was doing, to treat it like I was going on a truly epic quest. Battle Kimi Finds Herself.

But right now, I'm feeling about as far from epic as you can get. I'm crammed into a packed train speeding from the airport and into Kyoto, my suitcase jammed between my knees. I've made it through a sleepless fifteen-hour flight, a seemingly endless customs line, and a heart-stopping moment wherein I thought my suitcase was lost. (It wasn't, it got put on an earlier flight and was waiting for me at the little office next to baggage claim, its cheery floral exterior an insolent blotch against the sea of black and navy blue bags.)

I'm in a jet-lagged haze—I think it's late afternoon here? And I'm clutching the piece of paper with the instructions detailing where to meet up with my grandparents in my sweaty hand. I'm also starving because I was too nervous to eat on the plane and then I was freaking out about my bag being lost and the end result is that I haven't had food since breakfast. The train is packed to the gills, but eerily quiet. I remember this tidbit from the hasty reading I did on Japan before I left—that you're not supposed to talk loudly on the train, and you're *definitely* not supposed to talk on the phone. There are plenty of signs posted—complete with helpful cartoons—just in case anyone forgets. It amazes me that people actually *follow* this rule. I can't see this happening in the States, where talking loudly on your phone in public spaces seems to be some people's chief joy in life.

The quiet is nice, though, and I try to let it soothe me. To remind me that this trip is going to be my escape from the chaos of school and my messy life and the near silent treatment my mother's been giving me since our fight . . .

Okay, so thinking about all that stuff is *not* very soothing. I focus instead on the colorful presence of my suitcase, remember how I packed it full of my favorite outfits. The ensembles that give me confidence. After all, if I'm going to be finding my passion, it's best to start from a confident place, right? A place where even if I don't know what I'm doing, at least I sort of look like I do. A place where—

BZZZZZZ BZZZZZZ!!!

My phone chooses this moment to make the loudest noise in the history of ever. I nearly jump out of my seat. The noise pierces the peaceful silence and suddenly I'm frantically fumbling around, stuffing my sweaty piece of paper into one pocket and trying to get my phone out of the other.

"Oh . . . crap . . ." I murmur to myself, my heart rate ratcheting upward as some of the older people on the train turn to stare, casting irritated looks at me, then at the signs that forbid talking on the phone.

My phone slides around in my sweaty hands as I struggle to unlock it—it looks like someone's trying to call me on Skype?—and my face gets all hot and is this really the first beautiful memory I'm making in Japan?

I try to hit "decline," but my finger slips and lands on "accept," and suddenly Atsuko's and Bex's faces are filling the phone screen and really, there's no way this could get any worse. Maybe if Mom was with them? Although, at least then, she'd be talking to me.

"Kimi!" Atsuko bellows, and I wince alongside everyone else on the train. I look up and mouth "sorry," trying to make eye contact with everyone, but the train is so packed, it's impossible. "My mom told me that your mom told *her* that you went to freaking *Japan* for spring break?!"

"Without even telling us!" Bex chimes in. "What about our plans? I made *spreadsheets*, remember? Color-coded?"

"And . . . and what are you even doing in Japan anyway, Kimi?!" Atsuko says. "How could you not tell us *anything*—"

"SorryIhavetogobyeeeee!" I finally manage, hitting "end call" as firmly as I can.

45

I stuff the phone back in my pocket, mouth "sorry" again, and slide down in my seat, attempting to get my galloping heartbeat under control. I kept trying to find the right time to tell them I was flaking on all our plans, that I needed to go figure stuff out. That I couldn't be in the same room as my mom at the moment, couldn't take her silent, disapproving stares. With every stare, I felt the weight of her disappointment crushing me.

Somehow, it was never the right time. And as the days melted away, as my friends' excitement over big spring break fun grew . . . I just couldn't bring myself to tell them. It was yet another thing I couldn't stand to make real—but in this case, it was because I knew how awful that moment would be. They would ask me zillions of questions I didn't have answers to, then stare back at me in disappointment.

I couldn't deal with disappointing anyone else.

So, I'd retreated to my comfy continent of Denial. And I hadn't thought past that.

But now I guess I have to think about it, because my friends know what's up, my friends are *pissed*, and I need to figure out how to tell them I have basically no solid answers to any of their inevitable questions. Because I *am* on a quest of self-discovery and all.

Although it may not matter if I find the answers I'm looking for here in Japan. At the rate I'm going, I may not have anything—or anyone—to return to.

I want to catapult myself off the train as soon as it arrives at my stop, but I force myself to stand and walk out in a calm, collected manner, hauling my suitcase behind me. My stomach lets out an angry growl and I quicken my step, trying to call as little attention to myself as possible. As I step off the train, I am once again struck by how orderly everyone is—there's none of the usual pushing and shoving and jostling that inevitably springs from being part of a crowd. The sheer mass of people is overwhelming, though, and my stomach's growling intensifies, like it was just waiting for me to exit one embarrassing situation so it could cause another. I scan the train station wildly, but in my hungry, panicked state, it mostly just looks like a big blur of people.

"Sumimasen!" a young boy calls out as he scurries by me, his tiny backpack bouncing up and down. He doesn't even come close to bumping into me, but I jump back instinctively and nearly knock into someone else. I do a double take as I watch his tiny form winding its way through the crowd, on a mission. He doesn't appear to have a parent, guardian, or any other grown-up-type figure with him, and as I scan the station, I realize there are a bunch of unaccompanied kids, just going about their business like tiny adults. I am struck by the fact that Japanese schoolchildren are already way more responsible and mature and in control of their lives than I can ever hope to be.

My stomach lets out a particularly enraged growl and I nearly jump out of my skin.

My gaze finally lands on a food stand selling a variety of snacks, many of which appear to be breaded in panko. *Mmm, panko.* Suddenly I can smell its fried richness wafting through the air. Calling to me like a beacon.

I detour over to the food stand and even though I want to order everything, I restrict myself to a pair of perfect, golden-brown croquettes positioned at the front of the display rack. I manage to do the necessary yen/food exchange without making a total fool of myself. The chipper man behind the counter deposits my croquettes into a paper sleeve with gusto and passes them to me. I nod and say, "arigato," and then I cram one of the croquettes directly into my mouth. It's lava-level hot and I let out a little whimper as it burns my tongue. It's also so, *so* good—rich and hearty, the crunch of the panko giving way to that soft, potato-y center. I take another bite, even though I know I'm going to get burned again.

My stomach finally stops growling as I polish off one croquette and start in on another, and I feel better as I move through the crowd, heading toward the spot where my grandparents suggested we meet. A few people throw me odd looks as I stride through the station and I wonder if there's something I'm doing that gives me away as, well . . . super American. I suppose it could be the big freakin' suitcase I'm hauling behind me. At least my stomach isn't making noise anymore, and my friends aren't hitting me up on Skype in the most disruptive manner possible.

As I approach the designated meeting spot—near the train station's exit, next to a stand selling postcards—I spy a pair of figures I've only ever seen in old photos, and my heart starts to beat faster.

My grandfather sees me first. A slight smile crosses his

face and he raises a hand in tentative greeting—like he's not sure it's actually me. I raise a hand in return and quicken my step, trying to snarf down the rest of my croquette. I manage to pop the last bite in my mouth just as I reach them. I paste a big smile on my face, realizing too late there's a smattering of crumbs dotting the left corner of my mouth.

"Konnichiwa, Ojiisan, Obaasan," I say, bowing. "Grandpa and Grandma." I realize then that I'm not exactly sure what I'm supposed to call them. Atsuko calls her Japanese grandparents Ojiichan and Obaachan, but since I barely know mine, pretty much anything feels too familiar, too affectionate. But is the more formal address even weirder? Ugh, I don't know. I try to cover my awkwardness by stepping forward to hug them.

"Kimiko-chan," my grandmother says, leaning back a bit, just out of reach—as if to discourage the hug in the politest way possible. Oh, right: Dad told me being all huggy and affectionate—particularly in public—doesn't tend to happen as much in Japan, especially among older people. And hand shaking isn't really a thing either, which is probably for the best since I'm still clutching my greasy croquette wrapper. I attempt to crumple it further, to make it as small as possible, but of course *that* makes a loud, obnoxious noise and Grandma's brow crinkles.

Just like Mom's does, I can't help but think.

"Sorry," I blurt out. "I haven't eaten since breakfast and the flight was really long and I was starting to feel like I was going to, I don't know, eat my suitcase or something, so I stopped to get a snack and . . . sorry." I hastily stuff the wrapper into my coat pocket. I'm wearing a coat I inherited

49

from my paternal grandmother. It's light wool with a bright red-and-blue check pattern and was originally cut in a flowing style that overwhelmed my shrimpy frame. I reconstructed it to fit me better—giving it darts at the waist for a more tailored silhouette and adding little fake fur cuffs and a collar for maximum whimsy. It was my first legit Kimi Original. The coat is a bit too warm for spring in the States or Japan, but wearing it while traveling always makes me feel sophisticated and jet-setting. Grandma seems to be studying the coat—or maybe she's just studying me?—but her expression gives away nothing and I find myself shifting uncomfortably.

"Snacking is good for maintaining the healthy biorhythm," my grandfather says, smiling at me. "I change what is in my snack drawer every month—keeps life interesting, ne?" He holds out his hand.

"Oh . . ." I say, fishing around in my pocket. I pull out the croquette wrapper and hand it to him. He gives me a little nod and tucks it into his own jacket pocket and I feel a stab of warmth—he took the wrapper from me just to soothe my embarrassment.

"Let's go home so you can rest before dinner," my grandfather says, reaching for my suitcase. "I know that flight is long."

"Thank you," I say, passing the suitcase to him and giving him a tentative smile. "I definitely need to, um, freshen up a little. I've been getting some weird stares—I must have plane hair."

"It is more likely because you were eating while walk-

50

ing," my grandmother says. She's still studying me in a way I can't quite crack. "That is seen as impolite here."

"Mostly just to old folks like us," my grandfather says, gesturing for us to follow as he pulls my suitcase along behind him. "You will likely want to consult some of the young people around here, Kimiko-chan, on what is and is not considered 'impolite' these days."

"'Young people' are the last people you should consult about being polite," my grandmother grumbles, shaking her head.

My grandfather turns and winks at me, his eyes twinkling with mischief. I feel another stab of warmth so visceral, I nearly tear up. I already feel so lost. And clearly I'm making cultural faux pas all over the place—from getting a call on the train to walking and eating to trying to get all huggy—that highlight the fact that I came here completely unprepared. I wish I'd had more time to research . . . well. *Everything*. But especially customs and etiquette and stuff that would help me feel less out of place. It strikes me how discombobulating it is to be in a place where so many of the faces look like mine, but where I clearly don't belong.

My grandfather's gentle humor soothes me, though, makes me feel like maybe things will be okay. (Also, it must be said that the way he teases my grandmother reminds me a bit of my dad teasing my mom.)

I study my grandparents as we exit the station onto the street. My grandfather's twinkly manner is enhanced by his tufty white hair and his rumpled, mismatched outfit—polo shirt a few sizes too big, wrinkled khaki jacket, neatly tied

51

sneakers. I can totally picture him at the lunch counter at Suehiro, a no-frills Japanese comfort food place in LA's Little Tokyo that attracts a big cross-section of local Aunties and Uncles. Atsuko, Bex, and I sometimes eat there on weekends. One time, I thought an Auntie with particularly notable side-eye technique was judging me for taking a picture of my food. But then her food came, and she whipped out *an actual camera*—like, not a phone—to snap a pic, so maybe she was merely judging my not-very-impressive photography skills.

In contrast to my grandfather, I can't get a read on Grandma. Except that she still seems to be shooting me deep, probing looks, like she's trying to figure something out. She's not what I expected, though. I had drawn up a vivid image of a stern, faded woman with a steel-gray hair bun and a penchant for muted floral prints. Someone who, I guess, had certain elements of Mom's demeanor, but was also clearly opposed to the vivid, artsy way she lives her life. But I don't think that's Grandma. Her hair is short and snow white and she has sweeping bangs that fall over her forehead. She's wearing all black—an interesting, blouse-like garment with asymmetrical ruffles layered along the front and a long skirt.

"Obaasan," I blurt out, and she cocks her head at me. "I like your outfit."

I feel instantly dorky. I'm talking to my *grandmother*, not some fellow fashionista I chatted up at my thrift store job and then hearted on Instagram.

She studies me for a few moments more in that deeply uncomfortable way, her brow furrowed.

"This outfit, not so good," she finally says, waving a dismissive hand at her ensemble. "The skirt is old and frayed at the bottom."

With that, she sweeps toward the station's exit. I follow along, my sense of dorky out-of-placeness growing. And I realize I don't have to choose between having an existential crisis and making bad decisions—because I'm definitely *really* good at accomplishing both of those things at the same time.

Dinner is a fairly uneventful affair. Grandma and Grandpa cook together and then we all sit on tatami mats around a low table, eating fish and rice and miso soup. The flavors are gentle and familiar, and I allow my exhausted brain to luxuriate in their soothing qualities. I keep apologizing for my zonked-out state, but Grandpa and Grandma don't seem to mind. In fact, they seem comfortable in companionable silence, which is refreshing since I can't, for the life of me, think of anything smart to say. It's weird, I have this sudden desire to impress them. Maybe I want to show them that Mom's life turned out okay. That *I* turned out okay—since I am the result of all the decisions she made that they disapproved of so hard.

I keep wanting to ask Grandma about her cool blouse thing from earlier. But I feel shy even bringing it up since she dismissed my compliment so quickly. And anyway, she seems uncomfortable looking at me—whenever I try to catch her eye, she finds something else to look at.

Grandpa tries to ask a few questions about Mom, which makes Grandma stiffen and stare down at her bowl extra hard. So I answer in quick, clipped sentences, not giving much away. I realize I also need to divert them around the subject of my future, which seemed pretty set up until recently. But now . . . I don't know.

That's what you're here to figure out, remember? a little voice in the back of my head pipes up. *Battle Kimi. Get your self-discovery quest on, girl. Rawr!*

Ugh, I'm too tired to *rawr.*

Grandpa also enthusiastically shows me some tourist spots I should most definitely visit while I'm here, pointing them out in a clearly brand-new guidebook.

"Your grandmother and I have our boring old-people routines during the day," he says, his eyes sparkling again with that irresistible mischief. "I suggest you find fun young-people things to do, then come home for dinner and tell us all about your adventures." He taps a spot on one of the guidebook maps. "Maybe start with Philosopher's Path in Kyoto. Good for clearing the mind of a tired traveler, ne?"

Hmm. That *does* sound like the right place to start a quest of self-discovery.

Later, I collapse onto the futon in the guest room and pull the covers tightly around me, wrapping myself up until only my eyes are peeking out. My dad calls this "burrito-ing." It makes me feel secure and protected, although sometimes rolling over is a chore. I attempt to roll my whole burrito self over anyway, squishing into a corner of the bed. As I roll, though, I feel something weird—a lump right in the middle of the mattress. I disentangle myself from my burrito and feel around on the sheets, trying to locate this mysterious foreign object. My hand lands on something fuzzy—a stuffed animal of some kind? I pick it up and scrabble around for my phone on the nightstand. I flick on the flashlight app and hold the fuzzy thing up to my face. It *is* a stuffed animal—a tiny black and white pig with both eyes missing and a front foot that's been chewed within an inch of its life.

My heart stops beating for a moment. I *know* this pig— I've heard about this pig. It's Mom's favorite childhood stuffed animal, Meiko. She's told me the story a million times, how she couldn't take very much with her when she came to the States for school, and her parents kept telling her, "Don't worry, Meiko will be here when you get back." She assumed they'd eventually just gotten rid of Meiko, along with all the other things she was clearly never coming back for.

I realize then that I'm sleeping in my mother's childhood bedroom. And that Grandma and Grandpa have actually kept Meiko around all these years.

I cuddle the pig to my chest and burrito back up, tears pricking my eyeballs. I'm not sure what I'm crying for. Maybe for the years of misunderstandings between people who are supposed to love each other more than anything—and the fact that I'm carrying on that fine tradition by hurting my mother so much, she can't even look at me.

CHAPTER FIVE

The train to Kyoto is as packed as it was yesterday, but at least I don't have to maneuver my bulky suitcase. And I've triple-checked my phone—it's on silent. I won't be answering any rogue Skype calls.

Apparently I still need to find a way to bungle something up, though, so I get distracted and lost trying to follow the cool girl in the tiered skirt and end up on that random bench next to the food market, staring at my blank sketchbook and thinking about how I've just ruined everything with this ill-advised trip around the world.

Come on, Kimi. Think about something inspirational.

My mind wanders to that girl's tiered skirt again, and before I know it, I'm brushing my pencil over the page, drawing a longer version. I end up drawing dramatic, flowing tiers everywhere, until my creation takes up the whole page. I look up, gnawing on my lower lip, and see those beautiful cherry blossoms overhead, the sun falling on them so they look like they're sprinkled with tiny bits of light.

Hmm, there's an idea . . .

I add soft texture to my tiered skirt, making it look like

it's made of cherry blossoms. Then I flip to another page and start experimenting with drawing a dress that mimics the flow of the branch above me, giving the texture that same fluffy cherry blossom feel.

"Mochi, mochi!"

I look up and see a cute guy in an unwieldy puffy foam costume bobbing around a few feet from me.

What in the world? Does this market have some kind of . . . mascot?

The costume consists of a blobby pink sphere with holes cut out for the guy's arms, legs, and head. It has a mushy look to it, like it's been constructed out of a giant marshmallow. It's topped off with a matching pink hat affixed with comically large googly eyes that bounce around as he dances.

"Irasshaimase!" he says to some tourists passing by, raising his arms above his head and swaying his hips side to side. "Mochi, mochi!"

Oh. He's trying to get people over to a food stall selling mochi. He's supposed to *be* a giant piece of mochi.

"Why would mochi have googly eyes?" I murmur to myself, sketching a necklace made of round, mochi-like shapes on top of my cherry blossom dress. "Is it alive? Is it sentient? Have I been eating sentient mochi beings all these years and I didn't even know it?!" I make the necklace even bigger, rounder, more exaggerated.

I look up again and the guy is really getting into his dance, doing bouncy, intricate footwork and flashing major jazz hands.

"Mochiiiiiiiiii!" he sings out, like it's the chorus of a Broadway showstopper.

57

I burst into giggles. I can't help it. The whole thing is *so* ridiculous.

He whips around, distracted from his dance by my giggle (I've always had a loud, explosive giggle, I can't help it), then stumbles backward and falls to the ground. He rolls around for a moment, arms flailing, the foamy roundness of his costume making it even more difficult for him to get back up. He looks like a puppy who hasn't figured out how to use all of its limbs yet.

"Sorry!" I blurt out. I jump up from my seat, shoving my sketchbook and pens in my bag, and dash over to him—and now I'm giggling harder. "Sorry," I say again, extending a hand to help him up. I'm not sure if I'm apologizing for distracting him or laughing at him. Maybe both. "Oh, and . . . sorry, I don't know much Japanese. Which maybe means you don't understand a single word I'm saying."

"I know English," he says, giving me a thoroughly irritated look as he takes my hand. "Why are you laughing at me?"

"I . . ."

I'm suddenly at a loss for words. Because as I'm helping him up, as I'm taking in his dark eyes flashing at me with irritation, I realize three things:

1. This is the first time I've laughed—or even smiled—since I got to Japan.

2. He is *very* handsome.

3. Instead of just fantasizing about it . . . I actually did something! I made it real! I ran over here and helped him and now I'm talking to him and—

Wait. What have I just done?!

58

"Why are you laughing at me?" the cute boy repeats.

He's back on his feet now, but I'm still clasping his hand for some reason. And staring, let's not forget the *staring*. He's taller than me (I mean, most people are taller than me) and his dark eyes flash with a certain kind of intensity that pulls me right in and makes me want to stare at him more. His shaggy black hair is kind of squashed under that ridiculous googly-eyed hat, and his face is so *serious*, in direct contrast to his goofy costume. That contrast makes me want to giggle again, but I manage to stifle the laugh burbling up in my chest.

"Um, sorry, I'm Kimi," I say, pumping his hand up and down and then finally, reluctantly releasing it. I give a little bow and he does the same. "I'm visiting from America. Which doesn't actually answer your question. It's, uh . . . I just . . ." I clamp my mouth shut and sternly tell myself not to giggle. "Your dance was . . . funny. In a good way. I've never seen such a coordinated dessert before. Do all the vendors here have mascots?" I gesture around the market.

"No," he says. His stance has relaxed a bit and now he looks like he's sizing me up. I believe I detect a sliver of amusement creeping into his expression. "I suggested to my ojisan, my uncle—he owns the mochi stand over there"—he gestures to a stall in the corner of the market—"that he should try putting a more personal stamp on things. A unique spin, to really bring the customers in. Yuru-kyara—you know, mascots—are so popular in Japan they have their own festivals. But this market has not yet taken advantage, in my opinion. I thought Ojisan's mochi stand could be the first."

"Ah, yes," I say, thinking of colorful photos I've seen online of gigantic, googly-eyed baby chicks rubbing elbows with rosy-cheeked, anthropomorphized tomatoes. "So for max kawaii, you volunteered to dress up as a giant mochi?" I cock an eyebrow.

"Not volunteered," he says, one corner of his mouth quirking up. "I suggested the costume—for *someone* to wear—and then Ojisan said, 'Oh, so this is how you want to help me out this year on your spring vacation? I accept.' One of my sisters made the costume."

"And the, uh, routine?" I say, stuffing down another giggle.

"The routine," he says, "is entirely my creation."

"It's definitely an attention-getter," I say. "You totally accomplished the whole unique spin thing. And I do love the costume—very eye-catching, and well made. Of course, if I were designing it, I'd probably make a few changes . . ."

"Such as?" He crosses his arms over his chest and gives me a challenging look. Only the costume is so bulky and squishy, he can't quite cross his arms properly, and has to keep shifting around. Which takes away from any level of gravitas he might be hoping to project.

"Well . . ." I reach into my bag and pull out my sketchbook and one of my pens. I flip to a blank page and rough out a few lines. "I'd probably lose the hat. If you're going to give your mochi a face—which, by the way, raises its own set of possibly disturbing questions—I'd put it on the actual body of the costume. Otherwise, it's like, why are the eyeballs on top? And where does your human face come into this? Did the mochi eat *you*? Are we dealing with human-eating mochi here? I'd also use material that would give the body less of a rigid spherical shape—something lighter that moves with you when you're doing your dance. So you won't fall down. Even if some annoying American distracts you with her way-too-loud laugh." I've gotten more and more absorbed in my sketch as I talk, and I realize suddenly that I've started to draw this cute boy's face—flashing eyes, shaggy hair, and the ghost of a dimple that showed up briefly when he gave me that half smile—

"Um, anyway." My face flushes and I snap the sketch-book shut. "You get the idea."

Now he gives me a full smile and that dimple shows up for real. My flush deepens. *Argh.*

"Kimi from America," he says. "I'm Akira. From Japan."

"Nice to meet you," I say. "Uh, Nakamura. Is my actual last name."

He cocks an eyebrow. "Okamoto."

"Okamoto-san," I say, giving another little bow.

"Akira is fine," he says, dimpling again.

"Sorry again for the, uh, distraction. I really need to work on the volume of my laugh."

Akira cocks his head at me, grinning away. "On the contrary. I do not think you need to work on that at all."

What. Is this extremely handsome piece of mochi trying to *flirt* with me? Panic skitters through my gut like a tiny, freaked-out mouse and my flight instinct kicks into high gear. Now is the time to get out of here, while this—whatever *this* is—is still living in that space where it can be a perfect fantasy. I'll go back to my grandparents' place and dream about brushing his shaggy hair off his forehead and skimming

61

my fingertips over his ridiculously adorable dimple and skipping through this beautiful park together—

"My shift is almost over," Akira says. "What sights were you planning on seeing today, Kimi from America?"

"Oh, well, I just sort of wanted to . . . look around," I say. Ugh. This is already getting too real. I'm never this awkward in my fantasies. "I'm staying with my grandparents, not far from here. And actually, I should probably be getting back soon."

"May I walk you to the train station?" Akira says. "There is a nice scenic route through the park. I could show you some of the best spots to see the cherry blossoms. And you could advise me on further design improvements that might be made to the mochi costume."

"Well . . ."

Okay, so I *am* still kind of lost. I don't exactly know my way back to the train station. And one short walk won't completely destroy all the fantasy potential, right? After that, I never have to see him again.

And you really, really don't want to stop talking to him, a little voice pipes up in the back of my head. *His voice is so nice and deep and also you would basically murder someone just to get a look at that dimple again.*

Dammit. This little voice is starting to sound way too much like an unholy mix of Bex's dreamy romanticism and Atsuko's no-bullshit truth detector and I do not like it one bit.

"All right," I say.

He nods and grins, then gestures to his costume. "Let me go change," he says. "And I will meet you over by that bench where you were laughing at me."

"Oh, so you're not going to walk around wearing that?" I say, arching an eyebrow. "Cause, you know, that might help you attract even more customers within an even greater radius."

"No way," he says, his grin deepening into dimple territory yet again. "I don't need to give you any more reasons to laugh at me." Then he turns and heads back to his uncle's stand.

I walk back over to the bench and tilt my head up to look at the cherry blossoms again. I could still leave. Get out of here while he's changing. I'm sure I could find my way back to my grandparents' place on my own.

But as I stand there gazing up at the cherry blossoms, I realize the simple truth of the matter. That little voice in my head, the unholy mash-up of Bex/Atsuko, is right. I don't want to. I want to keep talking to him.

And yes, I would murder to see that dimple again.

Akira emerges from the mochi stand wearing black jeans, a black T-shirt with an abstract pattern of red and orange intersecting lines, and bright orange sneakers. It's a cool yet unfussy outfit and I try not to linger too long on the way the thin cotton hugs his arms—which, freed from his silly mochi costume, are very, *very* nice. I don't recall ever wanting to flat-out *stare* at someone so much. Even Theater Guy Justin, who was plenty cute and had reasonably stare-worthy arms, only provoked a few lingering glances. There were other things diverting my attention and I was fine being diverted.

Now . . . not so much.

"Hey," Akira says, giving me a little nod.

"Hey," I say. "I like your arm—*shoes*. Your *shoes* are very cool."

"Thanks," he says. "My parents think they are a bit, how do you say it . . ." He makes a gesture with his hands that seems designed to simulate a big movie-type explosion. "But I told them they will never have to worry about losing me in a crowd."

"Ah." I laugh—my loud, explosive giggle spilling out of me yet again. "My mom's an artist, so she understands my need to wear stuff that's on the dramatic side. Or sometimes on the just plain weird side."

"Which side is this on?" he says, gesturing to my ensemble.

"It's on the side that makes me confident enough to navigate international travel," I say. "Though I haven't been doing super well with that so far."

I instantly regret saying that. Akira is still a stranger, after all—no matter how cute his dimple is or how nice his arms are—and he really doesn't need to know the depth of the angst I was allowing myself to get all tied up in before I sat down and started sketching. I'm preparing about a zillion quippy remarks that will somehow brush aside what I just said, but he just cocks an amused, slightly intrigued eyebrow and holds something out to me.

"For you," he says. "It's our most popular item with tourists."

I peer down at the item in his hand. It's a perfect piece of green mochi—matcha-flavored, most likely—with a perfect strawberry perched on top.

"Oh, thank you," I say, taking it from him. I take a small bite, suddenly self-conscious because he's watching me, trying to gauge my enjoyment. I guess now the staring shoe is on the other foot. Or maybe . . . the other eyeball?

In any case, my self-consciousness melts away as soon as the mochi hits my tongue. That irresistible chewiness, that delicate sweetness, contrasts wonderfully with the firm, bold burst of strawberry. "Wow," I say, my eyes widening. "That is an absolutely perfect bite."

"I'm glad you like it," he says, smiling. "Now would you like to walk through the park? You need to go to the train station, ne?"

"Yes," I say, remembering the supposed purpose of our little jaunt. "Which is . . ." I try to subtly turn my body in what I think is the right direction. Akira gives me a funny look.

"In the other direction?" he says, turning to face the exact opposite way I'm standing.

"Right, of course," I say. I hastily pop the rest of the strawberry-mochi concoction in my mouth, marveling again at the flavors bursting on my tongue. "Like I said, I haven't been doing too well with all the navigating."

God, shut up, Kimi.

"I can navigate for both of us," Akira says. "This way."

We stroll under a canopy of cherry blossoms and I can't help but stare up at them—I love the way the branches intersect through all the pink and white fluff, threads of darkness

Stop for Monday

that make the overall beauty more complex. I'm already picturing adding that element to the dress I was sketching, perhaps by giving some structure to the bodice—

"Oi, watch out, Kimi from America!" Akira exclaims. My head jerks down and I realize we're stepping onto a small stone bridge that arches over a little pond. It's just a baby step up, but I'm so preoccupied by the cherry blossoms above me that I miss it and trip. Akira grabs my elbow, supporting me. "I've got you!" he says, helping me navigate the last of the nefarious step.

"Whoa, sorry! I mean, thank you," I say, giving him a grateful smile. The warmth from his hand on my elbow lingers, even as he lets me go. My gaze lands on our surroundings—the stone of the bridge has an aged look to it, old water stains coupled with moss growing up its sides. Its graceful arched shape is punctuated by squat columns topped off with peaked domes that look a bit like cupcakes or maybe mushroom caps. The water below reflects so many trees, it looks green. And it's all so peaceful, tranquil—the direct opposite of the bustling market we walked from. "Wow," I say, stopping at the edge of the bridge to peer down into the water. "This is so . . . untouched. It looks like something out of a fairy tale."

"You don't have ponds in America?" Akira says, his voice laced with light teasing.

"We do," I say, giving him an eye roll. "But where I live—Culver City, which is sorta kinda part of LA—things are always a little . . . louder."

"Los Angeles," he says, nodding thoughtfully. "Do you know any movie stars?"

"No," I say, and now it's my turn to be amused. "I mean, that's a common misconception, but—"

"I'm joking," he says.

"Oh," I manage, my face flushing. Wow, my turn was over so quickly.

"Do you want to sit for a minute?" he says, gesturing to a nearby bench. "Spend a moment in the not-loud place?"

"Okay." Somewhere in between gazing up at the cherry blossoms and tripping and almost falling on my face, I seem to have stopped trying to get to the train station—and to end this ill-advised encounter—as quickly as possible. I must be *really* compelled by the Power of the Dimple.

We step off the bridge and sit down on the bench, which is shaded by yet another beautiful canopy of cherry blossoms.

"So what do you do when you're not hanging out with movie stars and laughing at people in goofy costumes?" Akira says.

"Oh, well, I'm . . ." Dangit. Before I would have said: *I'm an artist.* It would have fallen off my tongue as easily as *I'm a human.* But now I don't feel like I can lay claim to that—and I *chose* not to, didn't I? Blew up my life because I didn't want to paint anymore but couldn't seem to figure out what was next. "I'm . . . working on it."

"Hmm. A mystery. And you want me to crack the case, I see." Akira nods thoughtfully. "I will figure this out, Kimi from America—I have picked up many excellent detective skills from American mystery shows. My mom loves the one with the really handsome guy who wears a trench coat and lives on a boat or something?"

"That . . . could actually be a few of them," I say. "But I'm not trying to hide anything, I'm just in the process of figuring myself out."

"Ah," he says. "So you are a mystery even to yourself. Very interesting. Well, what do you enjoy? Drawing?" He taps my bag. "The mochi costume you drew for me was very good."

"Thank you," I say. "Yes, I suppose I enjoy drawing. Though lately I haven't been drawing much of anything. Except clothes."

His brow furrows. "Clothes are something, ne? Or are you saying clothes are not a thing that exist in the world?"

"No, clothes . . . exist. Of course they do," I say. "But I mean, drawing clothes is just a silly thing I do, for fun. It's not important."

He leans forward, resting his elbows on his knees, and regards me keenly. There's that intensity flashing through his eyes again. He holds my gaze and I can't look away.

"If it's not important, why do you do it?"

"Well, not everything we do in life is important, right?" I say, twisting my hands together. "Some things are just . . ." I make a hand-wavey gesture, which just makes his brow furrow further. "I mean, is dressing up as a giant piece of mochi and dancing around in front of your ojisan's stand important?" I try to make my tone light.

His expression softens a bit. "Yes, it is," he says, his mouth quirking into a half smile. "I'm helping Ojisan grow his mochi empire, one customer at a time. Who knows how many people I've tempted over with my moves." He does a little hip wiggle on the bench and I giggle. Then he taps my

68

bag again. "Can I see some of these completely unimportant drawings?"

"Well . . . if you insist," I say, pulling out my sketchbook. I have the sudden, bizarre need to show him just how inconsequential my fashion scribbles are. If he sees them, maybe he'll get that they're a mere distraction, diverting me from the journey of self-discovery I'm supposed to be on.

I flip the sketchbook open to the page I was drawing earlier, the fluffy cherry blossom dress and chunky necklace made out of mochi shapes.

"I was getting inspiration from our surroundings," I say, gesturing upward to the cherry blossoms. "And I like to contrast shapes and materials. So this dress would be very light—almost like clouds, floating around your body—and the necklace would be heavy and solid. Maybe made out of some kind of polished stone."

"Ah, like this?" Akira says, tapping the rock ring I'm wearing on my index finger.

"Exactly," I say. "Only bigger. Bolder. But the point is, that contrast between light and heavy, soft and hard, makes for an interesting overall look. Just like the contrast between mochi and strawberry makes for an interesting bite."

"I see," Akira says. "And where would you wear this?"

"A party," I say immediately. "But not just any party—a special, fancy-but-not-too-snooty party. I imagine something like . . . I don't know, my friend Atsuko is being honored for her achievements as an advice columnist. Maybe we're a little older and she's working at some fancy magazine and they're throwing her this party . . ." I close my eyes, picturing it. "The desserts are all cute and tiny. Like little bite-sized

69

ice cream sandwiches in a rainbow of pastel colors. There are these sort of chiffon streamers draped everywhere and twinkle lights strung across the ceiling so it looks like we're in a fantasy wonderland. Like a freakin' unicorn could come galloping through at any moment."

"And you are wearing this dress," Akira says.

I open my eyes and beam at him. "Yes. I'm wearing this dress and maybe I've designed dresses along a similar theme for Atsuko and Bex—that's our other best friend—and everyone's having a great time and I'm just so proud of Atsuko. It's a perfect moment."

"Hmm." Akira studies my drawing again. "And you think all of this is somehow . . . unimportant?"

"Not exactly," I say, running my fingertips over the sketch of the dress. "But . . ." I flash back to my argument with my mother. "Drawing endless outfits and having endless fantasies about them isn't exactly something I can build a career on. So I'm trying to figure out what I *can* build a career on. I need to figure out where my future lies."

I meet his eyes. This is the first time I've vocalized what I'm actually doing here in Japan—you know, outside of my own head. And it feels unexpectedly good to say those words out loud, like I'm unzipping a too-tight dress after a night of not quite being able to breathe.

I expect him to ask more questions, but he's studying me intently again, like he's trying to figure something out. I shift uncomfortably.

"What about you?" I say, breaking the awkward silence. "What do you like to do? Besides perform as anthropomorphized food."

"I like eating," he says, grinning. "Playing video games. Exploring new places. And I'm hoping to become a doctor one day. I will be starting my studies in the fall, after I graduate high school."

"What, really?!" I exclaim, another giggle spilling out of me.

"Laughing at me again?" he says, looking perplexed.

"No, I'm sorry—again," I say. "It's just . . . most Asian American kids' parents dream of them becoming doctors. And most of us run away from that as fast as we can. I remember Atsuko telling me I was lucky that my mom 'only' expected me to become a world-famous artist who's a credit to Asian Americans everywhere. So to hear someone say that's what they *want* to do . . ." I shake my head in wonder. "Did your parents pressure you at all?"

"No," he says, still perplexed. "I've always been—how do you say it?—*attracted* to the very odd science of how the body works. When I was younger, I discovered this old set of medical texts at a secondhand shop. I didn't understand any of the words, really, but there were some . . . well, honestly, pretty disgusting diagrams relating to all the things that can go horribly wrong inside of us." He gives me a sheepish grin. "I was fascinated."

"That's so cool," I say, grinning back at him. "And, you know, being a doctor is like the most important profession there is. Your future is *set*."

"I suppose," he says, cocking an eyebrow. "But I don't think it's necessarily more important than anything else."

"Saving lives and stuff? Oh, it is. It *definitely* is," I say, hopping to my feet. "You'll be a credit to your family, your country, your generation—pretty much everything some-body can be a credit to."

Something about this exchange is making me itchy and I can't put my finger on what it is. On the other hand, it's not necessarily a *bad* itch, an unwelcome itch . . . ugh, what am I thinking? What the hell would constitute a "good" itch?! "I should be getting back," I say. "So . . . the train station?"

"Yes," he says, getting to his feet. "This way."

We walk through even more impossibly beautiful nature, Akira pointing out various mini-sights and points of interest as we go. Something about him puts me on edge and makes me at ease at the same time. I guess that's what I mean by a "good itch." I simultaneously want to run away and continue talking to him for as long as possible.

It makes no sense.

"Ah, and here we have perhaps the most important sight in all of Maruyama Park," Akira says, making an expansive gesture.

"The tree?" I say, my brow furrowing. "But there are tons of trees. What makes this one special?"

"Look below the tree," he says.

And I do. That's when I see what he must be talking about: an odd little stuffed creature wearing a purple-and-white haori, staring out at the world in semi-indignant fash-ion. He's not quite cuddly enough to be a legit stuffed animal and not quite creepy enough to be taxidermy. He's been placed there in the grass so he blends in with the park—if you were in a hurry, you'd probably mistake him for an actual critter and bustle right by.

"Is that a raccoon?!" I exclaim, laughing a little. "He's so freakin' cute!"

"A tanuki," Akira says. "Which is sort of like a Japanese raccoon dog."

"Who put that there?" I say, moving closer to get a better look.

"No one knows," Akira says. "He just appeared one day. All part of his charm."

"Adorable. I love how he looks like he has such an attitude—like he's totally offended by our presence or something."

"If you pay him proper tribute, he will give you advice about your future."

"What, really?!" I squawk. "I *need* advice about my future! How do I pay proper tribute?"

"Close your eyes," Akira says. "And clear your mind of all thoughts. Except the tanuki. Think only of the tanuki . . ."

"Got it." I squeeze my eyes shut and allow the stuffed tanuki's indignant furry face to fill my brain.

"Focus on him," Akira says, his voice deathly serious. "Focus on his greatness. His wisdom. The tanuki knows all."

"The tanuki knows all," I murmur.

"I think he's sending you a message," Akira says. "I'm getting it loud and clear."

"Really? Why is he sending it to you and not me—"

"He has a very clear view of your future, if you just do this one thing—"

"What is it?! Tell me!"

"The tanuki absolutely, one hundred percent thinks you should—"

"What?!"

"Give Akira your phone number."

My eyes fly open and I can't stop myself from punching him on the arm.

"What?!?" I explode. "I'm pretty sure the tanuki did *not* say that."

"Okay, maybe not," Akira says. "But it is still a good idea, ne?"

He gives me a full-on smile, his dimple firing on all cylinders.

I get that feeling again, that weird little itch—that *good* itch. And I can't help but smile back.

CHAPTER SIX

I wish I could talk to my friends.

That tiny thought bursts the fizzy, itchy bubble I'm in after parting ways with Akira. I ended up giving him my phone number and I can't tell if I really hope he'll text or I really hope he won't. I should be doing my usual thing, retreating into whatever fantasy I can make up about this boy with the perfect dimple and the strangely endearing obsession with old medical textbooks. But instead, I find myself just wanting to talk to him again. I crave that little burst of pleasure I got when he touched my arm . . . and I'm also afraid to feel it ever again.

Once again: None of this makes any sense.

Atsuko would give me some no-nonsense advice that cuts right to the heart of the matter. And Bex would probably just start planning our wedding, which maybe wouldn't exactly be helpful, but would at least make me laugh.

But I of course *can't* talk to them since our last interaction involved me hanging up on them in the midst of an argument that's entirely my fault. I heave a big, dramatic sigh as I trudge up to my grandparents' house.

"Kimiko-chan?" my grandmother's voice calls from the backyard. "Is that you?"

"Um, yes!" I call back, jumping a little. Well, now I know where my mother inherited her terrifyingly preternatural sense of hearing. Mom has the uncanny ability to pick up when you're passing by a room or shifting around in your seat or most especially when you're doing something wrong—or even just thinking about it.

I detour myself around to the back of my grandparents' house, following the sound of my grandmother's voice. I find her rooting around in her vegetable plot, her brow furrowed in ferocious concentration. I take a moment to admire her impressively giant sun hat. She doesn't look up when I shuffle into view and I briefly wonder if I imagined her calling out to me.

The backyard area of my grandparents' place is sprawling yet contained—the vegetable plot boasts at least a dozen rows of plants, neatly lined up like little green soldiers. The far left corner of the garden has a sectioned-off spot for a flower bed, which has bloomed in pink and red and yellow. I'm struck by how no space is wasted, but it doesn't look cluttered or messy. It looks like there's a *system*—though possibly a system only my grandmother can decipher.

Obaasan doesn't appear to be trying to engage me in any further conversation. But maybe if I just give her a minute to warm up to me, we'll be well on our way to bonding. I spy a small, rickety-looking wooden bench in the far left corner of the vegetable plot, so I shuffle my way over there, sit down, and take a moment to gaze out at the countryside. There are so many different shades of green, all juxtaposed against each other—it reminds me of how powerful a single color can be when you look at all its variations. In a way, every color has the potential to be its own little rainbow, and my fingers itch for my sketchbook, imagining how I'd bring that concept to life—I can see it as a sort of ombré effect, cascading over a full, flowing skirt. All of this green is dotted with the thatched roofs and gardens of other families who live in this little town. The peacefulness feels in direct opposition to the bustle of the market at Maruyama Park, and I allow it to soothe me for a moment.

"It's so beautiful," I murmur, almost to myself.

My grandmother turns and looks at me quizzically.

"Everything about this area is so beautiful," I say to her, feeling self-conscious underneath the weight of her piercing stare. "And your garden—wow. I love how many different things you're able to grow. I'm bad at growing anything—I mean, I somehow managed to murder the supposedly indestructible algae plant I was supposed to be studying for Bio, but even I can see there's a good variety of veggies going on here."

My cheeks heat as my babbling intensifies, but I can't seem to stop chattering. My grandmother's stony stare makes me feel like I have to keep talking until I get some kind of reaction out of her.

"Anyway," I say, forcing myself to wrap it up. "Your garden is really lovely."

"It is too small," she says, waving a hand and going back to her vegetables. "We can only manage a few crops at a time."

"Oh, well, clearly you've made those thrive," I say, struggling to find something that will net me even a modicum of approval. I feel like I'm grasping at random straws, desperate for something that will stick. "And, uh, I love your sun hat."

"Mmm, I need to replace it," she says, without turning around. "It is getting old—not protecting my eyes as it used to."

I'm pretty much striking out in every possible way here. I have the sudden wild urge to try asking her about Akira and all my weird, confusing feelings. But if I can't even make headway talking about her garden, I don't know why I think gossiping with her about boys is an option.

"Do you need any help?" I try instead. "With the gardening?"

"Didn't you just say you are bad at growing things?" she responds.

Good point. Funny how I came here to escape my mother's all-consuming disappointment, only to have it replaced with this thread of disapproval that feels just as potent. But what could I have possibly done to disappoint my grandmother? I've barely been here twenty-four hours.

Once again: I really wish I could talk to my friends.

"See you at dinner?" I say to my grandmother as I stand, gathering my things. She gives a sort of grunt in response, not looking up from her intense weeding.

I shuffle into my grandparents' house, shoving down another big, dramatic sigh. I don't *deserve* a big, dramatic sigh. It is, after all, my own fault I have no one to talk to.

"Kimiko-chan?" my grandfather says.

I turn and see him sitting at the table in the middle of

the living room, which is positioned by a big window that looks out into the garden.

"Oh, hi, Ojiisan," I say, forcing a smile.

"Come, sit," he says. "We will have dinner soon."

I cross the room and settle on a tatami mat at the table. The main living room in my grandparents' place is an open space sectioned off by shoji screens, giving it a soft, relaxing vibe.

Grandpa has a bunch of little plastic pieces of something spread out on the tabletop—there appear to be a few wheels? A gear or two?

"I like building the model trains," Grandpa says, anticipating my question. "But we don't have space to display a big collection, ne? So I take them apart when I am done. And then go back to the beginning and build them all over again." He cackles to himself, like that's a pretty funny joke.

I can't help but smile. "You don't get bored?"

"I get *better*," he corrects, picking up a tiny wheel and rapping it against the table. "I've built this one three times and I get faster every time. Soon, I'll be able to build it in five seconds."

"Amazing," I say, my smile widening. My gaze wanders to the window and to my grandmother, who's still digging through her garden with gusto. "Wow, Obaasan's working hard out there."

"She can never do anything less," my grandfather says with a chuckle. He picks up a piece of model train, snaps the wheel onto it, then scrutinizes his handiwork. "Did your mother ever tell you about how your grandmother and I ended up with this house?"

"No," I say. "She doesn't, um, talk about you guys very much."

"Ah." His smile is tinged with more than a little sadness. "I suppose this is understandable. Ano . . . let me share with you, then." He begins clicking other pieces of his train together—the sound is oddly meditative. "Your obaasan was the younger of two children—her older brother was supposed to inherit this house and the family farm that came with it. But he never showed interest. He was always going off and doing other things, trying to find something that would make him money very fast. Eventually he lost contact with the family entirely. Your obaasan, on the other hand, was always here. She loved the land, growing things. She stood up to her father—who had very traditional ideas about things—and made a case for taking over the farm herself. He wanted to try everything he could to track down her brother instead. But . . ." My grandfather smiles to himself as he painstakingly fits the tiny pieces of the train together. ". . . she was very persistent. As she usually is. She fought to make this place her home."

So much pure love shines through in his every word, my chest warms.

"And you moved in here when you got married?" I say.

"Hai, hai," he says, his smile widening. "But I did not work on the farm. I already had a job I loved, doing maintenance for Japan Railways—the Japanese railroad."

"That's where you developed your train fandom, isn't it?" I exclaim, feeling an unexpected surge of delight at uncovering this factoid.

"Sou da ne," he agrees. "I have always been fascinated

80

by all things relating to the railroad. Even when I was a boy. I believe your obaasan and I were attracted to each other because we both had very distinctive passions in life."

"So what happened to the farm?" I say, gesturing out the window. "Because Mom did mention you guys had a farm, and the crops Obaasan still takes care of out there are super impressive, but I always imagined it being bigger."

"It used to be," my grandfather says. "We ended up selling most of the surrounding land and keeping what your grandmother could maintain. As we got older and did not have any, hmm, eto . . ." He trails off for a moment, frowning at the half-assembled train in his hand. "Well, having a bigger farm made less sense. The money from selling the land helped us continue to live here, near Kyoto. And to be comfortable. Comfortable enough to send our granddaughter a plane ticket, for instance."

He gives me a slight smile and I smile back—but I can sense some of the things he's leaving unsaid. Not only were he and Obaasan getting older, they must have eventually accepted they didn't have any family to pass the house down to. They probably always expected Mom to take over the farm. And then she went in a totally different direction.

A tangled mess of emotions snarls through my chest. That familiar sadness that filled my heart last night, when I discovered Meiko. A melancholy over bonds so broken, they can never be mended. But weirdly, little sparks of joy and curiosity are part of that big tangle, too. Hearing about my grandparents and all the colorful details of their past gives me a bit of that strangely pleasant itch I felt with Akira. I'm dying to hear more and I'm also afraid to hear more, because getting more of my family story disrupts everything I've always known. There's a void in my understanding of my own history—a void I didn't fully realize existed until this moment, sitting here and picturing Mom's life before she came to the States. The life she barely ever talks about.

"Kimiko-chan, you should not be afraid to speak about your mother around us," my grandfather says, as if reading my thoughts. "I know your grandmother can seem . . . hmm, I'm not sure what the word is, eto . . . like a wall? But I believe she really does want to know about how your mother is doing."

"Really?" I say, my voice tiny. "I don't want to upset her. I remember the times when she and Mom have tried to talk on the phone. Well, mostly I just remember a lot of yelling from my side."

"Sou, sou," my grandfather says, a ghost of a smile passing over his lips. "That is just . . . how they are with each other. I do not think it would be as bad if they talked to each other more often. Or talked to each other at all—it has been a while. But it's hard for both of them to let go of things that have been said in the past."

"What about you?" I say, fiddling with a tiny plastic gear thingy. "You don't seem to be as . . . upset. About Mom. I mean, you even asked me about her last night."

I bite my lip, hoping I haven't overstepped. But my ojiisan just smiles again. "I wrote your mother a number of letters over the years. I never sent any of them. But they helped me realize I was angry with her for not following a path *I* had laid out for her. Her own path was meant to be different, ne?"

"You never sent them?" I say, stuck on this tidbit. "But why?"

"Your grandmother, ah, communicated enough anger for both of us," he says, clicking more pieces of his model train together. "I did not need to add on top of it. The act of writing the letters was clarifying for me—that was enough."

"Huh," I say, turning this over in my mind.

Grandpa snaps the last piece of the model train in place and hands it to me. "There," he says. "You see? I put this one together faster than I ever have. You can keep if you like."

"Thank you," I say. "But don't you want to take it apart again?"

"I do not think so," he says, waving a hand. "It looks good the way it is."

I smile, studying the tiny gears and bits of plastic that make up this minuscule vehicle. "Can you excuse me for a moment, Ojiisan? There's something I want to do before dinner."

It actually takes me until *after* dinner to work up the nerve, but I finally do. My heart hammers in my chest as I type the email address for Atsuko's advice column, Ask Atsuko, into the appropriate field. Unlike my ojiisan, I *am* going to send this letter, silly as it may be.

I start with an apology and explain why I chickened out and didn't tell my friends anything before I left. I try to convey how overwhelmed I was—how overwhelmed I still am.

I mention that I've met a boy who I really want to talk to more and am also scared to talk to more. I ask if the brilliant, insightful, totally famous Ask Atsuko has any advice on that front? Then I close by saying that even if she doesn't have any advice . . . well, I'd just really like to talk to her. To apologize face-to-face. I ask her to please show this letter to Bex, too. Then I hit "send."

Five minutes later, my phone buzzes.

Skype again, but this time I hit "answer" with gusto. And, you know, on purpose.

"Kimi!" Atsuko shrieks. She and Bex are both onscreen and I nearly burst into tears.

"Wait!" I yelp. "Isn't it obscenely early over there?"

"It is!" Bex exclaims. "But we're up early for our big Temescal Canyon hike."

"Yes, I don't think I saw the part about 'obscenely early' on the schedule spreadsheet," Atsuko says, giving Bex a vaguely accusatory look. "Anyway, we got your email and before we set off to conquer this hiking trail like the bold adventurers we are, we need to hear everything about this boy."

"But I need to apologize first!" I insist. "I'm so, so sorry. I love you guys so much and I'm sorry I hurt you and flaked out on all our plans, I just don't know what I'm doing right now—"

"Kimi, it's fine," Atsuko says with a hand-wave. "Asian Mom Math stipulates that the fallout from any Asian Mom Fight is terrible and all-consuming and may temporarily impair the judgment of the participants."

"We just wish you felt like you could talk to us about it," Bex says. "We're always here for you, you know?"

"Same—and thank you," I say, a warm glow blooming in my chest.

"Now tell us about the boy," Atsuko demands.

"Tell us everything!" Bex exclaims.

"His name is Akira," I say. "He has a cute dimple and he wants to be a doctor—like, actually *wants* to be one, no parental pressure required—and when I first saw him, he was dressed as a giant piece of mochi."

"Whoa," Atsuko says, holding up a hand. "Please go back to the very beginning and don't leave out a single detail. Let's start with the mochi."

So I do. I tell them the whole story of our afternoon, from mochi to tanuki.

"That's so cute!" Bex screams when I'm done, clapping a hand to her chest and pretending to swoon.

Atsuko casts a sidelong glance at her, then refocuses on me, her eyes shrewd. "So what happens next?" she says. Her tone is low and measured and doesn't give away even a scrap of what she's thinking, which is maddening.

"I don't know," I say, throwing up my hands. "I mean, part of me—like eighty percent—wants to keep this in fantasyland and never talk to him again rather than risk . . ." I trail off, gnawing at my lower lip.

"Risk what?" Atsuko prods.

"Risk actually liking him," I admit. "Because that's what will happen if we hang out again, I'm pretty sure. But then I'll have to leave in two weeks and who knows when I'm coming back here, maybe never, so what's the point? It's like dooming a relationship to fail before it even starts. And anyway, I shouldn't be letting myself get distracted from the purpose of my visit, which is to figure out my future and stuff now that I've totally tanked the whole important Asian American artist thing."

"Oh, Kimi." Atsuko shakes her head, a hint of amusement creeping into her expression. "First of all, I'm going to tell you something, and it will likely come as a big shock—but I need you to listen up." She leans in close, her face deathly serious, and sounds out each word. "You. Already. Like. Him."

"What!" I yelp. "I do *not*. I barely know him! I—"

"You've already internalized all kinds of tiny observational details about him," Atsuko says. "The dimple, the arms, the intense looks he keeps giving you that make you all swoony. Give it up, because that ship has sailed."

"Saaaaaaaaillllllled!" Bex sings out.

"And you want to hang out with him again because he challenges you," Atsuko continues. "He doesn't respond to stuff the way you think he will and that means you can't conjure up some fake-o fantasy version of him. You are . . ." She gives me a sly smile. ". . . *stimulated* by his real-life presence. That's the 'good itch' you're feeling, my friend." She shakes her head, amused. "Honestly, Kimi. You can be so KY."

"KY?" I sputter.

"Japanese slang—kuuki yomenai. It means you're clueless in certain situations. You literally 'can't read the air,'" she says, cackling. "You know, if you'd actually told us about your visit, I could have schooled you on—"

"Okay, okay. Back to the good itch situation. What do I do about it?" I grumble. There are a ton of things I want to fight her on, but somehow I know I'm not going to win this argument. "What does the great and powerful Ask Atsuko have to say?"

"Here's your official Ask Atsuko decree," Atsuko says, nodding sagely. "Hang out with him again. Try not to think about how this possible relationship has a limited shelf life. And Kimi . . ." She leans in close again, her face nearly taking up the whole screen. "Have *fun*. My god. You just met a cute guy who engaged in tanuki-related subterfuge to get your freaking phone number."

"And you already like him!" Bex shrieks.

I cover my face with my hands. I want to respond with some clever quip, but all I can manage is: "Blargh."

"Fun-having will totally *help* you figure out your future," Atsuko says. "Because you won't be obsessing over it and thinking about it and running your thought spirals into the ground. It's like how I usually come up with my best advice responses when I'm in the shower, *not* thinking about my column. My brain is relaxed and open and the right advice just comes to me."

"I guess I could try that," I say, gnawing on my thumbnail.

"That's the spirit," Bex says, laughing. "We have to head out to meet Shelby for our hike now, Kimi, but please let us know the *minute* you've made further contact with Akira."

"I will," I say. "I promise. Oh god, I miss you guys so much."

"Miss you, too!" Atsuko says, blowing me a noisy kiss.

And then they blink out of sight. I let out a deep, cleansing breath. Just hearing their voices, seeing their faces, makes me feel better. Even if I'm not yet totally convinced of Ask Atsuko's "have fun!" decree.

I'm just about to set my phone down when it buzzes again. I glance at the screen, wondering if Atsuko and Bex forgot to tell me something. But no—it's a new text from a number I don't recognize.

Konbanwa. This is the tanuki.

That little series of bubbles appears underneath the text, indicating another one is forthcoming.

Just kidding, it's Akira.

I can't help the smile that's already spreading over my face.

Do you want to explore a new and exciting tourist site tomorrow?

More bubbles.

With me. In case that wasn't clear.

Dammit. Now my smile is ear to ear and there's nothing I can do to stop it.

You. Already. Like. Him, Atsuko says in my head. *Have fun.*

I take a deep breath and type back a single word.

Okay.

CHAPTER SEVEN

Akira has taken me to a magical wonderland. I'm not even exaggerating.

"Wooooooooooow," I breathe out, craning my neck to get a better view of the soaring stalks of pure green surrounding us.

We've just entered the bamboo forest of Arashiyama, which, according to my grandfather, is one of the most famous sights in the world. He was very excited to hear I'd be visiting today and requested a full report later.

"Like another world, ne?" Akira says, gesturing toward the bamboo that's all around us. "This is what I thought of when you were describing the imaginary party where you would wear your dress. I know it's not exactly the same, but—"

"—but I'm still expecting a freakin' unicorn to make an appearance," I say, grinning at him.

"Let's keep walking," he says, nodding at the path ahead of us. "And keep our eyes out for unicorns."

We walk, and I try to balance moving forward with my desire to just keep looking up, up, up. The bamboo stalks are impossibly tall, enclosing us in a soothing sea of green punctuated only by patches of gorgeous, hazy sunlight glinting through. Wind rustles through the bamboo and it's as if it's whispering to us, revealing all its secrets. I feel sheltered, protected. Like I've entered a beautiful, otherworldly pod where time has stopped, and all my problems have melted away. The path in front of us looks endless, like this beautiful sanctuary just keeps going forever. It's kind of like being burritoed up in my cozy blanket—only on a way larger scale.

A burst of giggles disrupts my peaceful thought train and my head snaps down to see a group of girls dressed in beautiful, brightly colored yukata, snapping a group selfie. My eyes drink in the gorgeous floral prints, the elaborate obi tying their garments together. There are bright pinks and blues, greens and golds. Extremely contrasting prints that look impossibly beautiful layered against each other. Seeing this bold rainbow splashed against the soft green of the bamboo strikes a chord deep in my heart—I can't explain it, but I feel a sudden and undeniable bond of connection snap into place. For the first time since arriving in Japan, I recognize a little piece of my soul residing in its unfamiliar landscape.

"Kimi?" Akira says. "Are you all right?"

I force myself to turn from the girls and look at him quizzically.

"You are . . . ah . . ." He points to one of his eyes, then trails a finger down his cheek.

"Oh!" I realize then that my eyes have filled with tears. I hastily wipe them away. I don't know how to even begin to explain why this sight is moving me so much.

"Is this giving you ideas?" Akira continues, nodding in the girls' direction. "For drawing more clothes?" His mouth

90

quirks into a smile. "So many ideas, you cannot keep track of them? Is that why you are upset?"

"Yes," I say immediately. "I mean . . . no. I mean . . . yes, it's giving me *so* many ideas. My brain is actually kind of bursting right now. But I'm not upset, I'm . . ." I trail off, trying to find the right words. "I've always loved kimono and yukata—the colors, the shape." I swoon a little. "I love the contrasting patterns the obi usually have, too—so bold."

"Like the contrast you were talking about with your fantasy dress yesterday," Akira says. "Contrast in shape, contrast in colors."

"Exactly. I actually have a kimono and obi that used to belong to my mom—she gave them to me when I turned fifteen. The kimono is this really vivid red with white flowers and the obi is this gorgeous orange with gold embroidery. Red and orange aren't usually colors that people think of as going together—especially in those bright shades and especially with such elaborate prints on top of them."

Akira's brow furrows. "Why not?"

"You know, I'm not sure," I say, laughing. "I just remember posting a photo of myself from Obon Fest in the whole getup—and having this clique of supposedly trendy white girls from my school ask me why I was wearing 'clashing' colors." I smile at the colorful gaggle of girls across the way, who are still posing for selfies. "Watching them over there, having so much fun in all their beautiful, supposedly clashing colors—it makes me feel, I don't know . . . emotional, somehow."

Akira cocks his head, studying me, and I feel instantly self-conscious.

"I haven't had a whole lot of occasions to wear the kimono outside of Obon Fest, though," I say quickly, attempting to steer us back to more casual territory.

"Why not create an occasion?" Akira says, a smile playing over his lips. "It could be as simple as walking with your friends through a bamboo grove."

"I'll remember that," I say, laughing a little. "But I'm pretty sure we don't have any bamboo groves like *this* at home. Mom would definitely have taken me."

"Your mother is Japanese—from Japan?" he says. "I'm sorry, is that the right way to say it?"

"She is Japanese from Japan," I say, smiling at him. "My dad is Japanese, too, but Japanese American—four generations in. So I'm both Nisei and Gosei, which should be confusing, but somehow isn't."

"How did your parents meet?" he asks.

"At college—UCLA," I say. "That's one of the big schools in LA. Mom got a scholarship to study art—painting. And her parents allowed her to go, but only if she also learned some kind of practical trade she could use when she returned to their farm just outside of Kyoto. They didn't love the whole art thing, but I think they believed it was just a phase— something she'd get out of her system. They didn't have a ton of money, so Mom decided she was also going to take business courses—I guess with the idea that she'd be able to help Obaasan and Ojiisan run the farm way better. But things didn't exactly work out that way."

I've heard this story so many times, it has the feel of legend. Of course, after talking to my grandfather, it feels like the legend is shifting a little—becoming more blurry and shaded with different tones of gray. Still, my voice takes on a hushed, reverent quality as I talk—which, come to think of it, seems pretty appropriate for this beautiful bamboo grove. "She met my dad and they fell madly in love."

"Ah," Akira says, nodding. "And let me guess: This did not sit well with your mother's parents, ne? They disapproved?"

"Oh, did they ever." I cock an eyebrow. "They disapproved *so hard*. Especially when Mom and Dad got married and had a baby before they'd even graduated."

"The baby—this is you!" Akira exclaims, pointing at me.

"This is me," I agree.

"I told you, my detective skills are excellent," he says with a wink.

"Anyway," I say, rolling my eyes at him. "Somehow, they made it work. Mom held down a secretarial job during the day and took online graphic design courses at night while my dad got his restaurant off the ground. She even tried to help my grandparents and their farm out with some of the stuff she'd learned in her business classes—but my grandma really, really didn't want to hear it. She felt like Mom ruined her whole life." I pause, feeling a pang of sympathy for my grandmother—something I've never felt when I've told this story before. "And my parents raised me in between all that," I finish. "Against all the odds, they made it work." Somewhere in the midst of me relating my origin story, we've stopped in front of one particularly majestic stalk of bamboo. I gaze upward, following the flickers of sunlight playing through all the green. God, it's gorgeous. I wonder if I could create a textile with a pattern that mimicked that?

"Your parents sound cool," Akira says.

"They are," I say, my voice soft. I'm still gazing up at that flicker of light. "Honestly, I don't know how Mom did it—I think there were a few years of her life where she just didn't sleep. She's a total badass. Oh, that's a slang term—"

"You are afraid I'll think you're referring to an actual ass that is bad?" Akira gives me an amused look. "I know 'badass,' Kimi from America." He gives me finger-guns.

"American detective shows," we say in unison and then burst out laughing. I realize I feel light, buoyant—I am actually sticking to my Ask Atsuko directive to have fun. Talking to Akira is so . . . I'm not sure what the word for it is. I wouldn't say "easy." It's more like I'm getting used to the good itch. I'm enjoying it, even. I guess Atsuko would say I'm "stimulated."

Whatever the case: I feel like I can tell him anything.

"It sounds like you admire your mom a lot," Akira says. "Like she is your superhero."

"She is. And she understands me better than anyone." And just like that, my mother's disappointed face flashes through my mind and her words echo through my head: *I feel like I don't know you at all*. My light, fizzy feeling deflates. I stare up at those little flickers of sunlight again and try to brush the thought aside. "What about you?" I say, trying to direct our conversation elsewhere. "Any badass superheroes in your family?"

"My ojisan," he says.

I turn to face him. "The one who owns the mochi stand?"

"Yes. He started that stand from nothing. He's always made mochi from scratch for our whole family. We'd get together before New Year's and he'd try to show us how to do it so we would have a big batch for Oshogatsu."

"Ah, my dad makes mochi for my parents' Oshogatsu party, too!" I exclaim.

"Perhaps he would have been a better teacher than Ojisan," Akira says, smiling ruefully. "He would always get upset with us for not doing it correctly—apparently, there is some *very particular* technique no one could get. No one except him. He was determined that every single piece would be perfect, so we would always end up redoing the whole batch several times."

"Doesn't seem terribly efficient," I say with a laugh. "But I respect his artistic integrity."

"Me too," Akira says. "So, as soon as I was old enough, I asked if I could work for him at his mochi stand."

"Wait a minute." I shake my head, goggling at him. "I thought you said you *didn't* volunteer to dance around dressed as a giant piece of mochi!"

"That came later," he says, giving me a sheepish look. "At first, I had more of a, ah, *standard* job during spring, summer, and winter vacations. Taking orders and such."

"But still, you volunteered for something!" I say.

"I did," he says, nodding proudly. "And Ojisan's budget was tight, so I was not even getting paid at first."

"Wow." I cross my arms over my chest and study him. "What made you want to do that?"

"Ojisan and I have always been close and I admired his passion, his dedication," Akira says. His brow furrows and he gets that intense look in his eyes—which, I have to admit, I'm starting to find even more attractive than his dimple.

"He loves everything about mochi—the craft of making it, the taste. The process that goes into it. The way it brings people joy. It all gives him so much life. I want to be around people who *feel* things that way. Who run toward their passions with so much commitment."

"Is that the way you run toward being a doctor, toward—what did you call it—the odd science of how the body works?"

"Yes," Akira says, nodding firmly. "I do not see the point of doing anything less."

"I want to find that passion," I blurt out. I feel instantly embarrassed, saying something so personal, something that comes from so deep inside my gut. But now that I've said it, I might as well keep going. "I mean. Something that I can run toward in the same way. I want that for my future."

"You will find it," he says, looking at me with earnest conviction. And something about the absolute certainty in his voice makes my heart flutter. "I have faith in you. In fact . . ." He studies me for a moment, his expression turning even more serious. "Let's make that our mission this spring vacation. To figure out your future. That is our case we must solve—like on the American detective shows. And we *will* solve it before you have to go home."

"First you volunteer to work at your uncle's mochi stand for no pay and now you're volunteering to help some random American girl resolve her existential crisis?" I give him a teasing, incredulous look. "Are you for real?"

"I'm real," he says, giving me a puzzled look. "Though

for this mission I should perhaps assume some very manly American detective name: Jack? Chris? Dirk?"

"I like Akira," I say—and then blush a little when I realize how that sounds.

He gestures down the path of the bamboo grove, which seems to go on forever. "Shall we keep walking? See if we find any unicorns?"

Hmm. I cast a sidelong glance at him as we resume our journey. *A cute boy who I don't want to stop talking to . . . and who, for whatever reason, seems to want to keep talking to me, even when I blurt out deeply personal sentiments that are probably best left inside my head?*

I think I already *have* found a unicorn.

When we finally emerge from the bamboo forest, we're both starving, so we trek back to the Arashiyama train station and grab some takoyaki from one of the bustling food stands. I was running late when I arrived at the station this morning—and yes, okay, totally preoccupied, fizzing with anticipation over seeing Akira again—so I glossed over a lot of the atmosphere of the station. Now I allow myself to take a moment to breathe in the delicious mingling of food scents, to take note of the unaccompanied schoolchildren who are, once again, striding along with purpose.

"Was that you when you were younger?" I say to Akira, nodding toward a resolute little boy with a gigantic backpack.

"Yes, un," he says, grinning. "But probably moving much slower because of all the medical texts I wanted to drag around with me."

I smile at the completely adorable image this conjures up and take a bite of takoyaki.

"So good," I say, my eyes nearly rolling into the back of my head as I inhale the savory concoction of batter and octopus. "My dad has a version of these at his restaurant. It's cool to be able to just buy it at a train station."

"You do not have takoyaki stands in the States?" Akira says.

"We have food trucks. Kind of the same thing? I mean, it's not hard to find Japanese food in LA—we have whole sections of the city dedicated to it, even. But it's cool to be . . ." I gesture around. "Surrounded by all these food scents that are so much a part of my soul. Like they're sewn into the fabric of everybody's everyday life. I like being able to get takoyaki as easily as I can get french fries."

Akira smiles. "What is it like being here as—what do you say? The opposite of your mother, who is Japanese from Japan."

"Japanese American?" I say, laughing. "I mean, I suppose it's interesting." I stop and think about it for a moment. My first couple days here, I was too discombobulated and out of place to even think much about that question. But between the girls in their colorful yukata and this wealth of familiar food scents, I feel like I'm starting to locate little pieces of myself, and it makes me feel buoyed, moved—and curious to explore more. "There are things that are so familiar to me—like this." I hold up my stick with its two remaining

98

takoyaki balls. "But the, like, locational fabric around them is *so* different. It's a weird mishmash of feeling like there are these important 'home' touchstones, but they're wrapped up in the unfamiliar. And I really didn't do enough research before coming here because my trip was a bit . . . last-minute. I still feel kind of off-kilter and out of place."

"Ah, but you look like you fit in, ne?" Akira says, smiling "Because you are Japanese."

"Just in a different way," I say, laughing and thinking of my dad. "An Auntie *did* ask me for directions when I was walking to the train station this morning. She was extremely disappointed when she realized I didn't speak Japanese. I think Aunties are the same everywhere."

Akira laughs. "This, I believe, is true. And are you often surrounded by disapproving Aunties in the States?"

"Sometimes." I smile. "I mean, LA is so big and sprawling, it has basically every kind of person. I feel lucky to live in a place where I can be surrounded by Aunties if I want to be. Because there are plenty of other places in the States— or even pockets in and around LA—where I could be surrounded by people shocked that I can speak English or asking me where I'm from or telling me how much they love anime."

Akira's brow crinkles. "Do you love anime?"

"I've barely watched any!" I exclaim. "That's more my friend Bex's thing. But being Asian American means you don't fit some people's idea of what an 'American' looks like."

"That is odd," Akira says, studying me intently. "You seem very American to me. But there is no one way to be anything, ne? I have never experienced people thinking I'm not Japanese—but according to my parents, I also stand out." He gestures to his loud sneakers.

I smile, thinking that to me, he would stand out anywhere.

"Have you ever wanted to learn Japanese?" he says. "You know, to make the Aunties on both sides of the ocean more approving."

"Being here kind of makes me want to learn," I say, glancing around at all the signs I can't read.

"You know there are several things to learn—very complicated," Akira says, his eyes twinkling. "Hiragana, katakana, kanji. Perhaps you could start with some wasei-eigo?"

"I've heard that term," I say, nodding. "It's Japanese that's based on English words, right?"

"English made in Japan," he says. "Words made up of English pieces, but they may not make immediate sense to you. And we also use gairaigo—loan words. There is quite a bit of Japanese-style English. So you might hear things that sound sort of familiar. Like pepa-tesuto—paper test—to mean 'exam.' Or noto pasokon for 'notebook personal computer.' Like a laptop." He grins at me. "They are close, but not quite English? Somewhere in between. Perhaps that makes everything more confusing? Maybe you should go straight to kanji."

"My mom taught me a few kanji when I was younger—I had this little watercolor set and she showed me how to write the characters on paper. But I never quite had the patience or the focus to learn more than that."

Akira leans forward, resting his hands on his knees. "Ano . . . your mother is your superhero," he says slowly. "But when you talk about her, you also look . . ." He pulls a sad face. "Like you are thinking very hard about something."

"I . . ." I gnaw at my lower lip. Is this really something I want to talk to him about? I guess, in a way, I already am— by bringing Mom up so much. I must be very . . . stimulated. I can practically *feel* Atsuko smirking from all the way across the ocean. "There's a reason my trip was so last-minute. My mom and I had a huge fight about what I'm doing—or *not* doing—with my life and I felt like I needed to get away from . . . well, everything. For a bit."

I recap the whole sordid saga for him—Mom and Liu Academy and how I just couldn't bring myself to commit to painting forever.

"Ah," he says, nodding thoughtfully when I'm done. "Then our quest to discover your passion and what you will be doing with your future is especially important. We must commit ourselves to it one hundred percent."

He looks so serious—that intensity brewing in his expression again. I have a feeling he commits to *everything* one hundred percent. I find this both extremely attractive and extremely touching, and for a moment, I get wrapped up in being totally confused by my feelings—yet again.

"Are you in?" he says, meeting my eyes and giving me the full force of that ultra-serious look. "We will figure this out and make both your mother—and the Aunties—proud."

"I'm not sure *anything* will make the Aunties proud," I say, laughing. "But I *am* in. One hundred percent."

"Look behind you," he says, nodding. "These are those patterns and bright colors you like, ne? Perhaps this is a sign?"

I whip around to see that we're sitting next to a tall pole with a beautiful floral print: vibrant purple with pops of orange and sunshine yellow.

"That's . . . that's a kimono print, isn't it?" I exclaim, my eyes widening.

"Sou da ne. These poles are all over the station," he says, a smile breaking through his serious expression. "In all different prints. It's an art installation—a kimono forest, like the bamboo forest. There is a whole row of them all together up ahead, it is very striking—"

"What?!" I pop the last bite of takoyaki in my mouth and jump to my feet.

"You did not notice when you first came here?" he says, laughing.

"I was distracted," I say. "But I'm not anymore. I want to see this."

"Then let's go," he says, his smile widening.

As we approach the beautiful rows of the kimono forest and I see their bright prints standing side by side, my heart surges.

"Are you ready for this?" Akira says, giving me a concerned look. "I do not want you to become upset again."

"I'm ready," I say defiantly. And I realize I'm not just talking about the kimono forest.

I *will* discover my passion. I *am* in one hundred percent.

And I feel more determined than I have in a long time.

CHAPTER EIGHT

My ojiisan is sitting at his table again, assembling one of his model trains. I wonder how many times he's put this one back together.

"Kimiko-chan," he says, beaming at me as I let myself into the house. "Another day, another adventure. Come tell me about it."

I slip off my shoes and cross the room. I'm feeling energized after my bamboo grove jaunt with Akira. Having someone volunteer to accompany me on my journey of self-discovery feels reassuring—especially someone who takes it so seriously. It makes the whole thing feel more solid, somehow, like we're going to take *actual steps* to figure out my future instead of just wandering cluelessly around Japan. Which was basically as far as I'd gotten when it came to making a "plan."

And it doesn't hurt that the individual who wants to accompany me on this illustrious quest is so freaking cute.

I settle myself next to Grandpa and peer out the window. Grandma is out in her garden again, doing some ferocious weed-digging. Hmm. I seem to have settled into ping-ponging between calling them "Ojiisan and Obaasan" and "Grandpa and Grandma." The second feels less formal than the first, but not quite as intimate as Ojiichan and Obaachan. I can't quite get there.

My eyes wander back to the table and I notice an addition to the scattered model train parts: candy wrappers.

"Those are from my snack stash," Grandpa says. "They are special, the limited-edition Snickers—made with oats. I believe you can only get them in Japan."

"Oh, amazing," I say, and he passes me my own fancy limited-edition Snickers bar. "Thank you."

"Don't tell your grandmother we are eating these so close to dinner." He gives me a conspiratorial smile.

"My lips are sealed," I say, peeling off the wrapper. I realize then that I'm starving. After wandering through the kimono forest, Akira and I ate the most delicious ramen I've ever had—salty, brothy, hearty—then somehow, we ended up talking for another two hours. I texted Bex and Atsuko, but they haven't responded yet. Our time zones must be off.

I munch on the candy bar and reach into my bag, pulling out my sketchbook.

"Do you mind if I sketch while we talk, Ojiisan?" I say.

"Please do," Grandpa says. "Ah, that used to be your mother, too—sketching everywhere. She even tried to bring her sketchbook to the dinner table, but your grandmother put a very quick stop to that."

"Mom's told me she always wanted to be an artist," I say, flipping open the sketchbook. I start roughing out long, flowing lines that mimic the sweep of the bamboo stalks I saw today. "But she doesn't talk very much about, like, how she first started. What *made* her start?"

"Hmm," my grandfather says, shifting around his model train pieces. His brow furrows as he thinks it over. "I believe it was when . . . hmm, eto . . . She saw a photograph of an animal in a textbook. Or maybe it was an encyclopedia. A tanuki?"

"A tanuki?!" I exclaim, my voice twisting up at the end in a little squeak. Tanukis are really determined to make themselves a part of my whole Japan experience.

"Yes." My grandfather gives me a puzzled look. "She saw that photo and she could not stop looking at it, talking about it. She was fascinated. 'He is so creepy and so cute at the same time, Papa,' she'd say. 'How is that possible?'"

As he talks, I start sketching the tanuki in different outfits—an elaborate haori and a dignified blazer and a snazzy jumpsuit, inspired by the flowing lines of the bamboo stalks. Hmm, that jumpsuit is actually pretty cool. I sketch a human-sized version for myself in the margins.

"She found scrap paper and a pencil and drew thousands of tanuki," my grandfather says, smiling faintly. "He became like her own little cartoon character she would put in funny situations. He would steal taiyaki and eat too many, or spill tea all over the floor and blame it on his friend who was not there for some reason."

"Wow, the tanuki was a real troublemaker." I shade in parts of my cool jumpsuit and then smudge the pencil with my thumb, giving it a pattern like the sun blinking its way through the bamboo grove. "It's weird to think of Mom drawing something so . . . cute."

"Why?" my grandfather says, helping himself to another limited-edition Snickers.

"It's so unlike her work now," I say. "She does abstract painting with all these cool, bold shapes." I pull out my phone and scroll to a photo I took of some of Mom's more recent paintings displayed in her studio. "Like this," I continue, holding out the phone to my grandfather. "Amazing, isn't it?"

He takes it from me and squints at it over his spectacles. "Sou da ne," he says, a slow smile creeping over his face. "That's very nice. So interesting. It reminds me of her in a way—like I can almost *see* her speaking when I look at this. It has something of her stubbornness. The headstrong way she has about her."

"She's never sent you pictures of any of her work?" I say as he passes the phone back to me. "Her new work, I mean—the post-tanuki period?"

"No," he says, his smile taking on a tinge of sadness. "Ano . . . We do not speak much—and when we do, it is not with ease. I believe the time for us being able to do that has passed."

"Oh, I don't think so, Grandpa," I say eagerly. He suddenly looks so sad and I want to say something, anything, to make it better. "I know Mom can be stubborn and hard to talk to sometimes, but . . ." I trail off, fiddling with my pencil.

But . . . what, Kimi? Have you forgotten that you and your mom are currently very much not on speaking terms? That you can't figure out how to talk to her after living with her for the past seventeen years? Why do you think your poor grandfather's going to fare any better?

106

"Do you want to see more of her art?" I say, latching on to the only thing I can think of.

"Hai," he says, giving a tentative smile. "Yes, I would."

We spend the next half hour looking through Mom's paintings on my phone and I do my best to explain the origin behind each one, what inspired her various works. He listens raptly, munching his Snickers. We're so engrossed in our virtual art tour, we barely look up when Grandma comes back inside.

"I am going to start dinner," she says, surveying the scene and zeroing in on the empty wrappers scattered across the table. "I hope you did not fill up on too much candy."

"I will help you," my grandfather says, sweeping the candy wrappers into one pile and his model train parts into another. Grandma nods at him and heads to the kitchen.

"Grandpa," I whisper, leaning closer to him. "Did I do something wrong?"

"What could you have done wrong, Kimiko-chan?" he says, confusion passing over his face.

"I . . . I don't know. It's just, Obaasan . . . Grandma barely looks at me. And whenever I try to talk to her, it seems to go wrong. Like the other day, I wanted to tell her how nice her garden is, but she didn't seem too interested in discussion on that front. Or any front."

"Ah." My grandfather gives me a considering look. "So you were trying to say to her—what is the word?—something that spoke well of what she was doing?"

"You mean, was I trying to give her a compliment? Yes, I guess I was."

107

"Mmm." My grandfather looks like he's trying to suppress his burgeoning grin, but can't quite get there. "Did your mother ever talk to you about how, ah, 'compliments' are handled in Japan, Kimiko-chan? It is seen as boastful to accept—if you agree with the person complimenting you, you are bragging about yourself."

"Ohhhhh," I breathe out. Now my grandmother's dismissal of both my misguided garden comments and my praise of her outfit at the train station makes more sense.

"I also think . . ." Ojiisan hesitates, his smile fading. "You look so much like your mother, Kimiko-chan. You look like her when she . . . left us. I do not think your grandmother thought of how that might feel. Try to give her some time."

He gives my arm a little pat, then sweeps the candy wrappers off the table and rises, heading to meet Obaasan in the kitchen.

I stare down at my sketchbook and the images of the tanuki in his many dapper outfits stare back at me. I never imagined that Mom started out her illustrious abstract art career drawing cute, badly behaved raccoon dogs. I think again of my mother telling me she doesn't know me at all.

Apparently, there are some things I don't know about her, either.

I can't sleep.

There are so many thoughts whirling around in my brain and none of them will hold still long enough for me to grab on to them. So, I'm just lying here, clutching Meiko to my chest and staring at the ceiling. I probably look like one of those freaky, saucer-eyed children in a J-horror movie.

(Actually, when I was like twelve, this sour-faced white boy started calling me "Ring Girl," referencing this Japanese movie that was later remade in the US and featured a little girl with hopelessly messy, tangled black hair and a permanent death stare. Atsuko snarled at him for being an ignorant racist, and he probably was—but to be honest, I could sort of see the resemblance?)

I'm thinking about the near silent dinner I had with my grandparents, wherein Grandma still wouldn't look at me and Grandpa tried to pretend like he had a big appetite, even though he'd clearly filled up on candy. I'm also thinking about Akira's promise to help me with my quest, how he wants to make it a great detective case worthy of a crime procedural. And I'm pondering tanukis and my mother. I've always said my mother understands me better than anyone— she always seems to pick up on things I'm feeling and thinking before I've even had a chance to vocalize them. At least, she used to. I think of us as being so close . . . but did our connection only exist in painting, in the passion she thought we shared? I remember how happy she always was when we'd paint side by side, our brushes stroking in different but complementary rhythms on canvas. Maybe that's all we had.

Maybe we don't know each other at all.

I want to talk to Atsuko and Bex, but I can't remember what time it is over there. Although . . .

I sit up in bed, toying with Meiko's chewed-up paw.

My mom is a *way* tougher customer than my friends. But maybe I could try to reach her the same way?

I grab my laptop from the side table, open it, and hit "compose message." Then I stare at the cursor, a persistent blink against the bright white background. I feel like it's mocking me. I gnaw at my lower lip, trying to put my thoughts in order. What do I even want to say to her? I suppose, like my ojiisan, I can get my feelings out and then maybe not send it? I kind of want to snap the laptop shut and try to go to sleep, but for some reason, I'm convinced this is an important step in my journey of self-discovery. I need to do it *now* or I won't do it ever.

My gaze wanders the darkened room, finally settling on the shadowy shape of my blue-and-red-checked coat, draped over my suitcase. Hmm.

I take a deep breath, settle my fingertips on the keyboard, and start typing.

Dear Mom,

Before I left, you said you don't know me at all, and I can't stop thinking about that. It's weird not to talk to you. I keep wondering what you're doing: if you're in your studio or taking a meeting with clients or laughing with Dad over leftovers he's brought home from the restaurant. I'm having an interesting time in Japan and I hope I'll get to tell you all about it sometime.

But for now, I want to tell you about something else.

I don't know how you felt when Grandma—Dad's mom—died. I mean, I know you were probably sad. But most of what I remember is what a powerhouse you were, making all the arrangements and helping Dad and Auntie Aileen with everything and inviting people back to Dad's restaurant after.

It was my first real experience with death, and even though I was thirteen, I feel like I didn't totally get it. I didn't understand she was really gone and I'd never be able to talk to her again until the funeral.

If there was one thing Grandma could do, it was talk. She used to chatter my ear off about *everything*, and I loved every second. I remember how bubbly and funny and animated she was when she described, like, a week's worth of episodes of her favorite soap. She talked about those characters in obsessive detail, like they were real people—like they were her friends and she really, really wanted me to be friends with them, too. But she could also turn serious—she's the one who first talked to me about Japanese American internment, how her parents had gone through it during World War II. How she felt like there were pieces of her own history that were missing or lost forever, blank spots in her familial memory, because her parents had to give up so much when they were forced into the camps and—understandably—never wanted to talk about it. She didn't want me to feel like I had missing pieces. She wanted me to know everything she could tell me about her side of the family's past.

Anyway, I'm sure you remember what happened once we got to the funeral: I broke down sobbing next to the casket and you practically had to pick me up to get me to leave. It was embarrassing (probably for you, too). Later, when I'd calmed down, Dad gave me my inheritance from Grandma—her favorite coat, red-and-blue checked from the sixties and perfectly preserved. I'd always loved that coat.

I wrapped myself up in the coat like a cocoon and slept for hours. When I woke up, I looked at myself in the mirror and realized the coat was hilariously huge on me—like, I was swimming in it. I looked like a kid playing dress-up in Mommy's closet. For a moment, I felt devastated all over again. Like I couldn't even have this small connection to Grandma.

But then I stared at myself a little longer—and I got an idea.

I'd already been teaching myself to sew because clothes never quite hung right on me—I'm so shrimpy that everything was always too long or fit right in one place but nowhere else. I'd gotten used to altering things. I knew enough to take the coat's waist in so it had more of a fit-and-flare shape—then I altered it a little more, so the shape was even more dramatic. I asked Dad to drive me to the fabric store, where I got these little fur remnants and pretty pearl buttons. I added those to the coat and I had my very first Kimi Original.

Wearing the coat made me feel like Grandma was still with me a bit, like I was bolstered by her bubbly chatterbox spirit and her intense desire for me to live my life to its fullest. But it also did something else, something I didn't expect—it made me feel like the absolute best version of myself. Like I could take on the world and never be that sobbing girl by the casket ever again. Like I was Ultimate Kimi.

I know you think the way I obsess over clothes is silly, a waste of time. And you're probably right. But I wanted to give you a little bit of *why* I obsess over *certain* clothes and how I make them mean something to me.

Love,
Kimi

p.s. I've been hearing some very interesting things from Ojiisan about cartoon tanukis.

I search through my laptop and find a photo of me in the coat and attach it to the email. My index finger hovers over the "send" button. This is probably the most real I've ever been with my mom. It feels like opening up my chest cavity and letting her peer directly at my heart. That somewhat disgusting image makes me think of Akira and I can't help but smile a little.

My index finger is still hovering. With my other hand, I pet Meiko, hoping she'll give me some kind of sign as to what I should do. Then I think of my grandfather, his sad face when he said it was too late for him and Mom to ever speak openly to each other, as father and daughter.

I gather up every scrap of courage I have—and I hit "send."

CHAPTER NINE

In the wee hours of the next morning, I finally get ahold of Bex and Atsuko. It's afternoon back in the States and they're sprawled on Atsuko's bed, having just come back from yet another spring break adventure.

"Santa Monica boardwalk and the Ferris wheel," Bex says, resting her head on her arms. "Absolutely magical and we ate *so* much ice cream. But too freakin' hot."

"Also, they wouldn't let me ride in my own Ferris wheel bucket," Atsuko says, looking offended. "I wanted to soar through the sky like the strong, independent woman I am, and they told me single riders aren't allowed. Can you believe that?"

"What, why not?" I say, laughing. I feel like I'm sprawled out on the bed next to them, my skin overheated from the blazing seaside sun, my stomach slightly queasy from the combination of too much ice cream and carnival rides.

"I guess it unbalances the bucket or something?" Atsuko says, shaking her head in frustration. "Seems very discriminatory to me. The ticket lady told me I could 'find someone in line' to ride with, but how weird would *that* be?"

"Ugh, that's totally the start of your meet-cute, you just

refuse to see it," Bex says, poking her. Atsuko sticks her tongue out and scoots farther away from Bex on the bed. "There was an extremely hot guy totally scoping you out in line and you straight up ignored him!"

"I don't think 'no random carnival rides with strangers' is a bad rule to abide by," Atsuko says, rolling her eyes. "In fact, I'm going to put that in my next column: Ten Rules for Avoiding Hot Mess Meet-Cutes. Too bad you're not here, Kimi, you could've balanced my bucket."

"Awww, sweet," I say, reaching over to pat the screen—like I'm virtually patting her on the head. "So, you rode with Bex and Shelby?"

"Yes, and it killed my whole kissing at the top of the Ferris wheel fantasy," Bex says, side-eyeing Atsuko. "Since she spent the whole time complaining about how they wouldn't let her ride by herself."

"How romantic," I say, giggling.

"Speaking of romance," Atsuko says, raising an eyebrow. "How goes it with Akira of the Cute Dimple?"

"He took me to a magical bamboo forest yesterday," I say, my cheeks warming at the memory. "We talked for hours. And he made a . . . a declaration, I guess. To help me with my quest of self-discovery."

"Ohmygod, a *declaration*," Bex says, bringing a fluttery hand to her forehead. "I've always wanted someone to make a declaration for me. Or is it to me?"

"Maybe Shelby will make one," I say encouragingly. "The next time you guys go on the Ferris wheel. Um, by yourselves."

"I'll stay on the ground in the name of declarations,"

Atsuko says, letting out an overly dramatic sigh. "But Kimi, I want to know what it was like spending time *in real life* with a guy you like. Because usually that's something you run away from as fast as your tiny legs can carry you."

"First of all: *rude*, my legs are not that tiny," I say, holding up an index finger. "Second of all: I'm trying to follow your Ask Atsuko directive. You know, just have fun. And I did." A slow, dorky smile spreads across my face. "I really, really did. He's so fun to talk to. You're right, I can't predict what he's going to say next. And that means I can't seem to conjure up a fantasy version of him. And *that* means I want to see him again. You know, in real life."

"Mmm-hmm," Atsuko says, giving me the smuggest smile I've ever seen. She looks like a cat who's just eaten a thousand canaries. "Okay, so I'm going to give you your next Ask Atsuko directive."

"My *next* directive?" I squeak. "Why do I need another one? I'm seeing this one through so well."

"Exactly," Atsuko says, waving a dismissive hand. "You were so successful with the first directive, you clearly need another one. You've got to next-level all this fun-having with Akira of the Cute Dimple—you're only there for two weeks. Less than that now."

"I . . . I thought I wasn't supposed to be thinking about that part!" I exclaim, shaking my head. "Cause then I'll start thinking about how I'm setting myself up to totally like someone I can never *really* be with." Ugh. A little coil of dread winds itself through my stomach at the thought.

"Atsy!" Bex gives Atsuko a little shove. "Don't get her all freaked out about that. Let the romance *flow*."

"That's what I'm doing," Atsuko insists, shoving her back. "But it's not gonna flow if I don't give her a directive." She straightens her shoulders and points at me. "Kimiko Nakamura, it is time to . . ." She lowers her voice dramatically. *"Kiss him."*

"Guh." My face is suddenly on fire. "Atsuko. I've known him for, like, two days."

"And you already want to spend time with him *endlessly*," Atsuko says, waving her index finger at me.

"That *is* true," Bex says. "And don't forget the *declaration*. That's already taking things in a super romantic direction."

"Yes," Atsuko says, nodding emphatically. Then she hesitates, scrutinizing me. I shift uncomfortably. It's weird how I'm a whole freakin' continent away and Atsuko still seems able to pick up on my every thought. And through a computer screen, no less. "Kimi," she continues, looking at me intently. "Are you worried about, you know . . ." She lowers her voice again. *"Your first kiss?"*

"Shut up!" I yelp at the same time as Bex yelps, "What?!"

"It's not *technically* my first kiss," I say, shooting Atsuko a look. "I kissed Kevin Yee at eighth grade grad night."

"You mean when you got hopped up on the bottomless 'berry blast' Slurpees, tried to plant one on him, and totally missed his mouth?" Atsuko hoots. "Your tongue was *bright blue*, Kimi—he probably thought Cookie Monster was trying to eat his face."

"How have I never heard this story?" Bex says, shaking her head in wonder.

Bex didn't get folded into our friend trio until freshman

year, when she moved to LA from New Hampshire. Occasionally, there are embarrassing stories she's missed out on. Atsuko, on the other hand, has known me my entire life. There's pretty much nothing I can hide from her.

"That was not exactly an ideal perfect first kiss moment," I admit. "I've been waiting for another, way less humiliating opportunity—it just hasn't come along yet."

"So, you can have your *real* first kiss in a beautiful, romantic spot in Japan with your perfect, declaration-making boyfriend," Bex swoons. "That's *amazing*."

"It would be amazing," I say. "But . . . I mean, he's definitely not my boyfriend. And I don't know how to even . . . initiate that?" In my prior fantasies about perfect first kisses, I always imagined some over-the-top scenario out of a movie—like suddenly there's a rainstorm and my date and I have to run for shelter and we end up darting into a shadowy but not at all creepy alley and we're all breathless from running and we're standing *so close* that there's nothing to do but kiss. And then afterward we duck into some adorable thrift shop that magically has cute, perfectly fitting clothes for us to change into, so we don't catch colds.

"You'll know when the moment is right," Atsuko says firmly. "Although . . ." Her brow furrows. "Make sure you're not all out in public, like on the street in full view of judgy Aunties or something. My mom told me PDA isn't really a thing in Japan."

Hmm. Maybe my secluded, not-creepy alley would work just fine.

"I'm not getting ahead of myself," I say, shaking my head at Atsuko. "I will keep this Ask Atsuko directive in the back of my head—but no promises."

"*Yes*, promises!" Atsuko counters. "Kiss! Him! Kiss! Him!" She motions Bex to join in her chant and suddenly I feel like I'm the freaking football team, being egged on by two totally bananas cheerleaders.

"Good-bye!" I say loudly, hitting "end call" on Skype.

I push my laptop to the side and flop back against my pillows, laughing.

"What do you think?" I ask Meiko, patting her fuzzy head. "Should I kiss him?"

Her eyeless face stares back at me, providing no answers.

But somehow, I can't help but think she wants me to kiss him, too.

It's still early and my grandparents won't be up for another half an hour—after staying with them a couple days, I know they usually get up at eight a.m. on the dot. So when I get up to pee and use the last scrap of toilet paper, I go into a mild panic.

I have no idea where they keep the toilet paper and I don't want them to think I'm the kind of rude person who just leaves an empty toilet paper roll sitting there. I look in the cabinet under the sink. In the cabinet *over* the sink. Nothing.

I dart out into the hall to see if there's maybe a handy closet I haven't noticed yet right next to the bathroom? Nope.

The shoji screens that lead to my bedroom (aka, Mom's old bedroom) and my grandparents' bedroom line the hallway, and . . . okay, actually, the door at the end of the hall could be a closet, maybe? It's worth a shot.

I tiptoe past my grandparents' bedroom, doing my best not to cause any creaks or squeaks. Then I carefully open the mysterious door.

It's . . . wow, okay. It's actually *not* a closet. Although it's not that much bigger than one. It appears to be some kind of sewing room? There's a rainbow of scraps and bolts of fabric crammed into a shelving unit on one wall. A sewing machine crammed into one corner—a Bernina 560, I notice. That's a *really excellent* sewing machine. I move closer and run my fingers along the top of it reverently.

Then I turn and notice what's crammed into the opposite corner. It's a very simple dress form with a garment on it—but that garment itself is far from simple. It's one of the most beautiful, intricate yukata I've ever seen. It's still in progress, though—the sleeves are unfinished, and many of the seams are raw. "Wow," I say out loud, stepping toward it.

"Kimiko-chan?" I whirl around to see my obaasan standing in the doorway, giving me an odd look. "What are you doing in here?" She doesn't sound angry, merely puzzled.

"I'm looking for toilet paper," I blurt out, my cheeks flushing when I realize how ridiculous that sounds. "I mean . . . sorry. I was hoping this was a closet of some kind, but instead, well . . ." I gesture around. God. I'm pretty sure I'm only making this worse. I should've just left the empty toilet paper roll out and called it a day. She keeps staring at me with that confused look. "Um. Did you make this?" I say, gesturing to the yukata. "It's so beautiful. It's—"

Dammit. There I go, trying to give her unwanted compliments again.

"Yes," she says, stepping more fully into the room. She frowns at the yukata on the dress form and her expression shifts a bit—suddenly, she seems to be a million miles away. "It will never be finished."

Now it's my turn to look confused. "Oh, well, it looks like it's getting there? I mean, I don't know everything about constructing yukata and kimono, but I know *a few* things, I could help—"

"No." She shakes her head, her gaze still trained on the dress form. "It will never be finished," she repeats—and I realize it sounds more like a firm statement than a lamentation.

I decide not to pursue that further—at least for now. It really is beautiful, though, and it would be a shame if she never finished it.

"Obaasan, do you like to sew—to make your own clothes?" I say, deciding to take things in a more general direction. "Because I do, too."

"Your coat," she says, finally turning away from the dress form to face me. "The blue and red one. You made it?"

"I altered it," I say. "Customized it. But I've made tons of stuff since then—both from scratch and from existing garments."

"It is very nice," my grandmother says. "I like the fur on the sleeves and collar."

"Yes, I did that!" I say, beaming. I realize belatedly that I'm

121

not supposed to *accept* a compliment, either—that it's like bragging. "That's one of the ways I made it more . . ." I trail off, trying to think of the right words.

"More like you," my grandmother says. "More special. You are someone who likes to . . . eto, what do you say? Stand out in a crowd?" She looks at me appraisingly and I can't tell whether this is a quality she admires or not.

"In a way," I say. "I mean, I don't purposefully do things that are going to make a bunch of people look at me or cause a spectacle or something. But I love creating and wearing things that let me express myself. Does that make sense?"

"Hai," she says, offering no further elaboration. She's studying me in that intense way she did at the train station. And even though it makes me squirm a bit, I prefer it to her avoiding looking at me at all costs because I remind her too much of Mom. "And to answer your first question, Kimiko-chan: Yes, I do like to make some of my own clothes. I have tried to make them for your grandfather as well, but he prefers things more simple."

"Did you make that black blouse with the ruffles on the front?" I say, hoping I'm not pressing too much. "The one you wore when you picked me up at the train station? Because I loved it. It was so different. So not what I was expecting you to wear."

"You expected me to show up in some kind of boring flowered house dress, ne?" my grandmother says, cocking an eyebrow. "Some kind of old grandma clothes?"

"Um . . ."

My stomach drops as I realize I probably have pressed too much and offended her and ruined the nice moment we were just having. But then Grandma does the exact opposite of what I'm expecting. One side of her mouth lifts into an amused—I think it's amused, anyway?!—half smile and she lets out a gruff snort that I believe is almost a laugh.

"Kimiko-chan," she says. "Would you like me to show you how to make a garment like that—the blouse I was wearing?"

"Yes!" I say, jumping at the opportunity. "Yes, I would like that very much."

She gives me a little nod. "We can get to work after you get back from the tourist adventure you are having today. Come spend time with me instead of sneaking the candy with your grandfather."

"That sounds great." I tentatively return her half smile.

"Oh, and by the way," she says, heading out of the room. "Toilet paper is in the kitchen cabinet above the stove. Do not ask me why. Your grandfather came up with that system of organization."

I'm smiling as I head back to my room. I can't believe I'm on the verge of forging a connection with my grandmother. And I *really* can't believe I may have found someone else in the family who likes making clothes as much as I do. The combination of these two things forms a warm, giddy bubble in my chest.

My bubble only gets bigger when I pick up my phone and see a text from Akira, with an invitation to meet him at a spot that he believes will provide "case-cracking clues" in the mystery of my journey of self-discovery.

Of course, as soon as I send a reply agreeing to meet

him, half a dozen texts from Atsuko and Bex pop up on my screen, all saying the same thing.

KISS!

HIM!

KISS!

HIM!

How did they *know*?

I almost reply to tell them not to eat up my international data with separate texts for each word. Then I realize I'm smiling too much to care.

CHAPTER TEN

"Is this a clue?" I turn to Akira and put my hands on my hips, cocking an eyebrow. "Because if it is, it's maybe the most majestic clue I've ever seen."

We're standing in front of a giant, beautiful temple—it has a multi-level roof that swoops into curling flourishes and huge wooden doors and gives off the stately air of a building where Important Things Happen.

"It could provide us with a clue," Akira says. "It is also one of the most scenic spots in Japan—I thought just being here might help you get your mind in the right space to figure out your future. To find your passion."

"Do you think my passion could just be staring at this awesome temple forever?" I say, swooning a bit. "And if so, what kind of career do you think I could make out of it? Wait a minute." My brow furrows. "What about an architect—could I be an architect?" I roll that around in my mind, trying to see if it fits. Does the idea of designing buildings ignite some kind of flame inside of me? Does it—

"Kimi." Akira laughs a little. "Yes, that is a possibility. But why don't you relax a little and see what comes to you instead of trying to seize the answer immediately?"

"Right," I say automatically, even though I'm still stuck on the question of whether buildings are my passion. Suddenly I feel something cold and wet bump up against my hand and I let out a little shriek and dance to the side, my other hand shooting out to grab Akira's arm. I whirl around and catch the culprit in action—an indignant-looking deer, who snorts at me and trots forward, bumping my hand again with its cold little nose.

"Oh, right, I've heard about the deer in Nara," I say, relaxing. "They're just roaming free all over?"

"Yes," Akira says, giving me an amused look. "That one clearly thinks you have food to offer her." The deer cocks its head at us inquisitively. "The deer will pester you relentlessly if they believe you can feed them."

"Oh, can we?" I say, my face lighting up. "I mean, can we get deer-appropriate food and feed them? Because that sounds amazingly fun and adorable and . . . hey, maybe deer-feeding is my passion? Could that be a thing? I mean, I'm feeling pretty excited about the prospect. Maybe passion-level excited." My brow furrows again.

"Once again, I think perhaps you need to relax," Akira says. "Yes, we can feed the deer—that is actually one of the main attractions of Nara. There are vendors closer to Nara Park who sell these, ah, they are like . . . hmm, eto . . ." He makes a circular motion with his hands. ". . . cookies? Called shika-senbei. You feed them to the deer."

"Oh my gosh!" I exclaim. "Let's do that *right now*." The thought of feeding a deer fills me with such giddy glee—maybe that *is* my passion, is that so weird? But what kind of career can I get out of that? Maybe I can learn how to make shika-senbei? I could be the greatest shika-senbei maker in all the land—

"Kimi," Akira says, laughing, and I realize then that I'm still clutching his arm in a death grip. Somehow, I just can't bring myself to let go, even though the threat of the nefarious deer and her cold little nose are well behind us. She seems to have frolicked elsewhere—probably found someone who was ready with the shika-senbei.

Akira's wearing a light cotton jacket today and I can feel the warmth of his skin and the muscles of those incredibly nice arms through the thin blue material. My cheeks flush as Atsuko and Bex's chant wafts through my brain.

Kiss. Him. Kiss. Him!

No. Not yet. I mean, I want to. But the moment isn't perfect.

"Kimi?" he repeats. He turns toward me and raises his hand, his fingertips brushing my elbow—though I can't tell if that part is an accident. I reluctantly let go of his arm and sternly order my brain not to spiral into eight million fantasies of what that perfect moment might entail.

"I was thinking we'd feed the deer once we get to the park," Akira continues. "But first, why don't we walk through the temple? Maybe something inside will inspire you."

"Sounds like a plan," I say, falling into step with him and heading toward the temple's grand entrance. My brain feels like it's overflowing with amazing sights and we haven't even really gone anywhere yet. I can't help but imagine a sweeping gown based on the shape of the temple, maybe with a skirt that has some interesting texture to it— mimicking the look of the tiling on the roof. I'm also imagining a fun fabric with a cute deer print, something that could be cut into a variety of everyday silhouettes. Bex would absolutely *love* that. "What is this temple called?" I say to Akira, trying to get my head back in the present so I can be open to all the important inspiration I'm about to receive.

"Todaiji Temple," Akira says as we enter the giant wooden doors. "It is known for . . . well, you'll see."

We step into a huge, ornate room—really, it's so grand, "room" hardly seems like an adequate word for it. Its high ceiling is held up by red wooden pillars, which are decorated with green and gold flourishes. Pretty much every piece of this glorious room is breathtakingly beautiful on its own, but the clear main attraction is the massive bronze Buddha statue in the center. He must be at least fifty feet tall. His right hand is raised, his face is peaceful, and there's a pair of flat gold sculptures behind him edged in carvings that look like flames—like he's sitting in front of a pair of fiery suns. He's flanked by more golden statues—honestly, there's so much to look at, I feel overwhelmed. Like my eyes are totally excited to be receiving all of these stimuli, but also kind of can't handle it.

"Wow," I murmur.

"Daibutsu," Akira says, gesturing to the Buddha. "This is supposed to be the largest bronze statue of the Buddha Vairocana in the world."

"I believe it," I say. "It's . . . well, honestly, I can't even think of the right words to describe it."

We stand there for a moment, staring at the gigantic Buddha. There are tons of tourists milling around, making various noises of awe. But all of that fades to a burble and I

128

suddenly feel like Akira and I are the only people in the room. I allow myself to be swept up in the scale of this place, the impossibly high ceiling, and the huge Buddha staring back at me. I don't get caught up in thoughts of how this is helping us solve the mystery of my future or worry about the fact that neither of us have said anything for several minutes and could possibly be heading into Awkward Silenceville.

The thing is . . . it's not awkward. It doesn't feel weird standing here and being quiet with Akira and enjoying the awe-inspiring sight of something I can't imagine seeing back home. It feels . . . *nice.*

I wouldn't exactly call it a comfortable silence—it's more like there's this invisible energy crackling between us, goosing all of my senses and turning my awareness up several thousand notches. It's like I'm getting even more accustomed to the good itch from the other day. I *welcome* it, even.

I sneak a sidelong glance at Akira and see that he also seems to be deep in contemplative thought.

"What are you thinking?" I murmur.

He turns and grins at me. "Ahhhh. It's weird."

"I'm sure it's not weird," I say.

He rubs the back of his neck, his face turning sheepish. "I was thinking about how I came here with my parents when I was a kid and I couldn't stop thinking about what the Buddha's insides looked like underneath that shiny skin—you know, his guts, his organs, his heart. I wanted to know if it was like what I'd seen in those old medical textbooks I was so obsessed with, only on a bigger scale."

"You come to this beautiful, sacred place for the first

time and the only thing you can think about is Buddha's *guts*?" I giggle. "Okay, that *is* pretty weird."

"Excuse me," he says, putting on an indignant face. "You encouraged me to share and now you're laughing at me?" He leans in close. "Why do you enjoy laughing at me so much, Kimi from America?" His mouth is mere centimeters from my ear, his breath tickling my cheek. In spite of the warm spring air wafting into the temple, a little shiver runs through me. "Maybe *that* is your passion."

"Maybe it is," I say, my voice coming out thin and high. "Which means I'm also weird." I take a tiny step to the left, so I'm not quite as close to him.

"Hmm. Weird can be good, ne?"

"Definitely," I say, trying to calm my skyrocketing heartbeat and get my voice back into a normal vocal range. "It definitely can be."

"I have something else to show you," he says, his mouth quirking into a half smile. "Something else that may qualify as 'good weird.'"

He leads me around to the side of one of the gold statues flanking Buddha, to a particular pillar people are lined up next to.

"Whoa, what's this line for?" I say. "Or is that the good-weird—that people are lined up next to a random pillar for no reason?"

"Watch," he says, laughing.

The small child at the front of the line crouches down and—oh! Now I see. There's a small opening cut at the base of the pillar, sort of a square-shaped hole. As I keep watching, the child lies down on her stomach and carefully maneuvers herself through the opening headfirst. She wriggles through the pillar, her head popping out the other side triumphantly. It's a comical sight, like the pillar has swallowed part of her tiny body. Then she wriggles the rest of the way through and slides out onto the temple floor, grinning.

"Yatta!" she exclaims.

"The hole is the Daibutsu's nostril," Akira says.

"What!" I yelp. "Like the pillar is a giant *nose* or something?" It's such a funny juxtaposition, the idea of a big wooden nose plopped down in the midst of such a meaningful, reverent place.

"Not exactly," Akira says, giving me a slow smile. "The hole is the same size as the giant Buddha statue's nostril. If you can squeeze through, supposedly you will be granted enlightenment in your next life."

"*Next* life?" I say, shaking my head. "I really need enlightenment in this one."

We watch as a few more children squeeze through the nostril. Then a very tall, white, adult man is at the front of the line—he slides in more carefully and wriggles around, grimacing. It's another strange, almost funny sight, his arms and head emerging out of one end of the nostril, his feet dangling out of the other. He stops wriggling for a moment and his grimace deepens.

"Oh no," I murmur. "Is he *stuck*?"

"I think just resting," Akira says.

"This must have also fascinated you when you were younger," I say. "The idea of being able to crawl through someone's *nose*? Did you pester your parents with endless questions about that pillar and if it actually contained a complicated nasal ecosystem?"

"I did," he says, grinning at me. "So many questions. I think they were worried I was about to march over there and try to dismantle the entire pillar to see what was inside."

"Aww." I'm picturing a tiny Akira striding purposefully toward the pillar, his eyes flashing with that intensity he has, his shaggy hair sticking up in that mussed little kid way. The image is so cute, I almost can't take it. "So destructive and at such a young age."

"I didn't actually *do* it," he says, laughing. "But I thought about it."

We turn back to the pillar. The tall man has finally managed to squeeze through the nostril and his friends are patting him on the back in congratulations. His face is flushed from the exertion of wriggling through such a small, child-sized space, but he's grinning from ear to ear, his eyes shining with happiness. He doesn't look tired, he looks exhilarated. Like he'd do it all over again right now if he could.

"I want to do it," I say suddenly.

"Dismantle the pillar?" Akira says. "And *I* am the destructive one?"

"No, I want to squeeze through the nostril!" I say, smacking him on the arm. (Which, okay, gives me an excuse to touch him again.) "Maybe the Buddha will see fit to grant me a little enlightenment in *this* life—just a little bit?"

And . . . I mean, I don't want to say it out loud because it sounds super cheesy. But the look on that man's face . . .

well, he looks like Mom after she's just completed a particularly grueling painting. Like Dad after he's perfected a new experimental dish. I suddenly want to feel that so badly, I can taste it.

"Then let's get in line," Akira says, gesturing to the pillar.

"You want to do it, too?" I say.

"Absolutely not, no way," he says, waving a hand. "I passed through the nostril years ago; my next life's enlightenment is guaranteed. Now I am much taller. I think getting through might be more of a task. But I will wait in line with you and offer you my support."

We get behind a cluster of schoolchildren who seem to be part of a tour group, all wearing matching T-shirts. They're high energy, bouncing up and down and chattering among themselves.

Akira and I don't talk as the line moves forward—it's another moment of nice crackly silence and I feel a rush of gratitude. I like that he doesn't seem to think these patches of quiet between us need to be filled or explained. They can just be.

I watch as the tour group kids crouch down and squeeze themselves through the nostril one by one. And as we step closer and closer to the pillar, my heart rate ratchets upward, apprehension rising in my chest.

That hole is *really* small—even the tiny children have to wriggle to get through. What if I get stuck? I have a sudden, horrific vision of a crew of workers coming in to dismantle this beautiful, ancient landmark, all because some tourist girl was trying to claw her way to enlightenment. Maybe this is one of those things that's better left to fantasy—an experience I should most definitely *not* make real.

"Kimi?" Akira's voice snaps me back to the present and I realize the chatty kids have all squeezed through. Now it's my turn.

"I . . ." I stare down at Buddha's nostril. Which I have to say looks way, *way* smaller up close. My hands are all clammy and sweat beads my brow. I swallow hard.

"Kimi," Akira says again. "You don't have to do this if you don't want to."

"No, I . . . I do," I say. The tall man's triumphant, beaming face flashes through my mind. Dammit. I *do* want to. But I can't seem to make the first move toward actually doing it.

"Here," Akira says, crouching down. He sets his backpack to the side of the pillar. "It's okay. I'll go first."

"But I thought you didn't want to!" I squeak. "Y-you said you were taller now and it would be more of a *task*—"

He shrugs, smiles at me, and touches my hand. "I changed my mind."

Before I can protest any further, he turns and plunges headfirst into the nostril. He stretches his arms in front of himself, like he's diving. I watch him wriggle inside the pillar. The bottom half of his body twitches back and forth—all I can see are his legs and his feet, clad in those neon orange sneakers. He looks like an awkward mermaid, trying to swim through a particularly tough wave. This would be funny if I wasn't all freaked out about him getting stuck inside a historical landmark while doing something he didn't actually want to do. And he's doing it for *me*.

Now that's *a declaration!* Bex's voice crows in my head.

I feel so guilty and so swoony all at once.

His legs go still for a moment and my heart jumps—is he stuck? But then he starts wriggling again, his bottom half disappears through the pillar, and I hear a *thunk* on the other side.

"Kimi!" he exclaims, breathless.

I crouch down and peer through the nostril. Akira's grinning face beams back at me from the other side of the pillar. That adorable dimple is on full display and makes me feel momentarily soothed.

"Come on!" he says. "If I can do it, you can—ne? You have—eto, what's the expression?—you have got this!"

I think he's making a fist-pump motion, but the hole in the pillar is so small, I can literally only see his face.

I take a few deep breaths. Okay. He's right. I *can* do this. Didn't I travel halfway across the world to try to freaking find myself? Surely I can travel through a single pillar. I set my bag next to his backpack.

I stretch my arms in front of me, like he did. Then I plunge into the nostril. It's dark and snug and a little dusty, but I shuffle forward on my stomach and focus on plunging myself toward the light—which, once I'm inside, I realize isn't *that* far away. I wriggle through so that half of me is on one side of the pillar and half of me is on the other, the middle section of my body housed in the nostril. Having my head and arms sticking out makes me breathe a little easier. I look up and see Akira standing over me, smiling from ear to ear. There are also a bunch of people gathered around, cameras and phones at the ready—probably waiting for their own friends and loved ones to emerge from the nostril so they can snap a photo.

"Yes!" Akira says, nodding encouragingly. "See? You're almost there."

I settle my palms on the base of the pillar and push myself forward, trying to give myself leverage.

That's it . . . That's it . . .

It's a snug fit, but not unmanageable. Wriggle, wriggle . . . *thud.*

Suddenly, I'm not moving forward. Not even a little bit. Not *at all.*

Oh, crap.

Am I actually stuck? Did I, like, visualize this into being? And are all these people with their cameras cued up going to *take a photo of me permanently stuck inside Buddha's nostril*? I picture my hapless picture going viral, my mother covering her face in embarrassment. My heartbeat speeds up again and my palms get all slippery, sliding along the base of the pillar.

"Kimi." Akira crouches down, his brow furrowing. "Don't panic, okay? There's a bit of a tricky spot right there in the middle, but just be patient and twist your hips a little."

I take a deep breath. Meet his eyes. He looks so earnest, so concerned. That deep intensity is there again and even though I'm currently stuck in the most ridiculous position possible, I feel a rush of warmth. He's taking this so seriously, he believes so much that I can do this. He's not rushing forward, all manly-like, to pull me through with his brute strength. And he's not laughing at me for looking like a total dork. He just wants to help me complete my mission, this thing I suddenly *had* to do.

"You are a badass," Akira says, still earnest. Then his face softens into a little half smile. "You know, an ass that is bad."

I find myself smiling back.

I take a deep breath, twist my hips a little, and start wriggling again.

That's right, I tell myself firmly. *I am an ass that is bad, dammit! Battle Kimi, rawr! Look at me go!*

I wriggle with all my might and suddenly I feel the bottom half of my body slide through and my palms plant on the floor and I'm gasping for breath like I've been underwater.

"You did it!" I feel Akira's hand on my shoulder, giving me a triumphant pat. He holds out his hand and I take it and he pulls me to my feet. I finally look up and meet his eyes and he's grinning at me like I've just run a marathon or won an Oscar or some equally impressive feat of excellence.

A slow smile spreads over my face and I realize that . . . *yeah, I did it!* I pushed myself through Buddha's nostril. Next-life enlightenment will be *mine*, dammit! Yatta! Exhilaration blooms in my chest and giddiness fizzes through my veins and then I realize that Akira is still holding my hand. The warmth of his palm pressed against mine makes me even more giddy—he's holding tight, like he doesn't ever want to let me go.

We're standing so close to each other and it's another one of those moments where it feels like the rest of the room melts away and there's that crackle between us. Those dark eyes are searching mine with the same intensity he seems to give everything. My heartbeat is so loud, it seems like it's thundering through my ears, and all I want to do is close those last teeny, tiny centimeters of space between us and—

Kiss! Him! Kiss! Him! Atsuko and Bex chant in my head.

But . . . *no*. This isn't the perfect moment. I'm all sweaty and gross and . . . and maybe I'm imagining the way he's looking at me! Maybe he's just checking me over to make sure I didn't hurt myself or something. Maybe I'm being totally KY—totally unable to read the freakin' air. And anyway . . .

Are you worried about your first kiss? Atsuko's voice says in my head.

Argh. I mean, I said I wasn't. But now that it's actually within the realm of possibility, now that it's literally staring me in the face . . . what if it's bad? What if I, Totally Inexperienced Kisser, am bad *at* it? What if it's *so terrible*, it ruins everything?

"Kimi?" Akira says softly. He's still looking at me in that way that . . . I don't know if it's friendly concern or something more. I drop his hand and take a step back.

"Sorry," I say. "That was . . . Wow. Thank you for helping me accomplish that feat." I gesture to the pillar, where a new school tour group is pushing themselves through one by one, cheering each other on.

"Of course," he says. He tilts his head at me, his expression puzzled—or maybe I'm imagining that, too?

Ugh. I just don't know anymore.

"I think that could definitely be a clue in my whole self-discovery mystery thing," I say.

"Oh, really?" he says.

"Yeah," I say, nodding. "I mean, it's like I broke through that barrier so now I know I can break through other barriers. In my mind. Or something." Great, now I'm babbling. Filling up those formerly good silences with not-so-good chatter.

"That sounds like a good first step," Akira says. "Ano . . . this might seem out of nowhere, but are you hungry?"

"Starving," I say automatically—and then I realize it's true. Squeezing yourself through a minuscule, sacred nostril-space definitely works up an appetite.

"Excellent," Akira says, his puzzled look melting into a half smile. "I know just the place."

CHAPTER ELEVEN

"McDonald's? Really?" I put my hands on my hips and give Akira a look. "I thought you were taking me somewhere more . . . more . . ."

"What?" he says, feigning innocence. "You were expecting a place that is more . . ." He affects a bouncy, Valley girl–like accent, stretching out his vowels. ". . . like, totally authentic Japanese?"

"Is that supposed to be a California girl voice?" I say, my explosive giggle tumbling out. "I do *not* sound like that."

We took a long, meandering walk to get to this McD's, wandering through gorgeous green nature-scapes peppered with those adorable deer. A few of them tried to follow us, hoping we'd stop and feed them. But Akira marched on, determined to get to . . . an American fast food place? An American fast food place that, make no mistake, I enjoy greatly, but that I can also have whenever I want. Okay, okay: I'll admit maybe I *had* been expecting something more, like, totally authentic Japanese.

"We need french fry fuel before we go feed the deer," Akira says, opening the door for me. "And anyway, I believe our McDonald's has a few offerings that yours does not."

We step inside, and it looks like . . . well, a McDonald's. Bright lights and primary colors and the good ol' golden arches. But as I glance up at the menu, I realize Akira wasn't joking: alongside the Big Macs and Filet-O-Fishes, there are several unfamiliar items: a "Teriyaki Mac" burger, a fried chicken patty you shake up in a bag with spices, and something called an Ebi Filet-O.

"Shrimp burger," Akira explains when I point it out. "Shrimp smashed together into a patty and fried in panko. Highly recommended."

"You had me at panko," I say, holding up a hand. "I love panko maybe more than anything in the world. I haven't even tasted this yet and I'm all ready to start a petition to make the Ebi Filet-O a thing at McD's in the States."

"It is most definitely petition-worthy," Akira says, nodding solemnly.

We order a Big Mac for him, an Ebi Filet-O for me, sodas, and two large fries.

"Let me," Akira says, waving me aside when I pull out my money. "I am taking full responsibility for your first authentic Japanese McDonald's experience."

"Oh, thank you," I say. Then I lengthen my vowels and give him my own version of the California girl drawl. "I, like, so totally appreciate that."

He laughs. "Mine was better. More authentic California accent, ne?"

We get our food and sit at one of the plasticky tables, the scents of grease and salt mingling in the air surrounding us. I have to admit, there's something comforting about this heavy, greasy aura—it sinks into my bones and soothes me, reminding me of home and getting fries after school with Atsuko.

"Ah, smiling before you have even taken a bite," Akira says. "Already, my McDonald's is winning."

"Who said anything about a competition?" I say, arching an eyebrow as I pick up my shrimp filet and take a bite. *Holy crap.*

The flavor explosion of the Ebi Filet-O cannot be over-stated. Tender shrimp, crispy panko, and some kind of sauce on top that is sort-of-but-not-quite Big Mac sauce. *Wow.* It's rich and comforting and I can totally see Dad doing a killer version of this at his restaurant. I'll have to tell him about it.

"This. Is. So. *Good!*" I exclaim, pointing emphatically at my sandwich with every syllable.

"Ah, you see, Kimi from America?" Akira gives me a smug look and pops a fry in his mouth. "You were prepared to be disappointed by my lunch selection, but I have . . . what is the expression?" He puts his elbows on the table and leans forward, affecting an ultra-serious look. "Blown your brain."

"Blown my *mind*," I correct, laughing. "But you know what, my brain is pretty blown, too."

He grins and sits back in his seat, popping more fries in his mouth.

"You get so excited about things," he says.

"What, like food?" I say, taking another delectable bite of panko and shrimp. "Yeah, I love food. A lot of people love food."

"But you are always *exclaiming* over it," he says with a chuckle. "You seem to . . . how do you say it? Like, enjoy in an especially excited way. You . . . you *relish* it."

I shrug. "There's so much awesome food in the world. Why not relish it?"

"Not just food," he says. "You get excited about other things, too. The beauty of the temple earlier, or the girls in yukata at the bamboo grove the other day. Or when you were talking about where you'd wear that dress you drew— the imaginary party for your friend Atsuko with all the fantastical decorations. You got that same look as you were describing it, like you were relishing just thinking about such a party and such a dress."

"Is that weird?" I say, cocking an eyebrow.

"No." He smiles at me. "I like it."

I flush and look down at my food. Once again, I'm confused. Does he mean, *I like it and I like* you, *weird, overenthusiastic American girl* or *I like it as an element of someone I want to be friends with, full stop*?

Totally KY, Atsuko says in my head.

"You get excited about things, too," I say, polishing off my filet. "Creepy medical texts, American detective shows, Buddha's guts. And surely you have some outrageous fantasy you like to indulge in, much like my whole party thing."

"Ah, un, un," he says, his smile widening. "Sometimes I imagine I am already a successful doctor, spending my days cracking the medical mysteries of my patients and doing important research. I am making enough money to get my family all the things they have always wanted. I buy Ojisan a permanent mochi stand where he never has to worry about rent ever again. He can concentrate fully on perfecting all of his recipes."

"Is rent at the market expensive?" I say.

"It keeps going up," Akira says. "So far, Ojisan's profits have been enough to keep him going, but the margin gets smaller every year. Luckily he has the best employee in all of Japan to help him out." He grins and points to himself.

"Or the only employee in all of Japan who's willing to dress up in a mochi costume and dance around like a dork," I say, grinning back at him. "But you know, Akira: There's a big difference between your fantasy and mine."

"What's that?"

"Yours could actually come true," I say, making a face at him. "You're going to be a doctor. And you're so excited about it. That's *awesome*." I toy with my ketchup-stained napkin, tearing it into tiny little pieces. "My fantasy, meanwhile, is destined to remain pretty firmly in fantasyland."

"You could not make dresses for you and all of your friends for a party?" he says, his brow crinkling. "Or do you think such a party could not take place?"

"No, I have no doubt Atsuko will someday have tons of parties dedicated to celebrating her genius," I say, smiling slightly. "I guess I just assume that by then, we'll be actual adults and I won't have time to fool around with clothes anymore. Because I'll be doing . . . whatever I'm supposed to be doing with my life. Before all this, I thought I'd be painting. Becoming the great Asian American artist my mother was so convinced I'd become. But now . . . now, I don't know."

"Ah, but we are going to figure this out, ne?" Akira says, giving me an encouraging smile. "And I have to think: Someone who gets excited about so much in life shouldn't have too much trouble finding her passion. Surely it is lurking right around the corner." His face gets all serious for a moment and I lean in, wondering if he's about to impart some major insight. "Yes," he says, nodding. "I think I see it—"

I lean in closer.

"Right behind you!" he cries out, pointing dramatically at a spot just beyond my left ear, his serious face collapsing into a goofy expression of exaggerated shock.

"Ha-ha," I say, sticking my tongue out at him. "And here I thought you were about to offer me some life-changing words of wis—"

"Wait, but the *deer* is behind you!" he exclaims, making me jump. "The one who wanted food! She's back to—"

"Whaaaaaaaaaat?" I yelp, whipping around in my seat.

Of course, there's nothing there.

"Oh my god," I say, turning back around and throwing my napkin at Akira. He dodges easily, laughing.

"We do have some deer to feed, though, ne?" Akira says, sweeping our empty food wrappers onto a tray. He inspects his fry box, notes that it still contains a few precious golden potatoes, and tucks the box into the front pocket of his backpack. "Shall we get to that?"

The amount of hungry deer in sight is no joke.

They really are *everywhere*, roaming the green of the park. And they're aggressive, relentlessly seeking out tourists buying shika-senbei from vendors and nose-bumping them until they get fed. Some tourists are surrounded by entire packs of deer, pestering them for sustenance.

"Dang, the deer really love these cookies," I say, brandishing the pack of shika-senbei we've purchased. They're round, wafer-thin, and held together with little crisscrossing pieces of paper.

"Careful," Akira says, holding up his hand to cover the cookies. "They see you waving those things around and they'll be all over us."

But it's too late; I've given us away. A cluster of three deer frolics over, noses eagerly sniffing the air. They nudge the bottom of my dress and I hold the cookies up high so they can't reach them.

"All right, all right, calm down," I say, my explosive giggle spilling out of me. "Oh my gosh, you're all so cute."

I hand them cookies one by one, and they gobble them up eagerly. Akira purchases another packet of shika-senbei and starts handing them out himself. More deer, having heard the rumor of our cookie riches, trot up and sniff at us and before I know it, we're surrounded.

"This is so cool," I exclaim, laughing as one of the deer licks my hand. "I feel like a freaking Disney princess attracting a whole squad of woodland creature pals."

"They will be your 'pals' until we run out of shika-senbei," Akira says, cocking an eyebrow at me. He's looking at me like he was earlier, when he kept talking about me getting excited about things. A little amused, a little intrigued, maybe a little . . . tender? I can't tell if I'm imagining that part or not.

My cheeks flush and I turn back to my new deer friends, focusing hard on distributing my shika-senbei. One of the deer bumps my hip, almost like she's encouraging me to turn and look at Akira.

146

No way, little deer friend. We have to be more subtle than that.

I cast a surreptitious sidelong glance at Akira—and notice a deer nosing around in the open front pocket of his backpack.

"Oh—Akira!" I yelp. "Behind you—"

He gives me an amused look. "Trying to fool me like I fooled you earlier, Kimi? It will *not* work."

"No!" I say, gesturing wildly. "There is . . . the deer! It's behind you!"

The deer chooses that moment to get aggressive, craning its neck and plunging its snout more fully into Akira's backpack pocket. He must actually feel it this time because he gets a funny look on his face and turns his head to look.

"Wha—?" he says. "Oi!" He drops the rest of his shika-senbei on the ground and bats (very gently, I notice) at the backpack-plundering deer. "Stop that!"

I try to rush over to him, but there are so many deer between me and him at this point, and they're all poking at me for food. I start to wind my way through, bribing deer with cookies as I go, doing the best I can.

"Stop!" Akira repeats, trying to shake free. The deer, in response, head-butts him and he loses his balance and tumbles to the ground.

"Akira!" I cry, trying to move more quickly through the deer mass. "Shoo!" I say to them. "Get outta here, Bambi!"

The deer finally liberates the thing it was after from Akira's backpack—the McDonald's cardboard box half-full of french fries.

"Oi!" Akira yells as the deer runs off, fry box clutched

triumphantly in its mouth. Maybe it's my imagination, but I could swear it looks a little gleeful.

The other deer, sensing *that* deer has a cool new treat, take off after the fry thief, finally clearing my path to Akira. I run over to him.

"Are you okay?" I exclaim, crouching down next to him.

"Yes, fine," he says, grimacing. "Perhaps a little embarrassed that I cannot seem to stop falling down in front of you." He gives me a wry grin.

"Maybe we've had enough deer-related shenanigans for one day," I say, standing up straight and extending a hand to him. "Here, let me . . ."

He clasps my hand and meets my eyes, but stays still, making no effort to get off the ground. "We're always helping each other up," he says. His voice is soft and that quiet intensity is flashing through his eyes. It's almost like he's saying it to himself—turning it over in his mind, trying to figure out what it means. I'm suddenly very aware of the warmth of his palm against mine again, of the way my cheeks always seem to heat up—

CRAASSSSHHHHHHHHH

Suddenly, the sky opens up and rain slams down on us. There's no warning, nothing. One moment, things are pleasant and dry. The next, nothing but wet and cold and my bangs are getting totally drenched and sticking to my forehead.

"Wha . . ." I yelp.

Akira scrambles to his feet. "Come on!" he cries out, grabbing my hand.

And then we run.

I'm not sure where we're running to, I can barely see—my bangs are now in my eyes and dripping everywhere. Grass squishes under my feet as Akira pulls me to the right and then to the left, trying to maneuver around the deer. It's the kind of rain where there's no space between the drops, it's just like one big sheet of endless water.

We run and run and finally we reach a city street–like thing, wet concrete that doesn't squish as much underneath my shoes but still feels dangerously slippery.

"Over here!" Akira calls out.

He makes a hard left and pulls me into a small alleyway between buildings that appears to have some sort of tarp over it.

It's still cold, but at least we're not getting drenched. I guess technically, we're *already* drenched in pretty much every possible way.

"Oh, Kimi," Akira says, his brow creasing with concern. "You're soaked."

He sets his backpack on the ground, shrugs off his cotton jacket, and wraps it around my shoulders.

"Oh, uh . . . your jacket is also wet," I say, giggling.

"Guh." He laughs. "You're right. I'm sorry."

He smiles at me, flashing that dimple. He's holding the lapels of the jacket he's draped around my shoulders, pulling me closer to him. Even though we're both freezing, I suddenly feel very warm.

And *then* I realize we're totally in the fantasy of my first kiss: the rain, the alley, the adorable boy who's standing so close, there's nothing for us to do but kiss.

Only there are all these things that *weren't* in my fantasy

149

that are somehow even better: the sound of water pattering against the buildings, the way he's looking at me, the delicious scent of rain.

This is it. This is my perfect moment.

I don't think about ruining everything or being bad at kissing or whatever I was worrying about before. I don't even hear Bex and Atsuko chanting in my head. I just *know*. I part my lips slightly and lean in.

He needs to lean in the rest of the way. You know, meet me in the middle.

And he doesn't.

We just keep looking at each other, our gazes locked, me leaning in like I've thrown my hand up for a high five and am getting nothing back. He's still studying me in that intense, serious way. But he's not *moving*. It's as if we're trapped in a weird staring contest.

"Uh . . ." He shakes his head, like he's coming out of a trance.

Then he's carefully removing his jacket from my shoulders, avoiding my gaze, and putting some distance between us.

Well. That is *not* how I saw that going.

"Sorry," he says, giving me a tight smile. "I didn't realize, eto . . . my jacket is soaking you even more. We need to get inside, maybe find a store with some cheap sweatshirts to change into, so we don't catch colds."

"Oh, uh, of course," I say, my voice small.

He motions for me to follow him and I do. He doesn't grab my hand this time.

How did my perfect moment go so wrong?

CHAPTER TWELVE

Dear Mom,

Yesterday I climbed through Buddha's nostril.

It was an epic journey that forced me to push through a big barrier and it made me think of that time a couple years ago when we went to that tiny strip mall donut shop. I don't remember the name of it; we stopped there because it was the only snack-like thing we could find near the office where you were meeting your client. It was one of those places where everyone who works there has probably worked there forever and there are old, faded posters on the wall advertising ten-cent coffee and the tabletops are covered in cheap vinyl that's supposed to look like wood. And the people sitting there seem to come in every day, drinking the same cup of coffee for like twelve hours.

One of those people was this guy in the back—he had a big, bushy beard and bloodshot eyes and when he stood up, he was, like, ten feet tall. (Okay, probably not his actual height, but that's how it seemed at the time.)

We were picking out donuts—I remember you giving me a look and being like, "Kimi-chan, why do you like that awful pink frosting, it's full of chemicals" and I was like, "No, Mom, it's cherry-flavored, FRUIT, definitely all natural"—and that ten-foot-tall guy came lumbering up to us.

I don't remember the exact words he said. It was something about "our lumber" and "the Japanese" taking it. I do remember the way his face seemed to project these really pure feelings: anger, disgust. Hate. And those feelings were all for us.

You didn't say anything. You just stared at him while he ranted—your eyes were like steel, your spine straight as a rod. You had moved your body just a little bit, so that it was in front of mine. I remember thinking that if I touched you, I would probably fall down from that intense pure strength you were radiating. When he got tired of ranting, he turned and shambled back to his seat.

You turned back to the lady behind the counter and told her that you'd like two pink frosted donuts—and also, you were never coming in here again. She just kind of laughed uneasily and murmured something about the ten-foot-tall dude being drunk as usual.

It was one of those situations where all these confusing feelings piled up in me at once and there was pretty much no outlet for them—until we got outside and I blurted out: "Asshole."

I bit my lip, immediately worried you were going to punish me for swearing. But instead you said: "Yes."

Then you took a bite of pink donut and said: "Hmm. Does kind of taste like cherry. Shall we go to the Goodwill?"

You'd never quite understood my obsession with Goodwill (probably because you used to shop there out of necessity rather than desire and didn't get why I'd willingly pursue secondhand clothes with such zeal), so this was a huge treat.

As I zipped around the dollar bins, gathering various treasures, I remember thinking about how strong you were. Because I realized that you must have endured countless moments like that one with the dumbass drunk—and probably worse— when you first came to the States. And you met them like you meet every challenge, with that amazing steel. You pushed through that barrier like it was nothing, even though it probably chipped away at you every time it happened.

Later, I gathered all the treasures I'd gotten at Goodwill, cut them up, and pieced them together. A red, flared skirt chopped off an old figure skating costume. A long-sleeved sequined top liberated from an eighties ball gown. A few other glittery bits and bobs for extra flair. When I was done, I had a new Kimi Original: something that looked like a modern superheroine costume. Inspired by you and the superheroine you are.

Love,
Kimi

p.s.—Buddha's nostril is not an actual nostril, it's a hole cut in a big pillar.

p.p.s.—I kept waiting for the perfect moment to kiss the cutest boy ever and then I almost kissed him, but I don't think he wants to kiss me back, but maybe he does, but I can't tell and I'm really confused, how do you tell if

I stop typing and press the heels of my hands against my eyes until fireworks explode across my vision. Then I put my hands back on the laptop keyboard and make myself delete that last p.p.s. before I attach a photo of my modern superheroine outfit and hit "send."

Mom never responded to my first email, but for some reason, I feel the need to write her another one. Telling her about my first Kimi Original has made me want to continue the story, to tell her how I went on from there.

I have emailed a bit with Dad, who seems to go out of his way to tell me about everything *except* Mom. In addition to asking about how I am, his latest email notes that the first bill for Liu Academy tuition has come due. How do I want him to proceed?

I don't have an answer to that just yet.

I suppose I'm also writing this email to Mom so I won't have to answer that question. And, oh yeah, one more reason—to distract myself. I still don't understand what happened with Akira yesterday. After we slipped out of the alley, we found a souvenir shop and picked up cheap sweatshirts with NARA and cartoon deer printed on them. He was nothing but polite as we headed back to the train station and said good-bye. Polite, reserved, and most definitely *not* trying to kiss me. And he hasn't texted me since then. I guess my fears about reading him incorrectly were right on the money: He doesn't like me. Not *that* way.

But if that's the case, why is he always being so cute and charming and, yes, flirtatious? He used a stuffed tanuki to get my phone number. I mean, *come on.* And he keeps taking me to these beautiful, romantic places and . . . and . . . the declaration!

So why didn't he want to kiss me?

"Blaaaaaaaaaaah." I push the laptop to the side and flop on the bed, moping.

"Kimiko-chan?" Grandma appears in the bedroom doorway, giving me a quizzical look. "Are you all right?"

"Yes, Obaasan," I say, sitting up straight. "Sorry, I was just, uh, thinking about something."

"If you are not sightseeing today, I thought perhaps I could show you how to make that blouse you admired," she says.

"Oh . . . yes!" I say. "Let's do that."

She gives me a nod. "Please get ready and meet me out in the living room so we can walk to the train station."

"We have to go somewhere to make it?" I say, my brow crinkling. "I thought we could just do it in your sewing room—"

"Yes, Kimiko, that's where we will construct the garment," Grandma says, a hint of amusement creeping into her expression. "But we need to go somewhere for you to pick your materials. That is something you will enjoy, ne?"

"We're going to a fabric store?!" I jump to my feet. "Oh yes. That is *definitely* something I enjoy."

For a tiny moment, I forget my angst over Akira.

And for the first time, my obaasan and I exchange a look of understanding.

The fabric store is stuffed into one of the big shopping arcades in Kyoto—a long street covered by a tunnel-like structure. Light filters through the high, curved ceiling, illuminating the jumble of shops selling everything from cheerful rainbows of stationery to elaborately carved walking sticks to Buddha statues of every size imaginable (okay, not as large as the Buddha I saw yesterday, but I'm trying not to think about that, dammit).

I find myself nearly bumping into people as I attempt to maneuver my way through the dense mix of tourists and locals, my senses constantly overwhelmed by all the cool new things to see. I can't help but imagine myself here with Bex and Atsuko—Bex ferreting out whimsically printed notebooks and hard-to-find manga and Atsuko complaining that her feet hurt and coming up with excuses for us to stop at every snack shop along the way.

My obaasan moves through with ease, zigzagging her way through the crush of people, on a mission to the fabric store. When we finally reach our destination, the space looks deceptively small and gray and nondescript from the outside. But a low table boasting a tiny basket of brightly colored remnants sitting at the entrance catches my eye and my heart starts to beat a little bit faster.

Once we cross the gray threshold, my eyeballs are overwhelmed by the color and pattern explosion—there are shelves and shelves of beautiful bolts of fabric. And I haven't even gotten to the side displays of ribbon and yarn and buttons. My gaze darts everywhere, unsure of where to land. I'm practically drooling. Maybe this place keeps its exterior purposefully bland so the inside is more of a *wow*.

"I would suggest a lighter weight cotton," my grandmother says, guiding me toward a particular section of the fabric shelves. "This style will work with a variety of materials, but I believe the cotton provides the right weight and movement for the ruffled details on the front."

"That's what I was thinking, too—a lighter cotton will hold the shape without being too stiff," I say, studying the feast of fabrics in front of me. My fingertips brush over their soft textures. I love the possibilities contained in new fabric. It has the potential to be so many beautiful things.

My hand lingers on a bolt of bright pink with a pattern of white cherry blossoms and scattered gold threads. Something about it sparks immediate joy in my heart—it's so cheery, like a happy little song in fabric form. The gold gives it a sense of *drama*. And seeing it sandwiched between the bright oranges and reds of the fabrics around it sets my brain spinning—I'm already thinking about what I could pair it with, what kinds of "clashing" combinations I could come up with. Inspiration laces its way through my heart and I feel like I did when I saw the girls in their beautiful yukata and obi in the bamboo forest.

But this particular fabric is probably *too* loud. I should go with basic black for this blouse, like what Grandma has.

I already know that will look good; it's less of a risk. Plus, I've noticed Grandma likes to wear mostly black and white and gray—so she'll likely approve of that choice. I move my hand to a bolt of plain black cotton.

"This one," I say.

"Are you sure?" my grandmother says.

I turn to look at her, surprised. I expected her to give me an approving nod and motion for the salesgirl to pull the bolt from the shelf.

"You don't like it?" I say.

"It does not matter if I like it," she says, tapping the black cotton. "It is your blouse. You should get something you like. Something you *want*. Something that will speak to your soul every time you wear it. That is the point of clothing, ne?"

A slow grin spreads over my face. Somewhere deep inside of me, that's what I've always thought—but I've never been able to vocalize it quite so well.

"Yes," I say, with a surprised chuckle. "That is the point of clothing. That's why I *love* clothes. I mean, besides not being naked and stuff."

Oh, jeez. Why did I say that? Why did I have to ruin a perfectly nice moment?

But one side of Grandma's mouth quirks up and she lets out a little snort-laugh.

"Also a very good point," she says. "So is that the one you want?" She nods at the black cotton I'm touching.

I turn back to the fabric shelves. The black is cool. The black will go with everything. The black is what Grandma has.

The black . . . does not speak to my soul. It's not what I want.

I move my hand to the bright pink with little white flowers.

"I want this one," I say.

Grandma smiles. "Good choice."

When we exit the shop, I'm expecting we'll head immediately to the train station, but my obaasan turns in the opposite direction and motions for me to follow.

"Would you like to see something else here, Kimiko-chan?" she says, raising an eyebrow.

"I'd like to see *everything* else here," I say, my eyes scanning over all the cool-looking shops. "I could probably spend days here, in fact. Maybe I'll just move in?"

My grandmother gives me a quizzical look and my cheeks flush—why do I always insist on ruining our prospective nice moments by saying something weird?

"I am thinking of one thing you might like to see," she says. "It is a bit of a secret."

And then she takes off, effortlessly making her way through the crowd again. I follow, silently lecturing myself to *not* get distracted by the many, many potentially awesome things around me.

Obaasan leads me on a maze-like journey, taking me through a tiny side street, into another shopping arcade, and down a narrow, dimly lit corridor that looks straight out of a horror movie. I'm just starting to entertain the notion that my grandmother is an undercover evil mastermind who's leading me to my death (a notion I thankfully do *not* vocalize), when we emerge on the other side of the corridor and into a little courtyard shrouded in bonsai trees. A path of stones of all different shapes and sizes leads to a tiny red cottage with a huge front window that takes up most of its courtyard-facing wall.

I spend a moment just gawking. It's like something out of an old-fashioned storybook, a tranquil oasis hidden from the chaos of the shopping arcades.

"What is it?" I say, my voice full of wonder.

My grandmother motions for me to keep following her. And as we enter the tiny red cottage, I go right back to gawking.

I thought nothing could top the fabric store, but what's inside this cottage comes awfully close. The main attraction is a glass counter absolutely covered in different kinds of sewing needles, pins, pincushions—basically everything you need for sewing. And all organized in meticulous, precisely arranged clumps. If the fabric store felt like a glorious jumble, this feels more like a minuscule museum dedicated to the art of making stuff.

"This is Misuyabari needle shop," my grandmother says, nodding to the elderly Japanese man behind the counter. "It is four hundred years old—a true family business."

I'm so excited, I can't even form words. I approach the glass counter reverently, trying to take it all in. Pincushions are lined up in neat rows in a cute wooden box and tiny pins with colorful toppers pierce perfectly arranged squares of foam. I take a closer look at one of the clusters of pins and let out a squeak of delight. The tops are all little animals: a guileless-looking poodle with a bow on its head, a cranky frog with huge eyes. My eyes go to the next cluster, where the pinheads are all different kinds of flowers, like a tiny garden blooming right there on the countertop.

Something stirs in my chest and a lump rises in my throat. I can't quite explain why this sight moves me so much. Maybe it's because all of these sewing implements are displayed with such care and reverence—as if they're sacred, important, precious. It feels like whoever did this gets as excited about sewing and making clothes as I do.

"Are you all right, Kimiko-chan?" my grandmother says, and I'm so caught up in my reverie, I nearly jump out of my skin. I blink a couple times, getting my burgeoning tears under control.

"Yes," I manage. "This is amazing. Thank you for bringing me here, Obaasan."

"I thought you would like it," she says. "This is . . . eto . . ." She pauses, as if thinking it over. "This is a bit of what I think of as true Kyoto—a place for people who are passionate about making things."

"Like you," I say, turning to smile at her. I briefly wonder if this is skating too close to a compliment and decide to risk it. "You know, the way you like to grow things in your garden. And make clothes."

"And perhaps you, too?" she says, cocking an eyebrow at me.

"I'm trying to figure that out," I say, flashing to my failed painting career and trying not to wince. "But none of my

161

craftsman abilities are on par with this." I gesture to the adorable displays of pins.

"It is good not to have a big head," my grandmother says. "But . . ." She regards me shrewdly. "Do not be so fast to dismiss yourself."

"I don't think I'm meant to be an artist," I say, turning back to the pins and focusing on a bright scarlet ladybug. "Not like Mom."

The words are out of my mouth before I have time to think about them—or the fact that bringing up my mother to my obaasan is probably one of the worst ideas ever, no matter what Grandpa says. An awkward silence settles over us like a prickly blanket.

"Your mother had many steps on her journey," my grandmother finally says, her voice neutral. "I still remember how she struggled before she left for the America. She was not sure what it would be like when she got there and she was so afraid her English would not be good enough."

"She talks sometimes about how she had a hard time at first," I say, my voice soft. We're in uncharted territory, but I don't want to scare Grandma off from this line of conversation. "She'd mix up words all the time."

"That was a mistake she always made," my grandmother says. Maybe it's my imagination, but her voice sounds almost affectionate? "Back when we were taking our English lessons together."

"You took English lessons together?" I exclaim. *This* is a part of the story I've never heard before.

"Your mother, your grandfather, and I," my grandmother says. "It was something we did together, as a family. We always thought this would be useful—your grandfather and I hoped to save up enough to go to the America and attend her college graduation."

I can fill in the part of the story that goes unsaid: After my mom met my dad, after things deteriorated between my grandparents and my mother, this trip never happened. My grandparents have never been to the States. And my mom has never been back here.

I don't know if I've ever thought about how severe the break between them was, if I ever comprehended how much has been lost. I can't help but wonder if Mom ever feels cut off from an essential piece of herself, all those long ago memories that formed the person she is today.

"We have kept up the lessons—your grandfather and I," my grandmother says. "Our English is very good, ne?"

"Very good," I agree, surprised that she's sort of paying herself a compliment. Definitely not going to point that out, though. "And . . ." I cast a sidelong glance at her. Her tone is neutral again and so is her expression—she's studying the little set of animal pins, absently tapping each of them on the head with her index finger. "Maybe you can still come to the States one day."

Her expression doesn't change, but I notice her finger pauses on the tiny poodle pin. She hesitates, then gives it an extra little tap.

"Maybe," she finally says.

As we walk back through the shopping arcade, my phone lights up with messages from Bex and Atsuko—I haven't told them anything about my day with Akira and I guess they got tired of waiting for me to check in.

I really don't want to tell them what a non-event our non-kiss was. Just thinking about it brings down my mood.

"What's wrong, Kimiko-chan?" Obaasan says.

"Nothing," I say automatically. "I mean, uh, do I look like something's wrong?"

"You were swinging those bags around like you just won the biggest prize," she says, gesturing to my shopping bags—one containing my beloved pink fabric, the other containing a set of the bright flower pins I just couldn't resist. "Then you looked at your phone and stopped."

"I'm just thinking about something," I say, my gaze wandering to the ground.

"That is what you said earlier," she says, her brow furrowing. "When you were making that odd sound in your bedroom."

I keep my gaze trained on the ground. Can I talk to her about this? It seems like kind of a leap to go from tentatively bonding over fabric and sewing tools to talking out my boy problems. I mean, she just started being able to look me in the eye for more than two seconds—she seems to be slowly getting used to me, not being put off by the fact that I look so much like Mom.

And anyway, what is there to this story beyond, *I thought this boy liked me, but now I think maybe he doesn't?*

I look up from the ground, my eyes wandering the

street—and suddenly they land on something very interesting.

"Whoa, what's *that*?" I say, stepping forward to get a better look.

It's a little shop with the brightest, most beautiful garments in the window—they're interesting, modern shapes with kimono-inspired flourishes, like full, flowing sleeves. And they're all made out of rich-looking fabric in bold prints. They speak to my soul in an immediate, visceral way.

"Would you like to go in?" Grandma says, sidling up to me. "This is my friend's shop."

"Wh-what?" is about all I can get out as I follow her inside. My obaasan is just full of surprises today.

The shop owner greets my grandmother enthusiastically, bowing and talking to her in Japanese. She appears to be a little younger than Grandma and her black hair is swept up into a high bun, revealing dramatic streaks of white at her temples. She's wearing a garment like the ones displayed in the window—a bright red dress with an abstract pattern of blue streaks. The red matches her fiery lipstick.

She is quite possibly the coolest person I've ever seen.

"Sa-chan, this is my granddaughter, Kimiko," my grandmother says. "Kimiko, this is my dear friend Sakae Yoneyama. She makes all of these clothes."

"Yoneyama-san," I say, bowing. "You make all of this *and* you own this boutique? That's amazing."

"Arigato," Sakae says, beaming at me. Apparently she has no problem with compliments. "Would you like to try something on?"

"Uhhhh, maybe a few somethings," I say, my gaze scanning the wealth of beautiful clothes on display. "If that's all right with you, Obaasan."

"Hai," my grandmother says. "I would like to try on a few things myself."

Sakae laughs and says something in Japanese. My grandmother does her little snort-laugh.

"She said she has some things in black she put aside just for me," Grandma says, raising an eyebrow.

Sakae bustles into the back of the store and emerges with a pile of black dresses, which she hands to my grandmother. Then she turns to me.

"Hmm," she says, studying me intently. "Something brighter for you. Maybe this red?" She gestures to her own dress. "And shorter cut, ne?"

She goes over to the window and takes a dress I was admiring—red with dramatic sleeves—off the mannequin. Then she hands it to me and motions toward the curtained-off dressing rooms on the other side of the store.

"Go," she commands. "Try on."

I emerge from the dressing room a few minutes later to see my grandmother already in front of the mirror, scrutinizing her black-clad form.

"Wow, that looks awesome, Grandma," I say, sidling up next to her.

"Arigato," she says. "You look very nice as well."

I smooth the skirt of my own dress—it flows around my hips beautifully and oh, god, the *sleeves* on this thing. They make me feel like some combination of fairy princess and superhero. And it fits *perfectly*. I'm so used to having to alter things for my shrimpy frame, but the hang on this dress is just right. I glance around, looking for Sakae, and see that she's on the other side of the store, helping another customer.

"How do you know Yoneyama-san?" I say.

"We were in school together," Grandma says. "We both loved sewing." She smiles at the memories. "Sa-chan's parents wanted her to get married and settle down, but she refused. So they cut her off. Stopped talking to her. She struck out on her own and worked as a server in a teahouse and sewed her garments whenever she was not working. Built up a small private clientele and eventually saved enough money to quit the teahouse and open up her shop."

"Seems to have worked out pretty well, hasn't it?" I murmur.

"Sou desu ne," my grandmother agrees.

I gaze at our dapper reflections in the mirror. We're wearing spins on the same design and look adorably coordinated—like we go together. I feel a sudden rush of warmth in my chest.

"Grandma, I like a boy," I blurt out.

She turns to me. "Oh?" She's cocking her head to the side and there's no judgment in her expression, just curiosity.

"I like a boy and I can't tell if he likes me," I forge on. "I thought he did. But then he acted weird and now I'm not so sure. How do you tell? Is there a way to tell? How could you tell with Ojiisan?"

"Kimiko-chan." My grandmother shakes her head, looking

a touch exasperated. "You use so many words." She hesitates, studying me. "Did your mother ever tell you about the first time I made dinner for your ojiisan?"

"No," I say.

"He came to my family's home," my grandmother says. "I cooked fish in a special sauce, a recipe I was very proud of knowing how to make—because it was the *only* thing I knew how to make." She smiles slightly. "He ate so much of it. I was so happy. And our conversation was wonderful. My heart was—what do you say? Eto . . . full of butterflies. The only sour note was my father's dog, Yoshi, who kept hovering around the table, wanting to be fed. I kept trying to shoo him away." Her smile turns wry. "The dog was mostly staying around your grandfather, but toward the end of the meal, he came around the table to me. And proceeded to vomit a very large serving of fish right in my lap."

"What!" I exclaim. That's definitely *not* how I was expecting this romantic story to end. "Wait. Was Grandpa feeding the dog his fish all night?!"

"Yes," my grandmother says, her smile widening. "As it turns out, your grandfather hates fish. But he didn't want to tell me because I was so excited to make it for him."

Okay. *That's* pretty romantic.

"We had fish the other night," I say. "Is he still only pretending to like it?"

"He has learned to like it over the years. It has—what is the expression? Grown on him."

"So I should make fish and serve it to Akira and see if he feeds it to a dog?" I say, my brow crinkling.

"No," Grandma says. "I am saying: There are two ways

to tell someone something. One is to *not* tell them, the way your grandfather did—he didn't tell me he hated fish and he didn't tell me he cared for me. But he did tell me both of those things with actions rather than words. The other is to just come out and tell them." She turns back to face the mirror. "Personally, I prefer the second way. Less dog vomit."

"But how do I get him to tell me if he likes me—one way or the other?" I say, laughing.

"You don't," my grandmother says. "*You* tell *him*. After all, you just told me: 'I like a boy.' Why are you trying so hard to figure out what *he* wants when you already know what *you* want? If you want something, you have to say it out loud and to the correct person."

"It sounds so easy when you say it that way," I murmur. "But it might be hard to say in person."

"You are smart, ne?" my obaasan says briskly. "You will figure it out. Now. Do you want this dress?"

I smile at our reflections in the mirror. "Yes," I say. "I definitely want it."

Funny how that wasn't hard to say at all.

CHAPTER THIRTEEN

There aren't just butterflies in my stomach. There are butterflies having the freakin' party of the year in my stomach.

But after my talk with Obaasan, I realized I have to do this. I have to tell Akira I like him. Out loud and to his face.

It was kind of awesome to be so certain about something. When we got back to my grandparents' house, I texted Akira and asked if he wanted to meet up the next day. Then I waited for him to text back. Then I texted Bex and Atsuko and giddily explained what I was going to do. Then *finally* Akira texted back and said he had to work the next day—but maybe we could meet up at the market for ice cream?

I tried to parse the tone of his text, but it was pretty basic, not giving me much to work with.

My friends, of course, demanded a pre-meetup Skype session.

"You're doing it today!" Atsuko bellows, dancing across my laptop screen. "You're gonna tell him you like him!"

"That is sooooo awesome!" Bex chimes in. "Go, Kimi, go!"

I laugh and flash them a thumbs-up. They're trying to do some routine they've choreographed in my honor. They're dressed in pieced-together, mismatched cheerleader outfits they assembled from whatever they could find at Goodwill and Bex has constructed makeshift pom-poms out of strips of crepe paper. (How they had time to do all this, I don't know, but never underestimate Atsuko's pigheadedness paired with Bex's die-hard romantic nature.)

"Go, Kimi, go!" Bex repeats, waving her droopy pom-pom. She stops to swoon for a moment. "And now *you're* making the declaration. So romantic."

"Yeeeaaaaaah!" Atsuko bellows, flopping on the floor and trying to do the splits. She's not quite successful, so she just splays her legs out as far as they'll go and waves her pom-pom in time with Bex's.

"Thanks, guys," I say, giggling.

"Kimi," Atsuko says, pulling herself out of her awkward not-quite-the-splits position. "Are you okay if . . . I mean, you know it's not guaranteed he's going to respond in the exact perfect way when you tell him, right?"

"I know," I say—even though the very thought makes the butterflies in my gut start partying up a storm. "Believe me, I know. But if he doesn't feel the same way, well . . ." I shrug. The butterflies dance harder. "At least I'll know. And anyway, he's not the only reason I'm having fun in Japan. My grandma and I had such a great time together yesterday."

I briefly relate the tale of our adventures in the fabric store, the pins and needles shop, and Sakae's wonderful boutique. After we got home, and I'd managed to make a date with Akira, I spent hours sketching, drawing all sorts of new outfits inspired by the beautiful rainbow of fabrics I'd seen. I'm actually thinking of going back and getting more of that bright pink cotton. There's so much I can see doing with it. Maybe I'll pick up a few yards of a gorgeous purple silk that also caught my eye.

"Kimi!" Atsuko exclaims, laughing. "Did you hear what you just said? You're doing it! You're having fun in Japan!"

"Yeah, I am," I say, a slow smile spreading over my face as I realize it's true.

"Excellent," Atsuko says, nodding sagely. "Your next Ask Atsuko directive—"

"Wait a minute, I totally failed in kissing Akira—" I protest.

"Or you just haven't succeeded yet," Bex chimes in.

"Why am I getting another directive?!" I continue.

"Think of it more like a thing to consider, then," Atsuko says, her eyes turning thoughtful. "Try not to fantasize about all the different things that might happen when you tell Akira you like him. Because there's no way of knowing what he's actually going to say. And I know that's what you're going to *want* to do when you're on your way over to the market. Unless . . ." Her eyes narrow suspiciously. "You've already been doing that."

"No," I say. "Actually, I haven't."

Wait a minute. I cock my head to the side. I haven't done that, have I? And Atsuko's right—usually that's *exactly* what I'd do. Fantasize about all the possible perfect outcomes that might occur once I say those words to him.

But the truth is, I keep thinking about the way I felt when I touched that bright pink fabric. Proclaimed out loud that I wanted it instead of trying to hide my true feelings under a bolt of plain black cotton.

Akira is, of course, much more important than any piece

172

of fabric. But I don't want to hide my true feelings from him, either.

Even if it makes things real in a painful way.

Even if it ruins everything.

I take the train to Kyoto—and this time, I actually know where I'm going and don't get distracted. I stride with purpose toward Maruyama Park. Toward the mochi stand and the tanuki and Akira.

The market is just as bustling as it was the first time I happened upon it, but I spot the boy I like immediately. Akira is by the ice cream stand where he suggested we meet, stuffing his hands in his pockets and shuffling his feet around. He looks on edge. Unsure. Or maybe I'm imagining that, projecting that onto him? I have no idea what he's thinking. Maybe he's going to tell me he doesn't want to hang out anymore? A brand-new batch of butterflies parties its way through my stomach. God, *calm down*, butterflies.

I take a deep breath. Okay. Here we go.

I try to walk with purpose toward the ice cream stand. I decided to wear my new red dress, the one I got from Sakae's boutique, which makes my stride a little more confident.

"Kimi," Akira says, looking up. "Hi."

Once again, I have no idea what he's thinking. The look he's giving me isn't exactly happy, but it's not *un*happy.

"Hi," I say back.

And then we just stand there. This silence is *totally*

awkward, not at all like the nice silence we had going before. What shifted so dramatically between us in that rainstorm?

I'm all prepared to blurt out my declaration, but then he has to go and break the awkward silence with, "So. Ice cream?"

Hmm. *Guess what, Akira, I really like you* is probably not an appropriate response to that.

So instead I say: "Sure."

He seems to relax a little as we turn to the ice cream stand and scan the offerings—maybe because now we have something concrete to do. A task.

"This is sofuto kurimu," he says. "Soft cream. It's supposed to be like your American soft serve." He gives me a half smile and I relax a little, feeling like we're in more familiar territory. But I notice the smile doesn't quite reach his eyes.

"Great," I say, my voice loud and bright—a little too loud and bright. It doesn't sound like me. "I'll have—ooh!" I point to one of the bins. "Is that black sesame? I love black sesame frozen anything."

"You have black sesame–flavored things in the States?" Akira says.

"Of course," I say. "Whole lotta Asians in the States, you know." I poke him in the arm and finally, his smile reaches his eyes.

"Cone or cup?" he says.

"Cone. Always."

Akira orders for us, getting a black sesame for me and a matcha for him, and we sit down on a nearby bench with our cones. We eat in silence and it feels like that nice, crackly kind of silence again. I am momentarily soothed. The sofuto kurimu is delicious—light and sweet and somehow better than any soft serve I've ever had.

"You got home okay the other day from Nara? Sorry. Of course you did. I mean—sorry." Akira shakes his head. "I meant to check up on you later."

"My grandparents did wonder if all my fashion sense had deserted me when they saw the souvenir sweatshirt," I say, trying to keep my tone light. "But otherwise, yes, I was fine."

This is the perfect opening. We're talking about the other day, when we had that almost kiss moment. I can ease us into the topic and then tell him.

"Speaking of the other day," I say—and my voice suddenly has that too loud, too bright quality again. Also, the goddamn hard-partying butterflies are back. "Um. The rainstorm."

"That was quite the rainstorm," he says, nodding. "I was surprised. It does rain heavily in Nara, but not usually in the spring."

"Uh, yeah," I say, caught off guard. Why is he trying to go in-depth on the weather? "Anyway, so after we ran through the rainstorm—"

"I apologize," he says. "I did not mean to . . . pull you. Through the rain. In that manner. I was trying to find cover."

"Right, I got that," I say, frowning. He's acting all twitchy again, toying with what's left of his cone and looking at the ground. I'm trying to get my declaration out, dammit. "I didn't feel . . . pulled. I guess what I'm trying to say is—"

"And the deer," he interrupts. "They were so aggressive. I'm sorry about that, too, I should have remembered—"

"They were mostly aggressive to *you*," I say, exasperated. Why does he keep interrupting me and apologizing for random things? "Akira—"

"I have to go," he says abruptly. He stands, crumpling his cone wrapper in his hand. "It's almost time for my shift. I will see you later, Kimi."

Then he turns and takes off.

I sit there, dumbfounded, watching him hurry through the crowd, his shaggy hair bobbing with purpose.

What was *that*?

I pop the rest of my cone in my mouth, trying to process what just happened. Honestly, I can't make heads or tails of it. But as he disappears from view, annoyance bubbles through my gut, finally overtaking the stupid butterflies.

Why is he acting so weird? And why did he keep trying to talk about random bits of minutiae? And for the love of god, why did he keep stopping me from saying the thing I came here to say?

"Oh, no, Akira Okamoto," I mutter under my breath, my eyes narrowing. "I came here to make my declaration, and I'm not leaving until I make it."

I stand and toss my cone wrapper in the trash. Then I take off toward the mochi stand.

I half expect to see him out front, already doing his ridiculous dance. But the area around the stand is fairly empty; all I see is a man behind the counter who I guess must be Akira's uncle.

"Excuse me," I say to him. "Is Akira here?"

"Around back," he says, raising an eyebrow at me. "Getting ready for work."

"Arigato."

I stomp around to the back side of the stand. It's a tiny, sectioned-off area hidden from public view. And there's Akira, already dressed as a giant piece of pink mochi.

He looks so cute and ridiculous, I almost forget I'm kind of mad at him.

"Kimi," he says, his eyes widening with surprise. "What are you doing here?"

I put my hands on my hips and glare at him.

"Why won't you let me tell you I like you?!" I blurt out.

His eyes widen even further. "Wh-what?"

"Yeah," I say, crossing my arms over my chest and trying to straighten my spine like my mother always does. "That's right: I like you. Not in a friend way. In a *romantic* way. And this was not at all how I was planning to say it, but I *am* going to say it and you are going to listen and it's okay if you don't feel the same way, but I needed to tell you. So. Now I've told you. It's a *declaration*. What do you think of that?"

It all comes out in a rush. My cheeks are hot and adrenaline's blazing through my veins and I can't seem to catch my breath.

"Kimi." He takes a step toward me and I see that familiar intensity flashing through his eyes—that look I find so irresistible. "*Of course* I feel the same way."

His voice is so *serious*. Like this is the most important thing he's ever said. My heart lights up in about a million different ways all at once.

"Th-then why didn't you kiss me?" I sputter, falling out of my indignant pose. "After we ran through the rain and you put your jacket around me and . . . and it was so perfect! I mean, I *leaned in*!"

"I did not think you wanted me to," he says, taking another step toward me. His gaze is locked with mine and . . . *god*. I could just drown in those eyes. "Earlier in the day, there were several times when we got . . . close. And I always felt you pulling away."

"I was waiting for the perfect moment—so we could have our perfect first kiss." I take a step that closes the last bit of distance between us.

"I thought I imagined you leaning forward in the alley," he says. "After you seemed to pull away so many times that day, I did not want to make a mistake."

"You liked me *that whole time*?" I blurt out, shaking my head. I poke him in the chest—or where I think his chest is under that giant, squishy costume. "You wanted to kiss me that whole time?"

"I've wanted to kiss you *every* time we've been together," he corrects, covering my hand with his. "The bamboo grove. Nara. Even that first day, when we sat on the bench in this park. And when it seemed you did not feel the same way, I thought it would be best if I did not see you as much."

"Akira . . ." My voice trembles as he reaches over and strokes his thumb down my cheek. "We are both so . . . KY."

He laughs, surprised. "So KY," he murmurs. I see that tenderness lighting his eyes now—the tenderness I thought I had imagined. My heart lifts.

"What do you think, Kimi?" he says softly. "Is it finally the perfect moment?"

I respond by rising on my tiptoes and leaning in—and this time I'm not waiting for him to meet me in the middle. I brush my lips against his.

His arms go around my waist and he pulls me close. I don't think about how totally ridiculous we must look: a girl in a bright red dress kissing a giant piece of mochi. I don't even think about how this *is* a perfect moment, soft and sweet and wonderful.

I don't think about anything, because I'm too busy kissing him.

CHAPTER FOURTEEN

Kissing is *awesome*.

Seriously, I can't get enough of it. It's been two days since my declaration at the market. Akira and I have spent almost every minute together and a lot of those minutes have been devoted to kissing.

At the moment, we're sitting very close to each other at a table in the corner of a cozy café in Kyoto. It's the middle of the day and Akira has to work at the mochi stand later, so we agreed to meet here. We're supposed to be trying to finally crack the case of "What is Kimi's Future?" but we keep getting . . . distracted. Especially since there's no one else in the café and the one server on duty keeps disappearing into the back and our corner table is secluded enough to give us plenty of privacy. We are very nicely hidden from public view.

I've been trying to remain super mindful of not engaging in tons of PDA since, as Atsuko noted, that doesn't seem to be a thing in Japan. But Akira agrees that being all by ourselves in an adorable café is pretty private.

Although this adorable café boasts an extra feature that means we're never *totally* by ourselves.

"A pug café?" I squealed when we arrived. "I've heard of cat cafés and even owl cafés, but this is a whole new level of cute."

There are about a half-dozen pugs on duty today, wandering around the café premises wearing little numbered jerseys, like they're part of a sports team. You can order treats to give them and of course there's a ton of pug-branded memorabilia available for purchase, as well as Polaroids of the various pugs in residence plastered all over the walls. Rather than music, the café soundtrack is a medley of doggy snorts, whuffles, and snores.

"Akira." I giggle between kisses. "I think we're bothering him."

I gesture to an especially tiny pug who's sitting in front of our table, head cocked to the side, staring at us in what I can't help but think is a disapproving manner.

"Are we?" Akira raises an eyebrow, picks up my sketchbook, and holds it in front of our faces. "There. Problem solved." He kisses me again.

I let myself sink into it. Every touch from him makes me tingly all over.

"Gah . . . !" He breaks the kiss suddenly, looking down. I realize the tiny disapproving pug has jumped into his lap. "I am sorry," he says, patting its head. "Were we disturbing you?" He smiles slightly, dimple on full display, and I get a little flutter in my chest.

Cute Boy is distracting enough by himself. Cute Boy + Cute Dog? Forget about it.

"This pug is right—we should probably get back to work," I say, taking my sketchbook from him.

Since sketching always seems to relax me, Akira suggested I try doing some stream of consciousness sketching to see if it leads me any closer to figuring out what I'm supposed to be doing with my life.

I haven't gotten very far. Because of all the distractions . . .

"All right," Akira says, going back to his stack of papers. He's brought in some printouts of articles from recent medical journals—a lot of it is available digitally, but he prints it out because it gives him that same feeling he had when he was a kid, poring over those secondhand textbooks. These are nothing he actually needs to study for school. He says he reads them "for fun."

I find this mind-blowingly hot.

Akira looks down at the pug. "We will work for twenty minutes, ne? See what Kimi comes up with in her sketchbook. Is this acceptable to you?"

The pug snorts, flicks an ear, and makes himself more comfortable in Akira's lap, perhaps indicating approval.

I set my pencil on the paper and allow my mind to wander. I'm not supposed to think about what I'm drawing, just let the sketching flow. See where my pencil takes me.

These last couple days have been amazing. I've started working on my blouse with Grandma, snuck a few more limited-edition Snickers with Grandpa, and squeed endlessly with Bex and Atsuko over Skype. I've walked around Kyoto some more, taking in beautiful sight after beautiful sight. I've returned to the fabric store to pick up a few more textiles that inspired me. I never imagined I'd be having so much fun.

True, I still haven't heard back from Mom. I've taken to sending her an email every night, explaining the origin of yet another Kimi Original. I don't know if she's reading them, but I like writing them. In a weird way, writing out the memories associated with every outfit I've made makes me feel like I'm getting to know myself better, too. That sounds *so* dorky and I'm sure Atsuko would have a field day analyzing what it means for my overall psyche. But it's true.

I've Skyped a few times with Dad, but we still always manage to avoid the topic of Mom and what's going on with her. He's been trying to gently prod me on what to do about Liu Academy. So far, I've managed to avoid giving him an actual answer. Somewhere deep inside, I know I'm not going back to painting. But actually saying I want to cancel my attendance, my spot in the academy, and the future I thought I was going to have for so long . . .

It still feels wrong, somehow. Like a big, scary, amorphous blob of a thing I *really* can't stand to make real.

Besides, I haven't found that awesome, perfect thing that's going to replace it yet.

"Time's up!" Akira exclaims, pushing his papers to the side. He scratches the pug behind its ears and nods at my sketchbook. "What did you come up with?"

I look down at what I've been doodling for the last twenty minutes. My brain appears to have gotten stuck on my last trip to the fabric store and I've drawn a series of outfits made out of the delicious purple silk I picked up the other day.

"Oh no, more clothes," I say, laughing. "Sorry, looks like my brain wandered over to its distraction place. Let me try again. Another twenty minutes?" I glance down at the pug in his lap, looking for approval. But the pug has fallen asleep and offers only snoring.

"Hold on," Akira says, studying my doodles. His brow furrows and he gets that ultra-serious look I find so appealing. He taps one of my sketches, a skirt with a dramatic, exaggerated tulip shape. "Why do you always call this a distraction?"

I shrug. "That's what it is. Clothes have distracted me all semester. They distracted me from painting. They distracted me from figuring out what else I want to do with my life. Even now, they're distracting me when I try to sketch my way to enlightenment." I frown at the sketchbook. "Maybe I need to crawl through Buddha's nostril again. Save up some *extra* enlightenment for the next life."

Akira uses his index finger to trace the bold, swooping lines I've scratched onto paper. "There's so much in these lines," he says thoughtfully. "So much thought. So much, eto . . . happy." He gives me a slight smile. "Like I can tell you are happy when you're drawing them." His expression sobers again, and his eyes search my face. "And so much passion."

My cheeks warm. What is he trying to say?

"That first day we met, when we talked in the park," he continues. "You had that same passion when you were talking about where you would wear that dress you sketched. It reminded me of how excited I get whenever someone asks me to explain the alimentary canal."

"Do people ask you to explain that often?" I murmur, trying not to fixate on how he makes even the most clinical of terms sound sexy.

"The point is: Why won't you take this seriously? Because anything that inspires this deep a passion"—he taps my sketchbook again—"*should* be taken seriously."

"It's a hobby, not a career," I say automatically, parroting my mother. "Not something that will take me through life in a meaningful way. It's not important."

He sits back and studies me. "If it is important to you, then it's important," he says. "Simple as that."

"Not so simple," I say, trying to keep my tone light. "I can't get a job as a, like, clothes appreciator. At least, I don't think that's a thing that exists."

"There is nothing wrong with appreciating, but you don't just appreciate, you create," Akira says, paging through my sketchbook. "You make clothes, ne? From these drawings you have come up with. Like your grandmother's friend with the shop—Yoneyama-san."

"I make clothes for fun," I say. "That's all."

"Why does that have to be all?" He looks up from the sketchbook. "Just because something is fun doesn't mean it's nothing more than that. And anyway, fun is a great and wonderful thing that should be valued rather than—what do you say? Minimized?" He cocks a teasing eyebrow. "I thought you Americans were supposed to love fun the most."

"I'm *Asian* American," I say, giggling. "My love of fun is complicated by parental expectations and a burning need to not disappoint anyone."

"And I understand this as well," Akira says. "But don't you think finding joy in life is still important? We are having fun right now, ne?" He gently lifts the puppy in his lap, waving its paws back and forth. "See? The puppy agrees with me."

185 *Stop*

"The puppy does *not* agree with you," I say, giggling in spite of myself. "The puppy is currently giving you the most put-out look of all time because you woke him up from his nap."

Akira grins and sets the puppy back in his lap. It makes an irritated little whuffle-y sound and goes back to sleep.

"All I'm saying is that you may already have the clues you need to crack this case, Kimi from America," he says, tapping my sketchbook.

I glance down at what I've drawn, all those beautiful exaggerated shapes, and feel that familiar pinprick of excitement I always get whenever I come up with new designs. I'm already imagining how I'd pattern them out, how they'd look as I cut and sew them together, how I'd feel when I eventually wear them somewhere. Now it seems like there's something else they're trying to tell me, but I can't quite grab on to it.

Akira's phone buzzes, startling me out of my thoughts. The tiny pug raises its head inquisitively.

"Ah," Akira says, looking at his phone. "Ojisan needs my assistance earlier than I thought. We are doing the demonstration today."

"The demonstration?" I say.

"That's right, you have not seen this yet," he says. "Would you like to come watch? I think you will enjoy it."

"I would," I say, snapping my sketchbook closed. "Even though I have no idea what this 'demonstration' entails. But I'm a little disappointed our time together is getting cut short."

"We still have a few minutes," he says. He glances around

at the café to make sure it's still deserted, then leans in, giving me a devilish grin. "I am sorry," he murmurs to the tiny pug in his lap, playfully covering its eyes. "We are going to have to disturb you again."

Akira's uncle is already gearing up for "the demonstration" as we hustle up to the mochi stand.

"Ah, here is my nephew!" he announces in English to the assembled crowd. It appears to be mostly tourists, a mix of ethnicities with backpacks, fanny packs, and guidebooks. "He is going to assist me." Akira gives a little wave to the crowd.

"This is an usu," Uncle Okamoto says, gesturing to the thing standing next to him—a barrel-like wooden mortar. "And this"—he brandishes a large wooden mallet—"is a kine."

"Oh, he's going to demonstrate how to make mochi!" I exclaim.

"Yes, un, un," Akira says, grinning at me. "Mochitsuki—the traditional mochi-pounding ceremony. Have you done it?"

"Sort of," I say. "My dad doesn't always have the time or the man power to do a full-on mochitsuki—he tends to use those machines that form rice into mochi."

"Ah, but you still have to stir constantly when using those—ne?" Akira says. "Still much man power involved."

"Oh, definitely, but nothing like this," I say. "Anyway, I've helped him when he's using the machines—stirring the rice around—but not when he goes the whole mallet route. I've always been scared I'm going to smack something the wrong way. Or smack myself."

"The rice has been soaked overnight and steamed," Uncle Okamoto continues, gesturing to the hot rice in the usu. "I have given it the initial kneading, and it is ready to be pounded into mochi. Akira . . . ?"

Akira steps forward and kneels down next to the usu, dipping his fingers into a small pail of water.

"My nephew will wet and turn the rice while I pound," Uncle Okamoto says, holding his kine in the air like it's a mighty sword. "This is a dangerous task because if I swing wrong, I could smash my favorite nephew's precious fingers. And he wants to be a doctor someday!"

"Oi!" Akira says, pulling a mock worried face. "Maybe you should find some other favorite nephew to help you with this, Ojisan!"

"No!" Uncle says, shaking his head emphatically. "Must be you! But turn fast, I'm feeling extra strong today!"

The crowd laughs and I join them. Akira and his uncle clearly have an established banter, a routine—but the warmth between them is real.

Uncle lets out a yelp—a mochi battle cry, I suppose— and brings the mallet down on the rice with a hard *smack* that reverberates through the usu. Akira deftly slips his hand into the usu, flipping the rice and giving a little battle cry of his own. And then they get into a rhythm: Uncle smacking the rice, Akira flipping the rice, picking up the pace until I can hear the rice making that telltale thwacking sound that means it's turning into the gloriously doughy mass that is mochi. I find myself picking up on the rhythm of the kine's smack and swaying in time a little, as if it's my favorite song. *Smack-turn-smack-turn-SMACK!*

I love watching Akira and his uncle work this craft together, locked in a repetition they both know so well. Uncle's face is red from exertion, but he's clearly having the time of his life: swinging that mallet with gusto, his gaze trained on the glutinous rice mass as if it's both his greatest rival and his biggest love. And Akira occasionally steals a well-timed look up at him, grinning and sharing in his uncle's joy.

The crowd applauds, cheers, and snaps photos—they're enraptured. Akira and his uncle finally slow their rhythm and Uncle reaches down to touch the sticky mass now housed in the usu.

"Good texture," he proclaims, nodding his approval. "But I think it needs a few more pounds to be perfect, ne?" He hands the kine to Akira. "You try first, favorite nephew."

Akira stands and takes the mallet from Uncle, then looks over his shoulder and finds me in the crowd, giving me a wink. Then he focuses on the usu, as if sizing it up, and swings the mallet over his shoulder. His arm muscles ripple under the thin cotton of his T-shirt and sweat beads his brow as he brings the kine down hard, letting out a battle cry of his own. It makes the loudest *smack* yet.

Atsuko would probably say he's "peacocking," trying to impress me with an athletic display of brute strength. I would say "yeah, and it's totally working," because that's maybe the hottest thing I've ever seen.

As if sensing my thoughts, Akira looks up and grins at me. I blush.

"A good start, favorite nephew," Uncle says. "Shall we see if anyone in the crowd would like to help us give it that final pound?"

A nervous titter runs through the crowd, but no one steps forward. Probably they're all afraid of messing up that perfect mochi—which, in addition to worrying about smacking myself in the face, is usually what's on my mind whenever Dad suggests I take up the mallet. Surely one wrong smack from me and it will turn from a smooth, beautiful mass into something inedible.

"Do not worry," Uncle says to the crowd. "No one will be doing the mixing part while you have the kine, so there's no danger of you smashing anyone's fingers. It's just you and the usu, my friends!"

"I am pretty sure we can find someone, Ojisan," Akira says, cocking an eyebrow. He steps forward, swinging the kine around, scanning the crowd. And of course, his eyes land on me.

"Come forward, young lady," he says, giving me a teasing half smile and holding out the kine. "You look *very* strong."

I don't know what possesses me to take the kine from him. Normally I'd laugh it off and shoo him along to someone else. Maybe it's because I've been doing so many things I'd normally do my best to avoid this spring break: kissing cute boys and making *declarations* and shoving myself through the nasal canals of sacred national monuments.

I've been making a lot of things real instead of letting them just exist in fantasyland. And honestly, it's been pretty fun. So what's one more?

Or maybe it's because he's just that handsome and his arms look just that good, especially now that he's all sweaty and his T-shirt is sticking to him in all the right places, making for some *very* nice—

"Come, come!" Uncle bellows, snapping me out of my arm-appreciating reverie. "Give us that final pound!"

I step forward, brandishing the kine. It's heavier than it looks, and I take pains to steady myself in front of the usu before I even attempt to swing it upward.

"Do you need help?" Akira murmurs, coming up behind me. I get tingly the way I do whenever he's close, a shiver going through me as his lips nearly graze my ear. "I can show you a good stance."

"I know how to hold a kine, Akira Okamoto," I say. "I got this."

He steps away from me, grinning.

I stare down at the sticky, glutinous mass in the usu again.

You know what? I *do* got this. Er, have this? However you want to say it. I am going to swing the mallet and give the rice that final pound that will make it into perfect mochi.

I swing the mallet upward, putting all my muscle into it. Then I let out a roar that seems to come from somewhere deep inside of me. It sounds scratchy and guttural and not quite as cool as Akira and Uncle's battle cries. But so what? It works. And it feels so damn good.

I bring the kine down hard, satisfaction blazing through me as it connects soundly with the usu. The *smack* it makes reverberates through my entire body—my arms are on fire, my ears ring.

And suddenly I realize that making things real is more than just "pretty fun." Making things real means I feel so many things all at once and on a truly visceral level—deep in my bones and my heart and my soul. And right now, all of those things feel *amazing*.

CHAPTER FIFTEEN

I really need to tell Dad what to do about Liu Academy. The tuition deadline looms like a storm cloud, and you can only avoid a storm cloud for so long (okay, actually I'm pretty sure you *can't* avoid a storm cloud, really, unless you're starring in some kind of overblown disaster movie, and this is why I usually try to avoid nature-based metaphors).

Akira and I have decided to consult some ghosts for help. We're visiting an area of Kyoto where people supposedly go to meet spirits, figuring that maybe we can determine my future by visiting the past.

"Yokai Street," Akira says, gesturing to the narrow path in front of us. At first glance, it looks like a fairly ordinary Kyoto side street, lined with modest family businesses and tucked away from the hustle and bustle of the big shopping arcades. The pace feels gentler, less frenetic—more in line with the calming countryside where my grandparents live, or the hidden-away cottage housing the pins and needles shop. But just like those places, if you look closer, there's so much more to it.

"Yokai are like monsters—spirits, ghosts, demons," Akira says. "And as you can see, this street is full of them."

He gestures to the shops in front of us and I smile when I see what he's talking about. Every business on the street has some kind of statue or sculpture of a fantastical-looking creature standing guard. The flower shop in front of us boasts a green lizard-like guy with mournful yellow eyes and a helmet-esque hat made out of a planter. It lurks among the various blooms for sale, a bit of magic amid the mundanity.

"These are yokai?" I say, nodding at the sculptures.

"Yes," Akira says. "This is where people go to meet ghosts, and the street started to really embrace that idea and host functions about fifteen years ago. Now they have a big costume parade every year, people dressed as all kinds of monsters."

"How awesomely creepy," I say. "Are the little statues specific yokai, or do the shop owners make them up?"

"Some of them are based on actual creatures from Japanese folklore," Akira says. He gestures to our green lizard friend. "This fellow could be a kappa, for instance—a water-dwelling demon. But some of them"—he gestures down the way to a sculpture that appears to be a mishmash of a rubber Tyrannosaurus rex head, a dress made out of flowing scarves, and a scruffy wig of black yarn—"are most likely from the shopkeeper's imagination."

I laugh. "I'll take any useful advice I can get, even if it's coming from a strangely stylish dinosaur."

Akira gives me a little half smile—and I can't help but notice there's some kind of strain behind it. Come to think of it, his voice is a bit mechanical and he's not peppering his tour guide commentary with his usual asides, jokes, and teasing grins. He seems . . . off, somehow.

"Hey," I say, tugging on his sleeve. "Are you okay? You seem a little . . ." I search for the right word, then finally point to a funny paper lantern creature hanging outside a ramen restaurant. It's bright red and kind of an oval shape, with drawn-on eyes that look squeezed shut and pained and a big red tongue lolling out of its mouth. It basically looks like it's having the worst day of its life.

He lets out an amused snort. "Maybe not that bad," he says, finally cracking a grin. He hesitates for a moment, studying me. "I have some worries," he says slowly, drawing out each word. "About my ojisan."

I nod, encouraging him to continue.

"The rent may be going up at the market again," Akira says. "And we are not sure how much it's going to be."

"Oh no," I say, my brows drawing together. "Well, surely we can figure something out? Your ojisan's mochi seems very popular. And he's so passionate about it."

"That is part of my worry," Akira says. "The mochi is . . . everything he has. *Everything*."

"No partner?" I say. "No children, no pets? Or hobbies, even?"

"He has put it all into the stand," Akira says, giving me a slight smile. "He was married once, long ago, to a woman he adored, but . . ." His smile fades abruptly. "She got very ill— with cancer. And passed away."

"I'm so sorry," I say, my heart breaking for the vibrant, enthusiastic man who I witnessed taking such joy in mochi-pounding the day before.

"I was very young," Akira says. He moves closer to the lantern yokai with its outlandish tongue, studying it. A light breeze cracks through the warm spring air, ruffling his hair. I can't help but wonder if it's some sort of restless spirit, passing over him. "But I remember studying my secondhand medical texts, wondering if I could find a way to cure her. I remember wanting that more than anything in the whole world."

"That's part of why you wanted to become a doctor," I say softly—and it's not a question. I just know. I step closer to him, brushing my fingertips against his to let him know I'm there.

He turns and meets my eyes, giving me a soft, sad smile. "I cannot bear to see Ojisan lose another love in his life. I cannot bear to see him have . . . nothing."

"He has you." I squeeze Akira's hand.

Akira turns back to study the demon-lantern and we just stand there for a moment, staring at the pained-looking creature. It's one of our nice, crackly silences—but this time, it's charged with something extra, a deeper level of understanding between us. It feels like we're moving into uncharted territory and I'm not sure what to make of that.

"I am sorry," Akira finally says. "I do not mean to . . . talk about sad things. To take us off the path of your journey."

"We're on whatever this journey is together," I say. "You can talk about whatever sad things you want."

He turns away from the lantern-demon and smiles at me, then starts to continue down Yokai Street and motions for me to follow.

"I think I would like to talk about something else now," he says. He pauses, then meets my gaze, his eyes flashing with that intensity I love so much. "But, Kimi—thank you." His voice is so sincere, so layered with deeper meaning, I swear my heart skips a beat.

"So," I say as we move forward. "Let's see, what's a good something else we can talk about? Did you come here when you were younger—you said the street has only embraced its, er, extreme yokai-ness for about fifteen years?"

"Yes," he says, smiling a little. "Ojisan used to take me here, actually. I have three brothers and two sisters—"

"What?!" I exclaim, laughing. "How have we never talked about this before?"

"We have been busy doing other things, Kimi from America," he says, giving me a sly smile. "Things that do not involve talking."

"Mmmmmm," I say, turning bright red. I'm happy to see him perk up, even if it means my face is currently on fire. "Let me guess: You're the youngest?"

"How did you know? Is it my natural charm?"

"It's your ability to get anyone's attention no matter what the circumstances," I counter. "Makes me think you need all the attention-getting tactics you can muster."

"Perhaps," he says. "I often felt like I was getting lost in the shuffle. Ojisan took me under his wing a bit since he has no children. We are alike in many ways."

"I can see that," I say, flashing back to their affectionate routine from the day before. "I've always wondered what it would be like to have a bunch of siblings. I'm an only child."

"Because your parents got it so perfect the first time?" Akira says, cocking an eyebrow.

"I think because I was pretty much all they could

handle," I say, rolling my eyes at him. "My dad's restaurant was kind of like their second child, I guess. And then my mom's graphic design business was their third. But it's interesting . . ." I trail off, gnawing on my lower lip in consideration.

A new yokai catches my eye, an orangey-red dragon with three eyes and a winsome expression. It has some kind of cookie clutched in one hand—I can't tell if it's supposed to be offering it to me or clutching it possessively. Either way, it's cute and cool and striking. I love all the wonders lurking on this street, just waiting to be discovered.

"What's interesting?" Akira prompts.

"I've never thought very much about how my mom's an only child, too," I muse. "And talking to my grandfather—he told me about how my obaasan was kind of on her own in that way as well. She had one brother, but he basically abandoned the family." I crouch down so I can look at the little red dragon face-to-face. I tap the cookie in his hand. He's definitely clutching it possessively, I decide. It's something about his eyes.

Akira crouches down next to me. "And what do you think this means for you?"

"It gives me a more complete picture of myself—or it's starting to," I say slowly, thinking it over. I replay the various conversations I've had with my grandparents over the past week—conversations that revealed more about my mother and her life here than I'd ever imagined. "I don't think I realized how much I was missing, knowing next to nothing about one entire side of my family tree. Mom never wanted to talk about her parents. And I never pushed her to tell me—partly because I knew it would upset her, but also . . ." I trail off, staring into the dragon's three-eyed gaze, as if this will somehow give me all the answers I need.

"Also, what?" Akira prompts.

"Hold on, I think I'm getting a cramp from crouching down," I say. I stand, he follows suit, and I wave good-bye to the greedy little dragon as we continue our stroll down Yokai Street. "I think I didn't ask my mother more about her family because it seemed so complicated, so unresolved, so . . . *messy*."

"But all history is messy, ne?" Akira says. "Especially when it comes to families."

"Oh, for sure," I say. "And the weird thing is, somewhere deep inside, I already knew that. My other grandma—my dad's mom—told me the entire history of her side of the family. She told me about Japanese American incarceration during World War II, how her parents and their friends had to leave all their things and their homes and their lives behind. How they were treated like criminals and outsiders in their own country. How they never wanted to talk about it after. How they always thought it might happen again."

I picture my grandmother in her red-and-blue-checked coat, the one she passed down to me, the one she wore even inside the house because she was always cold and didn't want to "waste money" turning on the heat. I remember her regarding me very seriously as she sipped her tea and talked to me. She'd show me my great-grandmother's "citizen's indefinite leave" card and note that Great-Grandma is smiling in the picture because she was forced to.

"She told me she felt like her generation of Japanese

Americans had this innate, passed-down trauma," I continue. "So much was lost—in terms of possessions and memories and . . . well, everything. And she didn't want me to have that trauma, but she thought making sure I knew every detail of her parents' story was important—that it would help me understand myself better. Even though it's so painful."

"Did it?"

"Maybe not until now," I say. "Because the more I talk to my grandparents, the more I'm starting to understand that there are these huge gaps in my understanding of my own history. And I think, in a way, I sort of chose not to know about it. It disrupted the idea I had of my family: that Mom was cast out by her parents and after that they basically ceased to exist. Now I'm thinking about how my other grandmother—my dad's mom—fought so hard to learn all about her family history, to get her parents to share with her, even though it hurt so much. I kind of wish . . ." I pause, then swallow hard, vocalizing the wisp of a thought that's been dancing around the back of my mind since my first talk with Grandpa. "I wish I had fought harder for *my* family history."

"Maybe that is what you are doing now?" Akira says. He gives me one of those gentle smiles that seems to convey so many layers of meaning beneath his words and I feel that crackle pass between us again.

"Maybe."

Something off to the side catches my eye, a bright splotch of color. I turn and see a yokai that looks like a cat with long eyelashes who's standing up like a human—and dressed in a bright red kimono with a yellow obi and a pink flower behind her ear.

"Ohhhhh." I dart over to it. "I think this is my favorite yokai yet."

"Because of the bright colors!" Akira exclaims. "It is very you. Perhaps the most fashionable yokai on the block."

I smile. The color combination makes me so . . . *happy.* I flash back to seeing the girls in their yukata in the bamboo forest, how I was moved to tears. The surge of emotion I got in the fabric store, gazing at all those "clashing" patterns existing harmoniously together. My overwhelming excitement at the pins and needles shop and my obaasan talking about how Kyoto is home to people who like to make things.

There are so many little pieces of myself that have roots here, I realize. It's like finding answers to questions I never knew I had.

And maybe if I can put them all together, maybe if I fight to understand *all* of my history, I can finally answer the question that brought me here in the first place: *Who am I?*

"Hey. Kimi." I turn to see Akira looking at me, his gaze tender. He reaches over and his fingertips graze my cheek. "It is nice talking to you about our families like this. We have discussed things that are—how do you say it?— weighing a lot."

"Heavy," I say, my voice soft. "It *is* nice."

It is also the type of conversation I almost never have. Because talking about things that are "weighing a lot" inevitably opens you up to complications and messiness. It totally ruins things by making them *too* real.

But, in that moment, I don't care. It *is* nice to talk about these things with Akira. And I'm shocked to realize I can't even quite remember what I was so afraid of ruining in the first place.

Dear Mom,

Do you remember when you gave me your kimono and obi? I was fifteen and it was right before Obon Fest. (Also, do you remember how I used to pester you and Dad with constant questions about what Obon Fest was all about and Dad said, "It's about honoring our ancestors" and I was like, "But what does that mean??" and you said, "Shhh, Kimi-chan, there will be lots of good food and if you and Atsuko perform the Bon Odori well, I will buy you an extra taiyaki," and that usually shut me up pretty fast.)

Anyway, *my* memory of the moment when you gave me the kimono is made up of all these deeply sensory things that have been burned so far into my brain, I can still feel them now. I remember touching the silky fabric, in awe. I remember the texture of the embroidery on the obi. And I remember my eyes drinking in the sheer beauty of those bright colors layered next to each other, red and orange. I had never seen anything more beautiful. For a while, all my paintings were red and orange, red and orange. Over and over again. Seeing them paired so vibrantly made me so happy, spoke to something deep in my soul.

At that particular Obon Fest, Atsuko got mad because her mom told her she had to do the Bon Odori dance even though it conflicted with her taiko drum performance and then we totally messed up the dance and you bought me an extra taiyaki anyway and the combination of heat and dancing and too much food made me a little sick.

But nothing could ruin the joy I found in that kimono and obi and in their glorious color combination.

Later that summer, I made myself a dress out of a bunch of tiny, silky fabric remnants—all different shades of red and orange. It took forever to sew them all together, but in the end, I felt like a sunrise come to life. And like I had a sort of representation of that kimono/obi combo I could wear every day. Putting on that dress always gives me this giddy feeling that reverberates through my entire body, makes me smile no matter how bad a mood I'm in.

This is the kind of feeling I would have dismissed before as silly and frivolous. But being here, I'm starting to think it's connected to something deeper—some kind of pure joy that's an essential part of my soul.

I need to investigate this further. I hope you'll be interested in hearing about what I find.

Love,
Kimi

CHAPTER SIXTEEN

I've redone the same ruffle five times now. No matter what, it won't gather right, so I keep pulling out the stitches and starting all over again.

"Come. On," I grumble, feeding my bright pink fabric through the sewing machine. But my hands aren't steady enough and it gathers wrong yet again, the fabric crinkling into a cartoonishly uneven ruffle. Really, it's more like a crumple. "Uggggghhhhhhhh," I growl, pulling the cotton from the machine and preparing to pull out the stitches for the kazillionth time.

"Kimiko-chan?" My grandmother, who's situated across the sewing room, working on a project of her own, looks up from the garment she's hand-stitching. "Is everything all right?"

"Yes," I say, glaring at the uncooperative piece of fabric. I force myself to set it to the side and stand, stretching my arms over my head. "I think I need a break."

"It is good to take breaks." Obaasan nods approvingly. "Helps to reset the mind." She sets her own sewing to the side. "Your blouse is coming along very nicely, though."

"Thanks," I say, smiling at her. The beginnings of my

blouse are laid out on the cutting table in the middle of the room—body and sleeves are ready to be sewn together and I'm just trying to get these damn ruffles right before I assemble the entire thing. Akira is working at the mochi stand all day today, so Obaasan and I decided to spend the afternoon sewing. I'm hoping to finish my blouse project. I also need to tell Dad by the end of today what to do about Liu Academy tuition. I would feel better about it if, in addition to telling him to cancel the whole thing and not send it in, I could tell him what I had decided to do instead. But I still haven't figured out that part of it yet.

You may already have the clues you need to crack this case, Kimi from America, Akira says in my head.

And even though that makes me smile, I brush the thought aside for the moment.

"What do you usually do when you take breaks?" Grandma asks, walking over to the sewing table and idly straightening the pieces of my blouse project so they're in perfect formation. "Your grandfather says taking a break means doing absolutely nothing, just sitting with your thoughts. But I, eto . . ." She smiles slightly and gives the blouse pieces a final pat. ". . . can never manage to do nothing."

"Me neither." I pull my phone from my pocket. "I like to look through street style photos on the internet. It relaxes my brain and gives me inspiration for my own outfits."

"Street style . . . ?" My grandmother's brow furrows.

"Just what it sounds like: Pictures of people's fashion out on the street," I say. "Like a collection of what people are wearing in their everyday lives. There are actually a lot of awesome feeds and blogs out of Japan in particular."

205

I tap on my phone to pull up a few photos from a Tokyo street style blog I like and show Grandma the screen.

"Interesting," she says, scrutinizing the screen. She points to a photo of a girl wearing a gauzy, flowing sleeveless maxi-dress over a bulky sweater with puffy, fuzzy sleeves. "This mix of shapes and textures—very unusual, ne? Lots of contrast. She is expressing something of who she is."

"That's another reason I love looking at these photos," I say, nodding eagerly. "You learn so much about the people in them based on the outfits they've put together. You can tell that what they're wearing really speaks to their souls—like what you were saying at the fabric store." We share a smile.

"Show me more," Grandma says, waving a hand at the screen.

We scroll through photo after photo, commenting on interesting layering combinations and bold prints and stop to admire one girl in particular who's wearing no fewer than seven different patterns.

"Ah," I say, pausing on a girl clad in a high-waisted tulip skirt. "This is the kind of shape I want to play with—maybe using that purple silk I got at the fabric store. Only I want to make a full dress and the shape should be more exaggerated and echoed in the sleeves."

"Mmm, sou, sou, I can picture this," my grandmother says. "Would you make the sleeves as one piece?"

"I was actually thinking of constructing them out of several pieces," I say. "The skirt, too. I think it would give it more texture and movement all around." I set down my phone and open my sketchbook, which is lying on the cutting table next to my blouse project. "Like this?" I show Grandma the designs I've been sketching out.

"This looks good," she says, nodding as she studies it. "You will probably want to reexamine your draping at every step as you go, to make sure the garment is hanging correctly. Shall we start this after you complete your blouse?"

"I'd love to, but we may not have time to finish it before I have to go home," I say. I gnaw on my lower lip as I study my sketch, getting a little stab of trepidation at the thought of going home.

"We could try to do some initial draping, ne?" my grandmother says, crossing the room to the shelf where we've stored my purple silk.

"Is this what we're doing while we're supposed to be taking a break?" I say, giggling. "That *is* what we're supposed to be doing, right?"

"Hmm." My grandmother smiles at me as she pulls the purple silk from the shelf. "Perhaps we should just accept that we are not good at taking breaks. Do not tell your grandfather."

I laugh again as she brings the purple silk to the cutting table.

"I can be your—what do you say?—model," my grandmother says. "I will stand very still."

"Oh, thank you, Obaasan," I say, beaming at her. "But you know, I think it would be easier if we just . . ." My gaze goes to the dress form in the corner of the room. The one with the beautiful, unfinished yukata on it. I haven't brought up the dress form or the yukata since the day I accidentally discovered this room. They just sort of lurk in the corner like ghosts—never to be mentioned, never to be touched. Grandma, I've noticed, seems to pretend they aren't there at all.

Her gaze follows mine and a shadow passes over her face.

"No," she says, her tone brisk. "We don't need that. Drape your silk on me, Kimiko-chan." She pulls herself up tall and holds her arms out, looking at me expectantly.

"But . . ." My eyes go back to the dress form. "I might need you to help me drape."

"I can do that and model," she says, lifting her chin.

"Um . . . well, I think it would make more sense if we could . . ." I trail off, my eyes still locked on the dress form. I don't know why I'm getting so fixated on this. Maybe because Grandma usually seems to endorse a no-nonsense approach—like when she told me I had to "say it out loud and to the correct person" if I really wanted something. So why is she going out of her way to avoid the most straight-forward way of doing this? "What if I helped you finish the yukata first?" I suggest. "Then we could free up the dress form and—"

"*No.*" She drops her arms to her sides, frowning at me.

"But it's so beautiful," I blurt out. "Why *don't* you want to finish it? I can already see how it will be a totally amazing piece and then we can make even more amazing pieces—"

"I said no, Kimiko," she snaps. "It will never be finished."

"But *why*?"

"Because it *won't*." Anger sparks in her eyes. "I am not sure how many different ways I need to say it. It will never be finished, and we do not need a dress form to make a good garment." She turns to the cutting table and starts to shove bits of fabric and pins and buttons into piles. As far as I can tell, she's not really organizing, just angrily moving stuff around. "I think we are done sewing for the day," she says, her voice low and cold.

"I was going to finish my blouse—"

"You can finish it another time."

She turns her back to me and continues shoving things into smaller and smaller piles, quiet tension radiating from her every pore.

I take a step back, swallowing hard. Somehow I know not to argue—even though I have no idea what I've done wrong. I'm sure Atsuko would say this has something to do with Asian Mom Math, but it's an equation I'm completely unfamiliar with.

I stew in my room for a while, messing around on the internet. I think about calling Bex and Atsuko or texting Akira, but I don't really feel like interacting with anyone. The reminder I've set to let Dad know what to do about Liu Academy pops up on my screen and I dismiss it with a grumpy snort.

I search the internet for different colleges, poking around at various websites to see if there are any programs that spark an interest. (Not to mention programs I can still apply to and programs where I'll have a shot at scholarships. Kind of important.)

My gaze slides to my sketchbook, lying next to me on the futon. It's fallen open to the page I drew my first full day in Japan—that fluffy cherry blossom–inspired dress, the one I was going to wear to Atsuko's fantasy party. A slight smile touches my lips and I reach out to trace the lines on the page with my fingertips.

Normally, this is the kind of moment where someone would speak up in my head—I'd remember something inspiring Akira's said or think of the advice Atsuko would offer or imagine how my mom might guide me in her firm, loving way.

But nothing pops up. Instead I think of how good I've felt this past week whenever I've done something I thought I couldn't do. I think of the exhilaration blazing through me when I told Akira I liked him, when I pushed myself through Buddha's nostril, when I brought the kine down on the usu with a mighty *smack*. Or when I moved my hand to the bright pink cotton, the fabric I really wanted deep down in my soul.

And I think about all those little moments that have felt like discovering pieces of myself in Japan—those pieces that are starting to make more and more sense the longer I'm here.

I stare at the laptop screen. Take a deep breath and rest my hands on the keyboard again.

My heart is hammering like mad as I type "fashion design schools" into the search bar.

I click around, perusing different links that look interesting. As I explore, my heartbeat calms a little. And I find myself drawn into different websites, different program descriptions. I pause on a photo of a girl in clunky glasses draping fabric over a dress form, her brow furrowed in concentration. A warm glow spreads through my chest as I scroll through a gallery of the behind-the-scenes chaos of a student fashion show, bits of fabric flying everywhere. I feel a smile overtaking my face as I click to a picture of an older woman explaining a large sketch of one of her designs. She looks a bit like Sakae, I notice.

I realize then that I've been lingering on the same website for the last fifteen minutes. I scroll up to the name. West Coast Institute of Design. It's in San Francisco.

I click over to the Admissions page. They have rolling admissions based on an unconventional three-semester school year. You have to submit transcripts, essays—all the usual stuff. But also, a portfolio of sketches. And photographs and descriptions of one piece you're particularly proud of, as well as a statement about what it means to you.

Hmm.

I'm so focused on the Admissions page that I don't hear my grandmother come in.

"Kimiko-chan?" she says, looking a bit uncertain.

"Hi, Grandma," I say, my eyes still glued to the webpage.

She settles herself next to me on the futon.

"I am sorry about earlier," she says. "I should not have snapped at you. I, eto . . . have a hard time letting things go. At least, that is what your grandfather tells me." She hesitates. "That yukata has been on the dress form for twenty years now."

I set my computer to the side, my brain latching on to

this factoid. I'm no math whiz, but I immediately figure out what it means.

"It's Mom's," I say, the realization sending my mind spinning in about a thousand different directions. "The yukata was supposed to be for Mom, wasn't it?" I turn to face her. She's looking down, toying with some sort of book in her lap.

"Hai. We were working on it together. That is, mostly I was working on it while she pretended to help." She meets my gaze and gives me a slight smile. "She was never that interested in sewing. I was going to finish it and present it to her when she graduated from college. But . . ."

"But she never came back," I finish. "And you never went to the States."

"I just wanted her to complete school before she made any big decisions," my grandmother says—and there's so much frustration in her voice, frustration that bubbles up instantly after all these years. "Focus on what she went to the America to do instead of getting distracted by a boy. Learn something that would make her a good living or allow her to help with the farm. I'd fought my father so hard for the farm and this house. Our *home*. And she, eto . . . anyway. Mostly, I didn't want her to struggle. I didn't want her to hurt. I worked hard so any children of mine would never *have* to hurt. But she seemed so determined to make choices that would lead her there. I did not understand. And then . . . too many things were said between us. Things that could not be unsaid."

She falls silent and I turn that over in my mind. Grandma's kept Mom's unfinished yukata on that dress form for twenty years. I can see how it's both a source of pain and

212

hope—it can never be truly completed until Mom comes back.

"Kimiko-chan, what are you looking at?" my grandmother says, gesturing to my laptop. "Fashion school?"

"Oh . . . yes," I say, pulling the computer back into my lap. "Yes, I guess I was."

"This is where you are going?" Obaasan says. "After high school?"

"Not exactly," I say. "I mean. I don't know yet." We've never really talked about what made me decide to come to Japan in the first place. I try to avoid talking to her about Mom. And *so much* of that story is about Mom.

"Why don't you know?" she says, her brow crinkling. "This looks like what you love." She taps the laptop screen.

"It . . . it is," I say slowly. Have I ever actually admitted this out loud? That I don't design and make clothes "just for fun" or "as a distraction," like I keep saying? "I *do* love it. But . . ."

"But what?"

"I-I'm scared. I don't want to ruin everything."

She gives me a perplexed look. "How would you do that?"

"Mom worked so hard," I say. Then I remember who I'm talking to. "Sorry."

"You can talk about your mother to me," she says, her voice mild. I sneak a sidelong glance at her. It seems like . . . she really *wants* for me to talk about Mom. So I keep going.

"She worked hard *for me*," I say, my voice trembling. "She didn't get to be the artist she wanted to be. So she wanted me to have that chance and I . . . I . . ."

I blew it. Tears gather in my eyes and I swallow hard, trying to keep them at bay.

"Mom always likes to tell this story," I say, switching gears. "About how she took me to the dollar store when I was seven. She told me I could pick a toy—any toy I wanted. It was this big, incredible treat, because we didn't have a lot of money. And I went for this set of cheap watercolor paints— the kind that comes in that flimsy plastic holder with the little brush. She showed me how to brush color onto paper, how to clean my brush between colors, and when I gave her my first finished painting . . ." My tears threaten to fall again. "Her eyes lit up and she gave me the biggest smile I'd ever seen from her."

"What was the painting?" Grandma asks.

I smile a little. "A truly innovative, impressionistic take on the neighborhood cat, Oreo. He became my muse—the subject of my entire first art cycle."

"Sounds like quite a masterpiece," Grandma says.

"Oh, it was. The thing is . . . Mom didn't smile a ton when I was a kid. Money was so tight, she was barely speaking to . . . um, well, you and Ojiisan. Working all these jobs, not sleeping hardly at all. So that smile she gave me was a big deal. She actually started painting again because of me and my dumb little watercolors—I asked her to paint with me and I was apparently too cute to resist."

"I can see this well," my obaasan says, a slight smile in her voice. "And then you continued painting?"

"Yes. I just kept doing it. If you tallied up all the hours I've spent painting over the course of my life, it would probably be more hours than I've spent doing anything else. I mean, I like it. But . . ."

"But you don't love it," Grandma says. "It does not speak to your soul."

I nod quickly. If I say that out loud, I *will* cry.

I tell Grandma the rest, all about Liu Academy and how Mom and I had a huge fight before I left.

"So now you are afraid to claim this," Grandma says, tapping the laptop screen again. "Didn't I tell you, if you really want something—"

"I have to say it out loud and to the correct person," I say. "But I'm afraid that if I say *this* out loud . . . I don't know. I can't disappoint my mother. I don't want all her hard work and all her sacrifices to mean nothing. And I'm so scared . . ." I trail off and hiccup, a rogue tear sliding down my cheek.

"You are scared that you and your mother will say things that cannot be unsaid and barely speak to each other for twenty years," my obaasan says, and it's not a question. She *knows*. "You are scared of losing her."

I nod, more tears sliding down my cheeks.

"Kimiko-chan," my grandmother says, her voice more gentle than I've ever heard it. "Do you think your mother is sad about how her life turned out? After all of these sacrifices she's made?"

"N-no," I say, hiccuping again. "I mean, she's painting again, she has a great business. She and Dad are still in an over-the-top disgusting level of love."

"And she has you," my grandmother says. "Which is

perhaps the main reason I do not believe she would go back and do things differently."

I look down at my lap. I don't know how to respond to that.

"Your mother wants you to be happy, Kimiko-chan," Grandma continues. "I am very sure of that. It sounds like perhaps the two of you did not, ah . . . communicate well about some of the things you love and do not love. But there is still time for that."

"Maybe," I murmur, thinking of all the unanswered emails I've been sending.

"The two of you sound very close," my obaasan says. "If you go after the thing that you want, the thing that will make you happy—I do not believe it will be like it was with her and I."

I'm just sitting here silently crying now. All of these things I was so scared to voice feel like they're lying in pieces around me.

Obaasan gently moves the computer aside and slides something else into my lap. The book she was holding, I realize. I cock my head at it, trying to figure out what it is.

"I have been thinking you should have this," she says.

Then she gives my shoulder a small squeeze, gets up, and leaves the room.

I open the book and a cavalcade of grinning tanukis greets me. They're sketched out in soft pencil and tumbling across the page in various mischievous poses. One is cramming taiyaki in his mouth and raising a devilish eyebrow. Another is totally upending an entire pot of tea and snickering about it.

My eyes widen, my hands grip the book tightly, and the realization hits me like a ton of bricks.

This is my mother's old sketchbook.

I spend hours paging through Mom's drawings, scrutinizing every line and eraser mark. When I get to the end, I flip back to the beginning and start paging through all over again. The tanukis are as funny and naughty and whimsical as I imagined when Grandpa described them.

Eventually, Mom started adding color to her work—bright, bold shades. It's fascinating to page through and watch how she grew and changed in her style of drawings, how the avalanches of tanukis eventually morph into the flowing lines of trees that look like the wild abstract shapes that are so much a part of her current work. I realize I'm seeing her story, how she became the artist—and the person—she is today.

I remember what Akira said about how he could see "happy" and passion in my fashion designs. I see that here, too. Joy in every pencil mark, exuberance in every splash of color. I'm seeing my mother discover her love of art.

I think about everything I've learned about her past, her life with her parents, while I've been here. She must have felt so much pressure to take over the farm after Grandma fought so hard to keep it. Especially since she's Grandma and Grandpa's only child. Even though it wasn't singing to her soul. Even though it wasn't what she *really* wanted.

I wonder, if I had just talked to her when I started having doubts about painting, would she have listened?

I set her sketchbook next to mine, both open to pages in the middle. There is that same passion in both books, dancing its way across the pages and across art separated by two decades. And I realize that you can see my journey, too: The exaggerated shapes and textures and contrasts and bright colors I like to play with in my clothes recall the shapes and shadows I've always put in my paintings, going all the way back to my watercolor of Oreo the cat. (I mean, I gave him a *really huge* head and painted him hot pink and yellow. How have I never seen that as the obvious first steps of my artistic development?)

The story of discovering my passion is in the pages of my sketchbook, just as my mother's story is in hers. And I've already found the "artistic voice" my mother's always talking about. It's been there the whole time.

Now I just need to find the courage to express it.

I pull my computer into my lap and compose a new email to Dad.

> Don't send the tuition. I'm withdrawing from my spot at Liu Academy. You don't have to worry about anything else, I'll let them know. And as for what I'm doing instead . . . I have a plan, Daddy. I promise.

I take a deep breath and glance back at the two sketchbooks lying side by side on my bed. Then I hit "send."

CHAPTER SEVENTEEN

I have a plan. Or at least, that's what I keep trying to tell myself.

After researching all the ins and outs of the Institute's application process, I've determined I can make the latest deadline for fall admission if I complete my piece and my statement right after I get back from spring break. Somehow, I know it has to be a whole new piece; I'm not going to apply with a Kimi Original I've already created. I just have to figure out what garment is going to express absolutely *everything* about who I am and who I want to be as a designer.

No pressure.

I stay up most of the night, sketching feverishly. I discard nearly everything I draw. Nothing feels *right*.

As the sun creeps over the horizon, I realize I haven't heard from Akira since we parted two days ago. That's odd. I mean, I haven't texted him, either, but I've been super busy having important revelations about myself.

I force myself to put down my sketchbook and send him a text, asking if he wants to meet up later.

I think I've finally cracked the case! I impulsively add at the last minute. Can't wait to tell you about it.

I start sketching again and can't help but smile as I imagine talking to Akira about everything from the day before: my heart-to-heart with Grandma and looking through Mom's sketchbook and taking the first step toward pursuing something I love. He'll be so excited. I picture his face lighting up, that adorable dimple making an appearance. Him sweeping me into his arms and holding me tight. All of it just makes my smile get bigger.

I still can't figure out my application outfit, though. I frown at the page. What I'm sketching isn't right, yet again. I scribble over it and flip to a new page.

After a couple hours of this, I realize that it's breakfast time and I'm starving. I go eat with my grandparents. Come back to my room, sketch some more. Decide to try for a change of scenery and go sit at the living room table with Grandpa, who's working on his trains again. Sketch, sketch, sketch.

It's almost lunchtime and I still haven't heard from Akira. I frown at my phone. Where is he? I know he's working this morning at the mochi stand, but it's unlike him to be silent for this long. Especially since I have less than a week left in Japan and we'd talked about making the most of it . . .

I turn back to my sketchbook, but now I'm completely distracted. Well, I'm not getting anywhere with this amazing application outfit, anyway, so I might as well go see the cute boy I like. Maybe he'll say something that will spur me on, inspire me.

"I'm going to Maruyama Park to get lunch at the market, Grandpa," I say. "Would you like me to bring anything back?"

"No, Kimiko-chan, that is all right," he says, disassembling the train he's just pieced together. "Have a good time."

I head out and take the train to Kyoto, then scurry through the park, giving a little wave to the stuffed tanuki as I pass by. I expect to be greeted by the familiar sight of Akira dancing around in his mochi costume, but he's nowhere to be seen.

I frown, scanning the market, and finally spot him behind the counter at the mochi stand. No costume. I cross the market and wait patiently for him to finish helping a customer. Then I hop into his sightline, give him a bright smile, and throw my arms out, like *ta-da!*

"Hello," I say cheerfully. "Why are you being so mysterious? Trying to get me to solve an all-new case: Where's Akira?"

"Hi, Kimi," he says. "Sorry, what?"

He looks tired around the eyes and his demeanor is muted—like someone's turned his volume way, way down.

"Um." I drop my arms to my sides. "You didn't respond to any of my texts? I haven't heard from you in, like, days and that's pretty unusual in our current pattern of communication? Are you okay?"

"Oh. I apologize for not responding. I am . . . eto . . ." He pauses, like he's trying to figure it out. "I am fine."

"Are you sure?" I study him, trying to scrutinize every inch of his face. "What's going on?"

"Nothing. I—"

"Akira-kun!"

We both turn to see Uncle Okamoto bustling up to the stand. He says something to Akira in Japanese and makes

221

a hand-waving motion. Akira shakes his head vehemently and says something back. Uncle hand-waves more forcefully, like he's shooing Akira away. Akira moves to the side, still shaking his head, removes his apron, and exits the stand.

He comes to stand next to me, but his eyes are still trained on Uncle, who has turned his attention to an approaching customer.

"Hey," I say softly. I touch Akira's hand. "I was going to get some lunch. Are you hungry?" Maybe if we sit down and eat—one of our top five favorite things to do, after all—he'll relax and tell me what's bothering him.

He turns and gives me a blank look and I can't help but feel stung. It's so different from the way he usually looks at me—sweet and earnest and a little amused, but with that intensity playing underneath, hinting at all the deeper emotions I feel whenever he kisses me. Right now, it's like he's been leeched of all that and I'm a stranger. I could be anyone, standing in front of him.

I half expect him to turn me down, but finally he says, "Yes, all right."

We find an onigiri stand selling a variety of flavors. I opt for a salmon and a kakuni and we settle on a nearby bench to eat. We chew in silence for a few minutes.

"Akira." My voice is gentle. "Tell me what's wrong."

He shakes his head, picking at the rice ball he's eating. "It's nothing."

"Clearly it's something," I press. "You're upset." I've never seen him like this and it makes my heart ache. I kind of want to murder whoever made him look so downtrodden, so robbed of hope. "Is it about your ojisan and the mochi stand? Did the market raise the rent again?"

"I . . ." He sets the onigiri down on its plastic wrap. "I think maybe it would be best if we do not see each other anymore."

"What?!" I set my own rice ball down and goggle at him. He's staring down at his food, refusing to meet my eyes. "How . . . how can you say that? Did I do something wrong?"

"No." He shakes his head vehemently but refuses to meet my eyes.

"Then . . ." My brow furrows and I shake my head. I'm so confused. "Then why? What's changed since we saw each other two days ago?"

Since we had that achingly deep, soul-searching conversation about our families. Since I talked to you like I've never talked to anyone. Since you kissed me like you were putting your entire soul into it—I think that's how you do everything and it's one of the reasons I . . . I . . .

"Kimi." He finally meets my eyes. "You only have a few days left in Japan and you should enjoy them—"

"I want to enjoy them with *you*—"

"I am not good company right now."

"And I get no say in that?" Frustration bubbles up in my chest, thick and toxic. "Because I'm the one you're keeping company. I should be, like, the judge of how good the company is. And I do *not* agree with your assessment."

"I also do not have time for . . . for distractions," he says, turning away from me and glaring at the ground. "I just don't have time."

"I'm a *distraction* now?" Tears prick my eyes.

"I just . . . I think perhaps I've been spending time on the wrong things—"

"Y-you were the one who told me not to dismiss important stuff that way," I press. "Even if it's *fun* important stuff. Is that what you think of me? Of us hanging out? Of . . . of . . ." My voice cracks and I swallow hard. I don't want to cry right now.

"I . . . eto . . . I think I'm not saying it right. I'm sorry." He slumps back on the bench, his glare dissipating.

There are so many emotions crashing through me— anger and frustration claw for space and underneath it all, my heart feels like it's about to shatter.

"Akira," I say, my voice urgent. "Please tell me what's going on. *Please.*"

He lets out a long sigh and turns to face me. "They *are* raising the rent on the stands at the market again," he says, his voice dull. "It's worse than what we thought it would be. *Much* worse—twice the amount as usual. Ojisan can't afford it. He will have to close the mochi stand. His life's work, his dream: gone just like that."

"No," I breathe, my eyes going wide. "There must be something we can do."

"I can go work for him full-time, year-round," Akira says, his eyes getting that intense look. "It would allow him to keep the stand open at all times and he could make more money. If I do that, he might have a chance to make rent."

"But . . ." I frown, gnawing on my lower lip. "What about school? What about taking that first step toward becoming a doctor—that's *your* dream."

224

"It will have to wait," he says.

But I can tell by the way his expression dims further: If he does this, his dream will be waiting forever.

I lean forward, resting my elbows on my knees, and study him intently. As awesome as mochi is, it's not what he wants to give his life to. How can I get him to remember that?

"I actually came here to—well, mostly to see you," I begin, trying to find the words. "But I also wanted to tell you something. I realized that designing and making clothes is more than the 'distraction' I keep trying to describe it as. It's my passion. It's what I want to do with my life. I love it and it's fun and it makes me so happy and all of that's *important*. You were right, Akira, I *do* have all the clues I need to crack the case. And I finally figured it out, because of you and my obaasan and being here in Japan and looking at my mom's old sketchbook." I give him a small smile. "I'm applying to fashion design school."

"Oh, Kimi, that is . . . that is wonderful." He leans forward, that intensity flickering through his eyes, and squeezes my hand. "Truly. I am very happy for you."

"Thank you," I say, my cheeks warming. "I still don't know what's going to happen—if I'll get accepted or not, and what my mom will say and . . . and . . . well, who knows how everything will turn out. But I know that it's worth it to *try*."

Akira studies me, not saying anything. He doesn't look as blank as he did before, though, and I take that as a sign of encouragement.

"Don't you see?" I say. "You helped me realize it was important to go after what I want—that I had a dream right in front of me and I was totally ignoring it. And you . . ." I think of that little boy he described to me at Todaiji Temple, the one bustling over to Buddha's nostril to dismantle it and uncover its secret biology. "You've *always* known your dream. Your passion. And you pursue it so enthusiastically. Nothing holds you back, you just *do* it. I love that about you." I lock gazes with him, trying desperately to convey what I need to. "You can't walk away from it now."

"It's not that simple—"

"Why not?" I demand. "I mean, I know there are a lot of complications. But there are also other options. Your uncle could find a stand at a different market—"

"He's built that one up for years—"

"Or hire another employee—why does it have to be you?"

"I'm the only employee he can afford." Akira gives me a slight smile. "I can live at home; my parents will feed me—it just makes sense."

"It makes *no* sense," I insist. "There must be another way."

"Kimi." Akira scrubs a hand over his face. "Sometimes reality intrudes on what we want. That's just the way it is. I have to do this for my family. And that means I can't . . ." For a moment, it looks like his face might crumple, but he quickly schools his expression. "I can't be a doctor right now."

Now my heart really does feel like it's shattering.

Akira gives my hand another squeeze and gathers his half-eaten onigiri. "I should be getting back," he says.

"Wait." I lace my fingers through his, refusing to let go. "Is this really it? We won't see each other again?"

226

"I need to focus on Ojisan and the business," he says. "And you . . ." He reaches over and brushes my hair off my face, giving me a slight smile that's a ghost of the usual Akira. "You should have fun your last few days in Japan."

"Akira . . ." My voice shakes, and my eyes fill with the tears I've been trying to hold back this whole time. "How can you just . . . not want to see me anymore? How can you be okay with that?"

In an instant, he looks like all the life's been sucked out of him again. "I . . . I'm not," he says. "But as I said before, sometimes—"

"Reality intrudes on what we want," I finish, unable to keep the bitterness out of my voice. "Got it."

He stands and gazes at me for a moment, looking like there's so much he wants to say. "Good-bye, Kimi from America," he says finally, his voice soft and wistful. He reaches down and gathers my discarded onigiri wrapper, crumpling it with his own. And then he leaves.

I bite my trembling lower lip, choking back the tears that want to pour down my cheeks. If I can just get up and get back to the train, maybe I'll be able to hold it together until I get back to my grandparents' place.

Stand up, Kimi.

I get to my feet, my legs wobbly.

Now . . . walk.

I take a step forward. Then, out of the corner of my eye, I spy something furry. The stuffed tanuki. Sitting in his usual spot under the tree.

I burst into tears.

CHAPTER EIGHTEEN

"I. Will. *Kill*. Him," Atsuko seethes, pacing in and out of view on my laptop screen.

"Atsy, we've talked about this," Bex says nervously, twisting her hands together. "You can't get all murder-y over someone breaking your best friend's heart."

"Oh, you think I *didn't* have a hit squad all lined up, just in case Shelby broke yours?" Atsuko flops onto the bed next to Bex and cocks an eyebrow. "I know people in Japan. I just need to figure out the best way to get ahold of them."

Honestly. I can never tell when she's kidding.

"Atsuko, I'm fine," I say. My quavery voice reveals this to be a total lie. I mop my eyes with a soggy tissue and let out a long snuffle. "And anyway, didn't you keep warning me that there was no way of knowing how things were going to turn out? Well, I guess now we do know: They turned out *horribly*." The last word comes out as a sob and I start crying again. Really, I haven't stopped crying since yesterday in the park. My eyes are red and puffy and my head feels like it has a metal band around it, pulling tight.

"Oh, Kimi." Atsuko blows out a long breath. "Just because

I want you to prepare for the worst doesn't mean I want the worst to actually happen."

That just makes me cry harder. Bex taps on the screen and holds up a small bowl.

"We're having ice cream," she says. "Breakup ice cream? In your honor. It's like you're here."

"And you will be here in just a few days," Atsuko says, brightening. "You can put this whole Akira mess behind you."

"Maybe meet someone new," Bex says, waving her spoon around. "Shelby's been introducing us to all these cool people from her job at the comic book store." She dips her spoon back into her ice cream, leans forward, and puts on a theatrical whisper. "There's this guy, Naz, who's *totally* into Atsuko—"

"Okay, okay, we're getting off topic here," Atsuko says, her face turning bright red. I wipe my eyes again, momentarily distracted from crying. I don't think I've ever seen Atsuko *blush*. "In any case, Bex is right—you can always meet someone new. Or hey, Justin's still single. I bet he'd be more than willing to woo you with a few more rock rings."

"Yeah." I nod mechanically, but all I can think is: I don't want someone new. I don't want Justin.

I want Akira.

"You only would've had a couple more days with him anyway," Atsuko says. "Then what? You'd come back here, and you guys probably never would've seen each other again."

"Always harshing the romantic buzz," Bex says, rolling her eyes.

"Yeah, with *reality*," Atsuko snarks back.

"I hate reality," I snuffle. "This is why I like to keep things in fantasyland."

"You can do that, too," Atsuko says. "You don't have to actually do anything or try anything ever again if you don't want to. Just keep imagining experiences instead of actually having them."

"Atsy!" Bex admonishes, hitting Atsuko with her spoon.

"Sorry," Atsuko says. "That came out all wrong. It's just, reality does hurt a whole hell of a lot and I hate that you're in this heartbreak place, Kimi."

"Come home," Bex says, giving me a sympathetic look. "Come home and we'll figure it out."

"All right," I say, dabbing at my nose. "I'm gonna go now, guys. See you soon."

They wave to me and wink out of sight.

I push my computer to the side and flop back on the bed. Reality *does* hurt. Atsuko's right, I only would have had a few more days with Akira anyway.

And yet . . . all I can think about is how much I want to see him.

My phone buzzes and I glance at the screen. It's Dad, responding to my email about Liu Academy tuition. God. That seems like a lifetime ago.

You got it, kid. I look forward to hearing more about this plan. Love you.

Oh, right. My grand fashion school plan. Which I haven't thought of since I started my twenty-four-hour crying jag yesterday. I flip open my sketchbook and listlessly turn through the pages. I still can't think of a good design to apply with. I turn all the way back to the pages I drew my first full day in Kyoto: the cherry blossom dress, the redesigned mochi costume with the cute boy . . .

Dammit. Tears fill my eyes again.

Maybe I'll never think of a good design. Maybe wanting this whole fashion school thing is like wanting Akira: a dumb fantasy I should never make real. Because if it doesn't work out, it will hurt too much. I gnaw on my lower lip, staring at my sketches.

"Kimiko-chan?" My grandfather is standing in the doorway, looking concerned. He and Grandma have been giving me concerned looks since yesterday, when I came home with drippy, puffy eyes. "Are you all right?"

"I'm okay, Grandpa," I say, sitting up in bed.

He gives me a slight smile. "Then would you like to come with me to town? I am going to replenish my snack supply." He lowers his voice and gives me a conspiratorial look. "Do not tell your grandmother; I am saying we are going to have lunch. A very healthy lunch."

"I heard that, Hakaru," my grandmother says, coming up behind him and giving him a disapproving look. "You think you are being so sneaky, ne? But I know you're going out to buy treats."

"I could go to get some snacks," I say, my voice hollow. "Or to have lunch."

My grandmother takes in my disheveled, red-eyed appearance. Exchanges a look with my grandfather. Then turns back to me, arching an eyebrow.

"Let's do both," she says.

231

My grandparents take me to an incredibly picturesque district of Kyoto called Gion, which is apparently known for looking like a perfectly preserved bit of old-timey Japan. It has narrow streets and rickety old teahouses with thatched roofs. It's also known for being a "geisha district," and my grandmother tells me that tourists flock here hoping to see geiko walking the streets in elaborate kimono and white face paint.

"Many of the people you see in full kimono are tourists themselves," she snorts. "You can rent all of that gear by the hour."

My grandparents take me to eat the freshest-tasting sashimi I've ever had—thin and delicate, it practically melts in my mouth. For dessert, we go to a beautiful teahouse that also contains various collections of oddball antiques for sale. We sit at a table with a nice view of the Shirakawa River and I order a green tea shave ice that comes out looking like a gigantic head of lettuce.

"This place is so cool," I say, looking around. The combination of food and beautiful scenery has lifted my spirits a bit. There's so much to see, I barely have to think about Akira. At least, that's what I keep telling myself. "Is this where you get your snacks, Grandpa?"

"Oh no, for that, we must go to the best snack shop in all of Japan," Grandpa says, digging into his own dessert. "Just wait until you see it—you can tell your friends back at home about how your grandfather took you there."

"It's the convenience mart by the train station," my grandmother says, giving Grandpa a look. "Do not tell tales, Hakaru."

I giggle. The way they are with each other reminds me again of my parents—gently needling one another, so over-the-top in love after all these years.

"Well. It is still the best," my grandfather says, giving me a wink.

"That sashimi we had for lunch was definitely the best," I say, taking another bite of shave ice. "It's a good thing you learned to like fish, Grandpa, otherwise you would have missed out."

"Ah, hai," Grandpa says, casting a sidelong look at my grandmother. "So she told you the story of our first dinner together."

"I did," my grandmother says. "And I am also glad you came around, because I cannot imagine a life without fish." She glances around the café. "I am going to go look at some of these antiques. Sometimes there are interesting treasures to be had."

"Ooh, I want to do that, too," I say. "I'll join you when I'm done with my shave ice."

Grandma nods at me, stands, and heads to one of the other rooms.

"So, what caused the fish switch, Grandpa?" I say, scooping into the dregs of my dessert. "Did your taste buds change one day or was it more of a gradual thing over time or—"

"Oh, Kimiko-chan." My grandfather smiles at me and lets out an ornery chuckle. "I have *always* liked fish."

"Wh-what? But Grandma said—"

"Your obaasan's fish was *terrible*," he says, his laugh morphing into a full-blown cackle. "Oh my. She could not cook to save her life. It was not—what do you say?—not fit for humans. To eat."

"So, you fed it to the dog and then lied about why?" I say, incredulous.

"She was so proud to have made it," he says. "Her smile when she served it to me was so . . ." His expression softens, and he gets a faraway look. "And anyway, dog vomit aside, the fish was a small part of our evening. The rest was . . ." He trails off again and smiles. "I knew I wanted to be with her forever."

"Even though you were possibly resigning yourself to a lifetime of not-fit-for-humans cooking?" I say, laughing.

"I was not a very good cook, either," he says with a shrug. "We learned and got better together. And if we hadn't? Eto . . . I suppose we would have just gotten a dog." He laughs uproariously, like this is the funniest thing ever, and I can't help but join in. "There is always a little uncertainty when you love someone," Grandpa says, polishing off the last of his dessert. "Sometimes that's part of the magic. Sometimes it means heartbreak. But when you feel strongly enough about someone to endure their bad fish . . ." He smiles and pats his heart. "Nothing like it, ne?"

I find myself smiling and nodding back. I consider his words, turning them over in my mind. And as I do, a tiny spark takes root in my chest. I have no idea what it means, so for now, I just let it flicker.

After dessert, I wander through the teahouse's rooms of antiques for sale. Surprisingly, nothing is very expensive. Some of the price tags contain little handwritten notes—which are written in Japanese, so I can't read them, but Grandma tells me they're explanations from previous owners about the history of the items and why they need new homes.

There's a section that has a beautiful rainbow of yukata and kimono. Another with a collection of chipped teapots. And one that seems to contain everything that didn't go anywhere else—a bushel of silk flowers, a ceramic bear holding a camera, a mask with horns and a ghoulish grinning mouth. There's a little pile of old books propping up the mask, and I pick through them, noting that they're also for sale. I pick one up and page through it—even though, once again, it's in Japanese and I can't read it. Maybe I can take some Japanese classes when I get back to the States.

I flip to a new page and find a detailed black-and-white diagram of the human body, arrows pointing to different organs and systems. Ah. This must be a medical textbook of some kind.

That, of course, makes me think of Akira.

I take a deep breath and keep paging through. Weirdly, I feel like looking at this makes me understand why he was so enchanted by these kinds of gross diagrams. It's like looking at a gigantic puzzle and trying to figure out how all the pieces fit, how everything works together to create a perfect whole. It reminds me a bit of sketching a new design, trying to make the elements balance each other, trying to find that one shape or sweep or pattern that makes my heart sing.

I picture tiny Akira studying these diagrams in detail, face lit with wonder, and smile. I remember refashioning my grandmother's coat and feeling that same sense of wonder for the first time.

I run my fingertips over the intricate black-and-white designs on the page, thinking of my sketchbook.

Suddenly images from my sketchbook over the past week and a half flood my mind—along with all the memories attached to them. The flowing patterned jumpsuit and the bamboo grove. The tulip dress and my trip with Grandma to the fabric shop and Sakae's wonderful store.

The cherry blossom dress and Maruyama Park.

My eyes widen, a bright thread of excitement flowing through my veins, worming its way into my gut, and exploding in my chest.

That's it. I know what I have to do for my application design.

And yes, I am going to apply. It might not work out the way I want. It might even end in a way that hurts so bad, I spend weeks crying and eating ice cream with Atsuko and Bex.

But here's the thing: None of that *stops* me from wanting it.

I close the medical textbook, clutch it to my chest, and jump up and down a little bit. My fingers are already twitching, eager to start sketching and measuring and draping.

"Kimiko-chan?" I turn and see my grandparents approaching me, looking puzzled. "Are you okay?" my grandmother continues.

"Yes," I say, hugging the book. "I'm more than okay." I smile at my grandparents. "Can we go home now? After stopping by the greatest snack shop in all of Japan, of course. I have something to work on."

CHAPTER NINETEEN

I sketch for hours, filling up page after page with ideas for my design. I sketch until my fingers hurt and my pencil is worn down to a tiny nub and I almost run out of pages. And when I feel like I finally have it, I catapult off my bed and run down the hall to the sewing room, where Grandma is puttering around with a new black skirt.

"I've got it!" I exclaim, waving the sketchbook around. "My fashion school application design."

"Let me see," she says, moving next to me as I set my sketchbook on the cutting table.

"This is inspired by my trip here," I say, tracing the soft pencil lines with my fingertips. "I'm trying to convey all of my spring break—and how it's made me feel—in one garment. And I want to use an unusual material, which maybe you can get from what I've sketched here . . ." I point to a couple of spots on my drawing.

"Yes," my grandmother says, smiling faintly as she studies my work. "I see it. I think it's perfect, Kimiko-chan."

I beam. I'm so excited to get started.

"Have you talked to your mother yet?" my grandmother

says, moving some things around on the cutting table. "Does she know about your plan?"

"Not yet," I say. "She still hasn't responded to any of my emails. I'll tell her when I have more of the design completed. I think I can get started here, but I'll need to finish at home. It's a lot of work and this—"

"Will be too bulky to take on the plane once completed," Grandma says, nodding at my drawing. "How do you think your mother will respond when you tell her what you are doing—when she sees this?"

"I don't know," I say honestly. "Everything could still end in disaster. But even if it does, I still have to do this."

"How did you come to this conclusion?" my grandmother says, cocking her head to the side. "This morning, you seemed discouraged. A bit lost."

"I was," I say, remembering my puffy eyes. "I mean, that was kind of about something different, I guess. A boy."

"The one you like—or liked?" my grandmother says, raising an eyebrow.

"I still like him," I say, and the ache around my heart pulses. "And I'm not sorry I still like him. Even though it hurts. Today at that funky teahouse–slash–antiques shop, I saw something . . ." I picture the medical text, which is now sitting on my bed. "And it made me think of everything I've done here. All the amazing places I've seen, all the wonderful things I've eaten, all the awesome experiences I've had."

All the kisses that thrilled me down to my bones, all the looks and touches that made my heart beat faster.

"Thinking about all that made me realize . . ." I smile

down at my drawing. "Going out and doing all those things and being honest about my feelings and telling that boy I like him, moving beyond just fantasizing about those things and making them real—well, yes, it did open me up to hurting and being sad. Heartbroken, even. But I wouldn't give up those experiences for anything in the world."

My obaasan smiles at me. I can't help but picture her younger, smiling at my grandfather as he tried and failed to choke down her terrible fish.

"Let's get started, then," she says, tapping my sketchbook. "What do you think the first step is? Creating your unusual textile?"

"I'm going to do that when I get home," I say. "That piece of it will be too delicate to transport. I was thinking I'd start by creating the pattern for the base of the garment and then maybe starting on the pieces that are made from more conventional materials."

"We will need to go back to the fabric store," my grandmother says, nodding. "Do you want to start with some initial draping to see if the basic design has any immediate flaws?"

"Let's do that," I say, nodding. "We can use muslin. Do you want to be my model? You can stand very still, yes?" I give her a hopeful smile.

My obaasan hesitates, studying me for a long moment. Then she glances at my sketch. Then back at me. I shift awkwardly from foot to foot, wondering what she's working out.

"No," she finally says, with an emphatic shake of her head.

240

She crosses the room and stands in front of the dress form, allowing her fingertips to graze the unfinished yukata.

"Come help me, Kimiko-chan," she says.

I cross the room to join her. We don't speak as we carefully remove the yukata from the dress form. She folds it and places it on one of the shelves. Then she brushes off the dress form and turns to me.

"Use this," she says, gesturing to the empty dress form. "It's been waiting for you."

I work late into the night, draping and sketching and trying to figure out the finer points of my garment. The next morning, Grandma and I pop over to the fabric store and to a big used bookstore called Book Off, which is apparently a chain in Japan. Even though I'm going to create my unusual textiles back home in LA, I want to do a test run to see how they'll work out, and for that, I need books. I find myself gravitating over to the old, used medical texts and pick up a few of those. The ache around my heart pulses again as I pay for my books, but throwing myself into this project is helping. And even though I'm hurting, I realize I don't want it to just go away. I don't want to reset to before I felt like this, because that would mean forgetting Akira, in a way. And in spite of everything, I don't want to forget him.

We get back to my grandparents' place just as my grandfather is preparing lunch—which I notice includes fish. I give him a pointed look and he just cackles.

When we finish eating, Grandma and I adjourn to the sewing room and get to work. We cut and drape and I pull some pages out of the medical texts to use in my unusual textile experiment.

"I think making this work is mostly about soaking the pages enough so that they become pliant—but not so much that they are in danger of totally disintegrating," I muse, lining up a few of the pages I've tried soaking on the cutting table.

"Sou, sou, I agree," Grandma says, nodding vigorously. "Have you also thought about reinforcing them with something?"

"Like adhering them to an actual piece of fabric? Definitely," I say. "But I need to choose that fabric really carefully so it still works with the rest of the garment."

"And that is something you will do once you get back to the America?" my grandmother says.

"Yes. I think we've done all we can do here." I gesture to our work-in-progress on the dress form. "I'll finish it at home. Thank you so much, Obaasan."

"It was my pleasure," she says, giving me a gentle smile.

"Kimiko-chan?" My grandfather enters the room, toting a small package and a bag. "This came for you."

"What, somebody actually mailed me something?" I say. "I didn't realize I'd been here long enough for that."

"It was left on our doorstep," Grandpa says, shrugging. "I do not believe it came through the mail. Especially this part." He holds up the bag, which I now see sports grease splotches and the telltale golden arches of McDonald's.

I take the bag from him and open it. It contains a single Ebi Filet-O. I swear, my heart skips a beat.

I open the Ebi Filet-O and take a bite, relishing the luscious panko goodness. Then I take the package from Grandpa and turn it over in my hands. It's fairly flat and my name is scrawled on the front in big, looping script.

"Open it," my grandfather says, clearly dying of curiosity.

"Let her open it or not open it, Hakaru," my grandmother says. "It's her package."

I polish off my Ebi Filet-O, set the package on the cutting table, and slit it open with my fingernail.

"It's . . . papers?" I say, pulling a sheaf of papers from the package. "Printouts of something?"

I spread the printouts on the cutting table. My grandparents gather around me, peering over my shoulder. As I study the papers, I see that they're printouts from various fashion design school websites—including the one I'm applying to. I look closer and see that they're also marked up in blue pen, with long, detailed notes scribbled in the margins.

Lots of focus on the technical side of sewing with this one—maybe you don't need? reads one note.

This program seems to encourage the most creativity, but does it have enough structure? Think you would like the special sessions with famous designers, another one says.

I turn to the last page in the sheaf of papers and see a single note scribbled at the bottom.

Everyone online says this one is extremely challenging—

lots of dropping out. But I know you can handle it. I believe in you.

    —A.

"This is from Akira," I murmur. "Um. The boy I like."

I smile slightly, because all of this is *so* Akira. The print-outs, the extremely detailed notes. Him doing all of this even though he claims he has to spend all his time working at the mochi stand and helping his uncle. I can picture him poring over these, his brow furrowed in concentration, all intense and cute. Taking it seriously, putting his all into it—because that's the only way he knows how to do things.

"He is trying to help you pick out schools to apply to?" my obaasan says. "But you have already chosen where you are going to apply, ne?"

"Yes," I say, flipping through the printouts again. "I didn't get a chance to tell him that part. This is so . . ."

My eyes mist over. I don't even have the words for it. The ache around my heart is pulsing again, but I can't tell if it's because I'm moved by Akira's gesture or angry with him for claiming he doesn't want to see me anymore or sad because I may never see him again.

Perhaps all of those things at once?

Boys are *so* confusing.

My gaze wanders to my textile tests, those medical texts with their macabre illustrations. Some of the pages have crumpled after being soaked, some have dried into stiff, exaggerated shapes. I brush my fingers over them, my brain getting the tiniest seed of an idea.

"Let's take that off the dress form," I say, nodding at my

work-in-progress application piece. "I'll get it all nice and packed away to take back with me."

"You don't want to leave it up for now?" Grandma says. "Because . . . you may. If you like."

"Thank you," I say, giving her a smile. "But I'm going to finish it at home. I have an idea for a new project to put on the dress form." I run my fingers over my paper experiments again, marveling at their different textures. "And I definitely need to finish this one before I leave Japan."

CHAPTER TWENTY

Dear Mom,

I can't remember if I ever showed you my roller coaster dress—probably one of my most elaborate Kimi Originals. I've only worn it once and I think you were tucked away in your studio when I sashayed through the house, on my way to Trini Dinh's sixteenth birthday party.

The bodice was from a red satin gown I found at the thrift store where I work—halter neck, structured, water-stained in a couple spots. I hacked the top part off the dress, altered it, and water-stained it all over so it looked like a pattern. The skirt was one of the first things I ever made out of completely new material. The guy who runs the fabric shop I like had this large remnant of cream-colored cotton he couldn't do anything with. I remember spreading it out on my bed and thinking how it could be so many things—it was a completely blank canvas. It took me forever to figure out what I wanted to do with it because the possibilities were so endless—and because I was convinced if I made the wrong choice, I'd mess up this cool fabric that had been gifted to me. (I'm pretty sure the fabric store guy didn't really care what I made it into or if I made it into anything at all, so I don't know why I stressed so much. Except that I guess I always stress in that particular way, so . . .)

I finally decided on a skirt. At first, I made it in a pretty basic shape—fitted at the waist and flaring outward to glorious fullness. A good twirling skirt. But it wasn't quite speaking to my soul. So, I started adding on to it. I sewed on some ribbons, flowing along the hemline. I added sequins to match. And then I saved up and got myself some fancy fabric paints and painted this wild, multicolored . . . thing all over it. It was a lot like my paintings—abstract and dreamy with big, exaggerated shapes and bright colors that shouldn't go together. Then I did some more sewing on the skirt—taking it in here, adding a drape there. So that it was sort of a big, exaggerated shape itself. The whole thing came together when I found that red satin gown and realized it was the last piece I needed to turn this initially simple skirt into the beautiful dress it was meant to be.

When I put it on and looked in the mirror, I felt pretty. But the dress was also wilder and more over-the-top than anything I'd worn before.

Trini Dinh's sixteenth birthday party seemed like the perfect place for the dress to make its debut. Her parents had rented the back room of this pizza place, which doesn't sound super fancy, but to most of us, just the fact that they *could* rent the entire back room seemed pretty swank. And Trini had requested we all dress up.

I'll admit: There was another reason I wanted to look extra nice. Marcus Reyes, who'd been my big crush since junior high, was going to be there. For weeks I'd had this fantasy: I'd show up in this beautiful dress, he would notice me for the first time ever, and we would have a perfect romantic moment. Maybe a brushing of hands over cheesy pepperoni?

When Atsuko and Bex came by to pick me up, Atsuko went "WoooOOOoooowie!" and pretended like her eyes were popping out of her head. Bex just told me I looked amazing and no way would Marcus be able to keep his eyes off me.

The party was in full swing when we arrived. Predictably, someone had spiked the big bowl of usually harmless "orange drink" the pizza place provides for all its parties, so everyone was kind of loud and sloppy. (Um, Bex and Atsuko and I totally did not have any, in case you are wondering.)

Trini gave all of us a big hug and screamed in our ears how happy she was to see us. Atsuko scanned the room, looking for people we know. Bex looked like she wanted to leave immediately. It was so loud—music blaring, people yelling at each other, a few of the attendees trying to do some kind of dance routine in the middle of the floor. But everything faded to a burble when I saw Marcus standing on the opposite side of the room. He was wearing what was probably his dad's suit jacket and he looked soooo handsome and he was laughing at something.

I drew myself up tall and remembered how pretty I felt in my dress. I started to cross the room. I heard some loud yelling in my right ear and then I heard Atsuko scream, "AGH WATCH OUT," and then suddenly I was covered in sticky orange drink. I whipped around and saw Ben Kirkman trying to scurry away, empty cups in hand. "Sorry!" he yelled over his shoulder.

Atsuko and Bex were at my side immediately, napkins at the ready.

I looked down at my dress. The orange drink had stained the few parts of the skirt that were still cream-colored—I'd left some blank spaces between the painted bits for balance. And the painted parts were now smeared. It was totally ruined.

Then I looked up and saw Marcus Reyes making out with some girl who went to a completely different school. Maybe one of Trini's band camp friends?

I didn't cry. I just said, very quietly: "We have to go home now."

Atsuko and Bex followed me outside, to Atsuko's Mustang. Then Atsuko twirled her keys in her hand and turned to face me.

"We are *not* going home," she said. "Tonight can't be all about some asshole spilling on Kimi's dress and some other asshole making out with . . . with . . . well, someone who isn't Kimi. Let's go ride some roller coasters."

We drove all the way to Magic Mountain. Atsuko had some free tickets from her cousin who works there.

We rode roller coasters all night—the twisty one that goes upside down, the creaky old wooden one, the one where you stand up in the car and get strapped in and whirled around. We screamed at the top of our lungs. We ate a ton of junk food and laughed hysterically about nothing in particular.

"You know, this skirt kind of looks like a roller coaster," Atsuko said at one point, tracing the now-smeared shapes I'd painted onto it. "It has that feeling of moving really fast and every which way. That feeling of *excitement*."

When I got home, the dress had other stains on it, too— grease from buttery popcorn, dirt from sitting on the ground. I took it off and hung it up in my closet. In the back of my mind, I couldn't help but think somehow it looked more beautiful—a little weirder, a little more off-kilter. More interesting. Definitely containing that sense of excitement Atsuko was talking about.

But I convinced myself it was ruined. I never wore it again.

When I look back on that night, though, the main feeling I can call up isn't sadness or regret or disappointment—it's not about something being ruined. Instead I remember how hoarse my throat felt from screaming, how giddy I felt being whirled around on the roller coasters. How my sides hurt from laughing so hard with my best friends. I'd say the main thing I remember feeling is . . . exhilaration.

I think I'm going to wear that dress again when I get home.

Love,
Kimi

CHAPTER TWENTY-ONE

I stay up late finishing my new project. It's not as complicated as my fashion school application design, but I'm still
very proud when it's done. I feel like I've only been asleep
for a few hours when I hear someone calling through the
shoji screen. I roll out of bed and blearily slide open the
screen to see my grandfather. Who looks way too excited for
this hour of the morning.

"Kimiko-chan!" he exclaims. "I need to go to my snack
shop again!"

"Really?" I murmur. "But weren't we just there the
other day?"

"Hai, hai," he says, waving a hand. "But I forgot some
very important flavors of Pocky and I must go get them.
I thought you would like to come with me?"

"Um, sure, Grandpa," I say, rubbing my eyes and stifling
a huge yawn. "Let me get ready. I have to do another errand
later today, though—"

"Oh, I know," he says, winking. "A very important
errand. That is why we go early, ne?"

I give him a woozy smile, shut the door, and proceed to
get dressed.

A very important errand.

I've started thinking of it as *a mission,* even.

It's a good thing I'm so tired, or I'd probably be super nervous about it. Luckily, I'm totally calm. *Totally.*

My grandfather yells out my name again and I shriek.

Okay, maybe I am a little nervous.

"Just want to see if you are ready yet!" my grandfather yells through the screen.

We take the train to the convenience mart and Grandpa grabs a basket and starts running around, throwing things into it with glee. I smile, wondering if he wanted to come back because now that Grandma's not with us to give him disapproving looks, he can load up on the mass quantities of snacks he requires.

"Ah, Kimiko-chan!" he cries, waving something around. I run to catch up with him. "Look," he continues, "they still have the limited-edition Snickers! I will get you some to take on your return trip." He sweeps an entire row of Snickers into his basket.

"I don't need that much, Grandpa!" I say, laughing. "They're delicious, but just a couple will do me."

"No, no." He shakes his head vehemently. "Save them up for later. You will need lots of energy at the fashion school."

I smile, a warm glow blooming in my chest as Grandpa puts more Snickers in his basket and asks the checkout clerk for an extra bag as he's paying. He separates out the limited-edition Snickers, tucks them into the extra bag, and hands it to me.

"For you," he says, patting my hand.

"Thank you," I say, genuinely touched.

We walk around Gion with our treats tucked under our arms and I feel a stab of melancholy when I realize this may be the last time we do this. I go home in two days.

But first I have to do my "very important errand." My mission. My heart speeds up just thinking about it.

"Kimiko-chan?" my grandfather says.

I snap out of my reverie and realize he's led me to one of the many shrines in Gion, an ornate compound of buildings with beautiful pillars of dark wood and rows of paper lanterns and flourishes of gold and scarlet.

"This is Yasui Konpiragu and there is something on these grounds I wish for you to see," he says, uncharacteristically solemn. "First, we must pay our respects here, at the inner sanctuary." He gives a little bow. I mimic him. "Now come with me," he continues.

We walk out into a courtyard area and my grandfather quickens his step, eager to get wherever we're going. I finally spot what he's so excited about: a blobby structure covered in tiny strips of white paper. It's about five feet high and there's a big hole cut in the middle and the paper looks kind of like cartoonish fur. The whole thing resembles some sort of mythical creature: a headless woolly mammoth or maybe a very pale Snuffleupagus.

"This is the power stone monument of Yasui Konpiragu," my grandfather says, his voice hushed. "It is supposed to be good for breaking off bad relations and initiating good ones. Many young people use it to wish for their romantic hopes and dreams."

I try—and fail—to suppress the smile that's creeping over my face.

"I thought it might give you luck in your important errand later," my grandfather continues, giving me a heart-breakingly hopeful look.

"All right," I say. "Tell me how this works, Grandpa."

"I have already gotten a katashiro for you," he says, whipping out a slip of white paper like the ones covering the power stone. "Write down your wish. Then"—he gestures to the big hole in the middle—"you crawl through the hole, reciting your wish as you go. You come back through the hole the opposite way, doing the same. Then you stick your katashiro on the monument—anywhere you like."

Oh, man. Why have so many of my attempts at sightseeing involved cramming myself into tiny spaces? At least this one looks a *little* bigger than Buddha's nostril.

"Hold this," I say, handing him my bag of candy.

His smile widens and I feel a fierce stab of affection. He *so* wants this to work for me.

I pick up a pen on the table next to the monument, then pause. Hmm. What is my wish, really? Of course I have my fantasyland version, but I'm also okay if it goes the other way. The main purpose of my mission/errand isn't necessarily romantic, I just want . . .

What do I want, exactly?

Finally, I write:

I want both of us to have our dreams and be happy.

I clutch the slip of paper in my hand and crouch down in front of the monument. My grandfather gives me an excited thumbs-up.

"You have got this, Kimiko-chan!" he exclaims.

I take a deep breath and crawl through the hole, chanting

my wish under my breath. This hole feels positively roomy compared to the other one I've had the pleasure of shoving myself through. I make it to the other side with ease, stand, turn, and funnel myself back through the other way. Then, finally, I stick my slip of paper on the stone, right near the top.

"Excellent," my grandfather says, passing me my bag of candy. "Would you like to have lunch—or dessert? We can eat dessert before lunch, as long as your grandmother is not around—"

"Oh, I'm so sorry, Grandpa, but I really should be getting back—I want to make it to Maruyama Park before the market closes," I say, genuinely regretful. Given my limited time left in Japan, I would love to have a few more extra desserts with him. But I do need to complete my mission.

"Yes, yes, of course," he says, waving a hand. "I just thought . . . Ano . . ." He pauses, his eyes considering. We stand there for a moment, staring at each other, as if frozen in time. "There is something I have to tell you," he says abruptly.

"Okay . . . ?"

"I . . ." He looks at the ground, then back at me. "I am the one who sent you the letter," he finally says. "Inviting you to come visit."

"I know," I say, puzzled. "You signed it."

"Yes, but . . ." He shakes his head, frowning. "What I mean is, eto . . . I sent it without telling your grandmother. She did not know. Until you accepted our invitation."

"Oh." Realization crashes through me. When I first arrived, my grandmother was so standoffish—and it wasn't just because I paid her too many compliments or because I reminded her so much of Mom. It was because she never wanted me to come in the first place.

"I knew if I consulted her first, she would be against the idea," my grandfather continues, his words coming out in a rush. "But I wanted . . ." A bit of his usual impish grin crosses his face. "I wanted to know you."

"I'm so glad," I say, my voice faint. I don't trust myself to say anything more—my eyes are already filling with tears. *This* is why he brought me on this excursion. It wasn't about Pocky or the power stone. He wanted to tell me the truth. "Um. So did Grandma forgive you? Because it seems like things have worked out okay."

"Hai, hai," he says with a chuckle. "It is easier to be against something when it is an abstract concept, a thing you cannot quite see, ne? But when you were standing right in front of her, a real person . . ." He beams at me. "I knew it would be all right."

I want to hug him, but I don't know if that will offend him—so we just stand there for a moment, smiling at each other.

"Kimi-chan," my grandfather finally says. "When you return to the States, I know you will be very busy with school and other young-people things. But I am wondering . . . eto . . ." He hesitates, his gaze wandering.

"What is it, Grandpa?"

"May I write to you sometimes?" he says. He looks so serious. "And would you write me back and let me know how you are—how life is treating you?"

"Of course!" I say, my eyes widening in surprise. "I just

assumed we'd keep in touch, Grandpa. These last two weeks have been . . ." I trail off. I can't even put it into words. Finally I just say: "Arigato, Ojiichan. For everything."

Grandpa nods, and he looks so relieved, my heart breaks. He really thought I was going to say no. "No, arigato to you, Kimi-chan. I will send you a first correspondence next week. I know how to use the email." He chuckles to himself, reverting to the Grandpa demeanor I'm more familiar with. "And the internet. That is how I found out when your spring break was—the Google!"

"Hey, Grandpa," I say, as we walk back toward the train station. "You should consider using the email to write to other people, too."

"I do," he says proudly. "My friend Shin and I exchange weekly updates about the weather and what team is ahead in football. And sometimes I send your obaasan a message that just says, 'Hi, I am in the other room.'" He cackles to himself. "She tells me to cut it out, but I know she secretly thinks it's funny."

"No, I mean . . ." I stop and laugh. "Okay, that is actually pretty funny. But I think you should try writing to Mom again, Ojiichan. A lot has changed over the years. I think she'd like to hear from you."

"Mmm." My grandfather's eyes soften, but his sadness is tempered with the tiniest spark of hope. "Perhaps you could put in a good word for me?"

"I'm not sure how far my 'good word' will go at the moment," I say. "But someone really smart gave me some good advice recently: If you want something, you have to say it out loud and to the correct person."

"Hmm," Grandpa says. "Who gave you this advice?"

"Grandma," I say, laughing.

"Ah." He smiles at me. "Then I agree, it is the best advice ever."

The hour has arrived. I am about to go on my mission.

I'm nervous, but actually kind of excited, too?

Grandma helps me pack up the project I worked on all night into a nice gift box and wishes me luck as I head off to the train station. I wend my way through the now familiar environs of Maruyama Park, my package tucked securely under my arm, my heart beating a kazillion miles per minute.

It speeds up as I approach the mochi stand and goes into hyperdrive when I spot Akira. He and his ojisan are both working the counter, helping a long line of eager customers.

I reach the mochi stand and position myself off to the side, not wanting to interrupt. After a few minutes, I start to feel incredibly awkward. Some of the people in line are giving me funny looks, probably wondering who this random girl is and what she's waiting for and why she has a gigantic box tucked under her arm. I shift from foot to foot and try to project a confident feeling—like, yes, I'm just standing here, what of it? I most definitely have a purpose, a *mission*, even if you don't know what it is, Mr. Random Tourist Person, and I intend to—

"Kimi?"

I whip around to see Akira standing there, giving me a quizzical look.

"Oh, uh, hi," I say, my face getting hot. Of course I've rehearsed this moment a million times in my head. Imagined the perfect speech I'd give. Pictured how he'd be gazing at me with surprise—but also affection, amazement, and appreciation for how cute I look. (I'm wearing my new pink blouse—the one I made with Grandma. And jeans and white ankle boots with fringy bits. I look *very* cute.)

For now, he just looks surprised. Also, *really* hot, which I didn't anticipate but probably should have. Under his apron, he's wearing the cool T-shirt with the abstract design on it— the one he was wearing the day we met. Tending to the mochi stand with such a big crowd is clearly hard work and his shirt is sticking to him various places in sweaty patches, especially his chest and those nice arms. My eyes linger and I very sternly remind myself to *not* get distracted by him the way I usually do. I'm on a mission, after all.

"What are you doing here?" he says.

"I brought you something," I say, brandishing the gift box at him. "Something I thought you should have."

He takes it from me curiously, examining it from every angle.

"Open it," I blurt out. "I mean, if you want to."

A flicker of amusement crosses his face and my chest warms. Ugh. Focus, Kimi. *Mission!*

"Let's sit down for a minute," he says, gesturing to a nearby bench.

We sit and he opens the box with care, keeping the flat

cardboard surfaces pristine. My eyes are glued to his face, waiting for his reaction.

"Wow," he says, his eyes widening to the size of dinner plates. "It's . . . wow."

He sets the box on the bench and pulls the garment inside free, holding it up in front of him.

"Kimi," he says softly. His voice has that sweet tenderness that always makes me blush. "Oh, Kimi."

He can't take his eyes off what I've made for him. I watch as he takes it all in: the old pages of medical texts I carefully soaked and treated and sewed together into a jacket. I cut it in a style inspired by the haori, so it's loose and cool and he can wear it over lots of stuff. I used Grandma's suggestion to reinforce it with another fabric, a light cotton I sewed the treated pages onto. And I made sure that plenty of the pages I used featured those ultra-detailed medical diagrams he's so fond of.

"This is the most thoughtful thing anyone has ever given me," he says.

He still can't stop looking at it. He's studying every detail.

"I know what it's like to want to do something for your family," I say. "To feel like they've worked so hard for you and you love them so much, you can't imagine doing anything else." I think of my mother's exhausted face when I was younger, working hours on end and pulling me tightly into her arms at the end of the day. "But that doesn't mean you have to forget what *you* want. Your ojisan knows what it's like to have a big dream. And I think—no, I *know*—he would want you to have yours." I lean forward, trying to get out what I want to say. "Spending time with you has given me so much courage, Akira. I love how much passion you have, how seriously you take things . . . and how you kept telling *me* to go after what I want." I brush my fingers over the jacket, smiling at the diagrams I know he loves so much. "It's totally scary. There are no guarantees. But when something speaks to your soul . . ." He finally turns and looks at me, but his eyes give nothing away. "You can't give up on it. Please don't give up on being a doctor, Akira. I know it's what you want more than anything in the entire world. I know it speaks to your soul. And I just wanted to remind you of how you felt when you first discovered that."

Something flickers in his eyes—I can't quite tell what it is, but it seems like he wants to say a million things at once and isn't sure where to begin. We gaze at each other for a few moments more and it feels a bit like those crackly silences we used to have with each other.

But it also makes that ache pulse around my heart again and I can only take so much. Anyway, I've accomplished my mission: I just wanted to get him to remember his dream— and to remember that because it's important to him, it's important. Simple as that.

So finally, I stand.

"Good-bye, Akira," I say, squeezing his hand. "And thank you so much for the printouts and the Ebi Filet-O. I really appreciated them."

I turn and manage to walk away before I start to cry. And when the tears begin to fall, I walk faster, motoring my way through Maruyama Park as quickly as I can. I pass by all the food stands, the gorgeous cherry blossoms, the fairy-tale bridge where Akira and I sat just last week. But it feels so much longer ago than that.

I'm walking so fast, concentrating so hard on getting to the train station, trying so much not to cry more, that I don't hear my name being called until someone taps me on the shoulder. I turn around and a young woman in an all-black ensemble says something to me in Japanese, her eyes wide and urgent. I think I catch the word for "boy," but I don't understand anything else.

"I'm sorry," I say. "I don't understand . . ."

"Ah, English," she says, switching over. "Ahhhh . . . boy? That boy. He is chasing you, I think?"

I turn my gaze to the spot she's gesturing to, just before the bridge.

And there's Akira. Running, out of breath, the jacket I made for him thrown awkwardly over his T-shirt–apron ensemble. He's waving his arms over his head, apparently trying to get my attention. He looks almost as ridiculous as he does when he's dancing around in his mochi costume.

"Kimi . . ." he gasps out.

"Are you in danger, miss?" the young woman says, her eyes narrowing.

"N-no," I stammer. "No, I don't think so."

Akira reaches us and the young woman gives him the stink-eye and nods at me.

"Please yell if you are in danger," she says. "My all-female advanced kendo group is meeting just across the bridge and we will all come to assist you if you need."

"Uhhh, that's so freaking cool?!" I blurt out as she strides off. "I will totally do that."

I turn to Akira. "Wh-what are you doing?" I manage, my voice faint.

He doubles over, out of breath, resting his hands on his knees.

"I am coming after you," he wheezes out. "I have been— how do you say it? An ass that is bad." He looks up at me. "And not in the good way."

"Akira." My explosive giggle escapes. I'm so overwhelmed with emotions, I don't know what to do but laugh.

He straightens up all the way and locks his gaze with mine. "I am sorry about the other day," he says. "When I said I couldn't see you anymore. Kimi, I don't want to do anything *but* see you. I just . . ."

"I understood," I say gently. "I mean, eventually. I do know quite a bit about family obligation and such, remember?" I arch an eyebrow at him. "Although I think I also should take you to task for always just *deciding* these things. Like when you just decided not to kiss me."

"That was partially your fault, too!" he exclaims. His lips twitch. "We have been over this. But Kimi . . ." He gestures to his jacket. "This is amazing. *You* are amazing." He steps closer and cups my face in his hands. "You made me speechless. For a moment."

"So are you going to talk to your uncle, to your family?" I say, leaning into the warmth of his hands. "About still going to school?"

"Yes," he says. "But for now . . ." His face softens. "I

already talked to Ojisan about needing tomorrow off. To spend time with you before you leave."

"And what did he say?"

"He said . . ." Akira flushes. "That he does not need me as much as I seem to think he does and I should stop being a fool and go after the girl who pounded the usu so well."

There's so much happy fluttering around my heart, I can barely stand it.

"Wow, she sounds awesome," I say, giving him a teasing look. "But, you know, she might be super busy. After all, tomorrow is her last day in Japan."

"Oh . . ." he says, his face falling.

"I'm kidding," I say, laughing. Then something off to the side catches my eye. "Oh, look. We're by the stuffed tanuki again. The one who told me to give you my phone number."

"Ahhh, yes," he says, smiling. Oh god, that dimple. I've missed it so much. "I am hearing him again. This time, he has a message for me."

"What's that?"

He leans in closer. "He's telling me to kiss you."

"Akira!" I shriek, because we're about to engage in some pretty massive PDA and I see quite a few old people giving us disapproving looks.

"Come here," he says softly. He pulls me behind the tree with the tanuki, out of sight.

"The tanuki can see us," I murmur against his mouth.

"The tanuki approves," he retorts.

And then he kisses me so thoroughly, I forget where we are in the first place.

CHAPTER TWENTY-TWO

It's my last day in Japan.

I'm trying not to think about it too much, honestly. I have breakfast with my grandparents, then putter around my room, getting ready for my date with Akira. I force myself to start packing and can't help but get a little misty when I stow away the bag of limited-edition candy Ojiichan got for me yesterday.

I felt so lost and discombobulated when I first got here, wondering if I'd made a huge mistake. Now I don't want to leave. Especially since I'm not totally sure what's going to happen when I return to the States, my mother, and all the uncertainty I left behind.

But I'm not going to dwell on that right now. I want to enjoy my last day with Akira. I know that after today, there's a very real possibility we'll never see each other again. I want to savor every second, every touch, every memory I'll take back with me. I want to be in the moment with him and have as much fun as humanly possible.

In other words, I'm going to pretend like it's totally *not* my last day in Japan.

Akira and I meet up that afternoon in front of his pro-

266

posed spot for a last bit of sightseeing: Fushimi Inari Taisha, one of the most famous shrines in Japan.

"How is it you have you not been here yet? It is maybe the most popular site in Kyoto." Akira grins at me.

I'm too busy being in awe to respond. My jaw literally drops as I stand in front of the big red gate that stands at the entrance of the shrine. It's a torii, a traditional Japanese gate usually found at Shinto shrines. It's actually kind of an orangey-red—scarlet? Vermillion? Some gorgeous, vibrant color I haven't seen anywhere else. The gate consists of two tall poles connected by a pair of long bars on top of them—like two letter Ts that have been joined together. And all in that bright, beautiful shade of red. A curving black swoop sits on top of the structure, giving it a dramatic accent. The whole thing is a vivid splash of color against the breathtakingly blue sky.

"There are supposed to be ten thousand torii gates on these grounds," Akira says. "Although I have tried to count them and I always lose track before the first thousand."

I take it all in, giddiness bubbling in my chest at the thought of another adventure. I turn to him. "Before we go in: Can I ask you for something?"

He gives me a smile, flashing that dimple. "Anything."

"Can we pretend it's just another day? Not my *last* day. I want to feel like . . . we could just keep going after this. And if I keep thinking about it being my last day, I'll get too sad."

"Uhhhhh, okay," he says, his eyes shifting back and forth.

"What?"

"Nothing," he says. "Except . . ." More eyes shifting back

and forth. "I might have, ahhh . . . got you something. To remember your last day by. Do you still want it?"

I smile. "I'll never turn down a present."

He reaches into his backpack, pulls out a small box, and hands it to me.

"What is this?" I turn the box over in my hands. "Another Ebi Filet-O in a cunningly designed package?"

"No," he says, grinning. "Open it."

I carefully remove the lid to reveal . . . mochi. Four perfect, round blobs of it, each one nestled in its own square of the sectioned-off box.

"Ojisan helped me make those. They all have different fillings," Akira says. He's talking fast and looking at the ground, like he's suddenly unsure as to whether I'll like it or not.

As if I'd ever *not* like any gift involving food.

"I love it," I say, giving him a reassuring smile. "And I'm starving, so it's extra perfect."

"Wait!" he exclaims as I reach for the piece in the upper left corner. "Eto . . . There's an . . . order. Eat that one first." He points to the lower right.

"Your gift comes with detailed instructions?" I cock an eyebrow and reach for the correct piece. "That's very *you.*"

"*One* instruction." He rolls his eyes. "I would not call that 'detailed.'"

I giggle and pop the mochi into my mouth—red bean paste. A little sweet, a little earthy. A lot of yum.

As I'm chewing, I glance down at the box and see there's a slip of paper where the mochi was—it must have been nestled underneath. I pick it up, turn it over, and see a carefully written kanji character.

"That means 'climb,'" Akira says. He gestures to the shrine gate. "Which is what we are about to do."

"Ah, yes. I'm glad you filled me in on that part beforehand." In addition to being a revered shrine, Fushimi Inari also offers something of a workout: Visitors can hike up Mount Inari, passing through those famed rows of ten thousand torii gates. Those who make it to the top are ultimately rewarded with an amazing view of the city. At least, that's what I've heard. I've worn comfortable shoes, packed light (I even left my sketchbook behind), and am prepared to climb like I've never climbed before. Especially now that I have mochi.

"And let me guess, there's a different kanji under every mochi," I say, eyeing the box.

Akira smiles. "I thought it might be fun for you to learn a little more Japanese before returning to the States. You know, try to impress the Aunties."

"*Nothing* will impress the Aunties," I say, laughing. "But thank you—I've been thinking about taking some classes when I get back."

I reach for another piece of mochi and he covers my hand with his. "Do not reveal them all yet. There are, ah, specific places where it will make the most sense for you to uncover them. Which I have planned out."

"Of course you have," I say, giving him a teasing look. "But hey, that's at least *two* instructions. Definitely counts as detailed."

He pauses, his hand still on mine, and his face goes all serious. "I want to make your last day special," he says earnestly. "I tried to include kanji that will mean something to you."

Oh. *Dammit.* Here I am trying to pretend like it's *not* my last day, and of course this adorable boy wants to go out of his way to make it special. Where does he get off being so perfect? I almost say that out loud.

"But of course it's *not* your last day." His expression morphs to teasing. "It is just another day, ne?"

"Just another day," I murmur, my eyes going to the box again. Now I'm really dying to see what's under the last three pieces. "Are you sure I can't eat these now?"

His mouth quirks into a half smile. "Yes." He inclines his head toward the shrine. "Now we go. Now we climb."

Akira leads me to a spot to the left of the main gate, a concrete basin filled with water and topped with an interlocking bamboo contraption containing rows of ladles with long, skinny handles.

"Oh, Ojiichan told me about this," I say. "It's a cleansing ritual, right?"

"To purify the mind and body before entering the shrine." Akira nods. "Like this." He picks up one of the ladles. "Pick it up with your right hand and pour water over your left. Then switch and pour over your right." He demonstrates. "Then take some water from the ladle"—he pours it into his palm—"and use it to rinse your mouth." He does this, then spits the water out next to the basin. "Do not swallow the water," he says, grinning. "Some skip this step because they are not sure of . . . you know, bacteria. Germs. The things that can exist in water. Then tip the ladle so the water runs down your arm and put it back."

"I'll take the chance and rinse my mouth," I say, stepping

270

forward and picking up a ladle. "I want to be as cleansed as possible."

"Do you need me to help you?" he says, leaning over my shoulder. He's close enough that his lips practically brush my ear and I flush. This is definitely one of those memories I want to take home with me.

"I think I've got it," I say, filling my ladle with water. I turn and give him a sly smile. "Also, I *might* have watched like a million YouTube videos to make sure I didn't mess up such an important part of visiting a shrine."

"Ah, why did you let me go on with my demonstration, then?" He pulls a mock offended face. "You already know what you are doing, ne?"

"Yours was *much* better than YouTube," I assure him. "Also, much cuter."

He shakes his head and gives me a look. I just grin at him.

I go through the purification ritual, carefully rinsing my hands and mouth. Then we proceed up the steps and through the elaborate gate—which is an amazing structure in and of itself. It's flanked by two green fox statues, who gaze down at us with fierce, watchful expressions. Foxes are the messengers of the god/goddess Inari and therefore a big theme throughout the shrine.

When we enter the grounds of the main shrine, I am once again overwhelmed by so many amazing sights. This is one of the things I'll miss most about Japan, I realize. I feel like my eyeballs are constantly drinking in about a zillion beautiful things at once. We pay our respects at the main shrine by putting coins in one of the offering boxes, then ring the bells and go through the basic prayer ritual. I'm especially drawn to a small temple off to the right of the grounds featuring a long wall of paper cranes. They're every color imaginable and strung together in flowing chains— they look like elaborate rainbow streamers.

"Ohhhhh," I breathe, moving in for a closer look.

"Let me guess," Akira says. "This will inspire a dress?"

"It could inspire many dresses," I say, my eyes glued to the cranes. "So many. Dresses for *days*."

"I cannot wait to see," he says—and I can't help but feel a little pang.

"But you won't see, will you?" I murmur, almost to myself.

He'll be an ocean away. And we haven't really talked about whether we're going to keep in touch. I mean, it makes the most sense for us *not* to talk anymore, probably. Talking to him without being able to touch him, to see him, to be together . . . it might hurt too much.

"Hey. Kimi." He reaches over and brushes my bangs out of my eyes. "Today is just another day, ne?" His expression is so tender, I nearly lose it right there.

Ugh. Be in the damn moment, Kimi.

"So can I eat another mochi now?" I say, trying to make my tone light.

"Not yet," he says, laughing. "We are only at the base of Mount Inari—still miles to go."

"Let's go, then."

He leads me up the stone steps, to the beginning of our climb. The endless row of torii extends in front of us, a winding tunnel of scarlet gates. There are quite a few people on the path and I smile as I watch them trying to walk and take everything in at the same time, heads turning this way and that. I make a mental note to try my best not to get so absorbed by the scenery that I trip over my own feet.

"This gets even more packed at New Year's," Akira says as we begin our walk. "It is a mass of people, just trying to pass through these gates."

"Still quite a few people here right now," I observe. "And yet it's so peaceful."

The tunnel of torii is surrounded by lush greenery, a beautiful foothill forest leading into the mountain. The contrast of those bright red gates against the tranquil green is striking, and I'm so swept up in it, I'm able to briefly forget my worries about what happens after today. Soon, we reach a spot where the line of torii splits into two side-by-side paths.

"Whoa, this feels very momentous," I say, stopping in front of them and putting my hands on my hips. I cock an eyebrow at him. "Surely this calls for another piece of mochi?"

"You are so impatient," he says, giving me an amused look. "Can you wait until we have gotten past this first section of torii—the first thousand—and reached the inner shrine?"

"Well, that sounds very fancy," I say, pretending to consider very carefully. "I guess I can wait."

"To the right, then," he says. "Both paths will take us to the same place, but you generally enter to the right because it keeps the flow of foot traffic going in the most efficient manner."

The torii in this section are packed so tightly together, we're surrounded by nothing but that brilliant orangey-red. It's a bit like being in the bamboo grove, suddenly enclosed in this gorgeous pod that's a whole world unto itself. But the feeling this pod gives me isn't soothing—it's *energizing*. My creative juices flow, my brain overloads with inspiration. My fingers itch for my sketchbook and I almost wish I had opted to haul it up the mountain with me.

"More dresses?" Akira says, gesturing around us.

"More everything," I say. "This is amazing."

We walk for a bit with that crackly silence between us. I savor it the same way I savored the mochi earlier, trying to commit each tiny moment to memory. I'm almost disappointed when we emerge from that first row of torii and into the open space of the inner shrine. I don't want this feeling of enchantment to end.

"Shall we get ema?" Akira says, nodding toward a stand piled high with small, triangular wooden plaques.

"Show me what these are," I say as we move closer.

"Oh, you did not watch a YouTube video on this?" he teases, raising an eyebrow. He points to the plaques—which I now realize are shaped like pointy little fox faces. "You write a wish or a prayer on the back of one of these," he says. "Something you are hoping for, perhaps? And then we go hang it on the shrine wall as an offering." He gestures across the way, to a bright red wall festooned with countless tiny fox plaques. "And because these are shaped like foxes, sometimes people draw a face on them as well."

"Let's do it."

We purchase ema and the woman at the stand offers us markers to write with.

Akira flips his ema over and starts writing immediately. I hem and haw over my wish. It seems like anything I actually want to wish for would require me to admit that this is my last day.

"Maybe I'll just draw a face," I say, toying with my marker.

"You must wish for something," Akira insists. He taps my ema with his marker. "That is the rule." He smiles at me. "You do not have to tell me or anyone else your wish— remember, it's on the back. Just write something that is in your heart."

I think about that for a long while. Akira finishes scribbling out his wish and turns the ema over to sketch a face.

What is in my heart? Like, the deepest, darkest places that I'm afraid to show anyone? What would I wish for with no limitations?

Finally, I write something down.

Then, before Akira can sneak a peek, I flip my ema over and draw a stylish fox face with long eyelashes and a jaunty hat.

"Even your ema is fashionable," Akira says, smiling at my handiwork.

"And yours is so cute and inquisitive," I say. "Look at those googly eyes."

We cross over to the wall and hang our ema among all the others. There are so many different faces, so many styles of drawing. There's one I can tell must have been drawn by a small child, crude scratchings and a big curvy line of a smiling mouth. Another one looks like it was done by a professional manga artist—so much detail contained in such a small canvas. I find myself wondering what kind of ema Mom would draw, if it would practically leap off the wall with her trademark big, bold shapes.

"Would you like to have another piece of mochi?" Akira asks.

"Yes!" I exclaim, my train of thought immediately diverting to what flavor I'm going to get, what kanji is about to be revealed. I pull the mochi box out of my bag and open it.

"This one," Akira says, pointing to the lower left corner.

I make a big show of plucking it free and take a bite. This one is black sesame, rich with deep, savory flavor.

"So good," I murmur. I gently extricate the slip of paper underneath and flip it over.

"This is 'hope,'" Akira says. He gestures to the wall of ema. "Because that's what this wall is full of. And . . ." He hesitates, turning to face me. His eyes have that earnest cast. "Because that is what you gave me, Kimi: hope. The incredible jacket you made for me helped me remember what it is like to dream of the future I really want."

"Does that mean you talked to your ojisan, your family?" I didn't want to press the subject until I knew he was ready to talk about it.

"Ojisan called me a fool again," he says, smiling. "Said he can manage just fine without me. I think he is going to try to set up at another location—perhaps not as well trafficked, but the rent is much cheaper."

"Not as well trafficked *yet*," I correct. "Once word gets out about your uncle's mochi, that place will be *mobbed*."

"And he may try to expand into mail order," Akira says. He taps my mochi box. "Doing boxes like this one."

"That's a great idea!" I exclaim. "Ooooh, if he gets a website set up—I mean, I see so much potential."

"And with this, I can still help him," Akira says. "Whenever I am on break from school."

"So you're definitely going to school?" I say, smiling.

"Yes." He returns my smile. "I am going to start my journey to be a doctor. And whenever I feel discouraged, I will look at the amazing garment you constructed for me and remember when someone believed in me more than I did. I will remember you giving me that hope."

A lump is slowly but surely forming in my throat. I swallow hard, tears pricking my eyes. I clutch the slip of paper in my hand, holding it close to my heart.

"Akira . . ." I say, my voice full of way too many emotions.

"Too much—how do you say it? Heaviness?" He gives me a gentle smile and reaches over and squeezes my hand. "I know, I know: It is just another day."

"Just another day," I murmur.

But as we walk away from the wall of ema, I hold his hand extra tightly, unwilling to let go.

CHAPTER TWENTY-THREE

Night begins to fall as we continue our journey, the sunlight sparkling through the cracks between the torii gates giving way to soft dusk. The climb gets steeper as we go, and my legs start to ache, but I'm determined to soldier on to the top, to get the full scope of this experience.

We stop for an early dinner at a little restaurant on the trail and eat inarizushi and kitsune udon—named for the fox-guides because the mouthwatering fried tofu that sits on top of hearty udon noodles is supposed to be their favorite food.

"My dad called this 'pocket sushi' when I was a kid," I say, holding up a piece of inarizushi. "I guess because he thought that concept would make it extra fun or something? Of course he meant because it's a little tofu 'pocket' stuffed with rice. But I thought he was saying, like, you could put it in your pocket."

"How many did you stuff in your pocket before he realized?" Akira says, a smile playing over his lips.

"I think six?"

We laugh and I feel a surge of warmth as the vibe between us resets to something lighter again.

"This is beautiful," I say, gesturing out the window. We're in that moment where it's not quite day, not quite night. The sky softens into something gray and magical and all the mountain greenery blurs into shadows. "But is it okay for us to keep hiking in the dark?"

Akira nods as he slurps his udon. "The shrine is open twenty-four hours—the crowds will thin out considerably the darker it gets, but you'll still see people climbing. You might even see an evening runner or two jogging up the steps." He sets down his bowl and studies me. "The feeling of the torii tunnel is different—I wanted you to have both experiences. And . . ." He hesitates, his gaze going to the window. "There is something I wanted you to see right about now. Let's go find out if I timed it correctly."

We pay for our meals and head back outside.

"This way," Akira says, leading me off the path to a spot slightly away from the steps and the torii gates. "Right . . . here."

"Ohhhh," I breathe out, taking in the scene around me. We're still surrounded by the wilderness of the mountain— even in the dark of early night, I can see the shadowy shapes of trees. But just beyond that is a stunning cityscape of about a million sparkling lights set against the clear sky that's slowly fading from brilliant blue to velvety black. And the stars are just beginning to wink into sight. "This is incredible," I say.

"This is Yotsu-tsuji—the crossroads," he says. "Possibly the best view on this hike. And even better at night."

We stand there for a few moments in silence, taking it in. We're the only two people in this spot right now and it feels like we're locked away in our own world.

"Would you like to sit for a moment?" Akira says.

I nod and even though there are a few benches scattered around, we sit on the ground, huddled together. We're almost fully plunged into night now and it's getting cool. Akira takes his jacket off and wraps it around both of us, pulling me closer. (I do have my own jacket tucked away in my bag, but I don't object.)

We sit there in silence for so long, I lose track of time. The city looks so vast and the sky is endless. I lean my head against his shoulder and try to commit every detail to memory once again: the solid warmth of his arm around me, the fresh laundry scent of his jacket. The way we don't have to say anything and it still feels like we're saying everything.

After a while, he whispers: "Do you want another piece of mochi?"

"What? I mean . . . yes!" I giggle way too loudly, puncturing the serenity of our surroundings, and clap my hand over my mouth. "This is such an amazing view, I actually forgot about the mochi."

I manage to stay under the jacket with him as I reach over, pull the box from my bag, and open it.

"This one," he says, pointing to the upper right corner.

I take it out and pop it in my mouth—mmm, chocolate. The perfect sweet treat after our savory meal.

"Wow," I say. "That is *good.*"

He smiles and hands me the slip of paper that was underneath the chocolate mochi. I flip it over, but it's so dark out, I can't actually see what's on it.

"Oops!" He laughs and fishes his phone out of his pocket, turning on the flashlight app and shining it over the paper.

"I should have realized reading up here at night might present a problem." He points to the kanji, which I can now see more clearly. "This means . . . well, there are a few meanings. Unlimited. Endless. Boundless."

"Ah, so this view," I say, gesturing to the incredible landscape before us, that combination of nature and city that seems to go on forever. "Once again, a perfect match of kanji and location—I guess I'm glad you made me wait before inhaling the entire box."

I give him a teasing look, but he's not laughing—he's regarding me seriously, his eyes searching my face. "It is not just about the view," he says. He turns off the flashlight app, tucks his phone back in his pocket, and meets my gaze. "It is also about you."

My breath catches. "What?"

"When you go home, I want you to remember that *you* are boundless," he says. "That your dreams are not limited by anything—not uncertainty. Not what someone else thinks or says. Not what you think you *should* be doing versus what makes your heart light up." He cups my face with one of his hands, his thumb stroking down my cheek. "Watching you embrace your passion is beautiful. And I hope you keep doing that, no matter what else might get in the way. You are so creative, so talented—the way your imagination overflows when you're inspired . . ." He shakes his head, smiling slightly. "You have this endless well of passion and when you love something, you love it so fiercely. I am in awe of that. I am in awe of *you*."

The lump in my throat will one hundred percent not go away this time. Ditto the tears that fill my eyes and start to trickle down my cheeks. No one has ever made me feel so *seen*.

"Oh, Kimi, no. Don't cry." His brow crinkles in concern and he brushes my tears away with his thumb. "I am sorry. I . . . I ruined it again, didn't I? The 'just another day' thing. I didn't mean—"

I cut him off with a kiss.

I'm feeling so many things I can't express in words and that seems like the only real way to show him. My palms press against his chest and his fingers tangle in my hair, pulling me close. We're still wrapped up in the cocoon of his jacket, and the dark cover of night really does make it feel like we're the only two people in the world, locked away from anything that's not this moment. I revel in every sensation: his lips on mine, his hands stroking down my back, all the places where our skin touches. I could live in this kiss forever.

When we finally pause for a moment, we're both breathless. He brushes away the last of my tears, his gaze exploring every inch of my face.

"Kimi . . ." he manages.

"It's not just another day," I interrupt. "It is my last day, my last night, my last everything—in Japan. And . . ." That lump rises in my throat again. I swallow, determined to continue. "I *am* sad. But I'm also so . . . so *happy* that I've had such an amazing time here."

I think about what I said to my obaasan the other day— about how even though making things real opens me up to hurting and heartbreak, I wouldn't trade all the experiences I've had here in Japan for anything in the world. All those experiences have led me to this place, right now—and I suddenly realize that I want to embrace that, not ignore it. It *is* my last day. And I'm with the sweetest, most passionate, and yes, *hottest* guy I've ever known.

"So much of that amazing time has been because of you, Akira," I say, reaching up to touch his face. "Thank you for wanting to make my last day special." My fingertips skate down his cheek and I feel him smile, his dimple appearing under the soft touch of my thumb. "Back at the inner shrine," I continue hesitantly, "I wished that we could have another day like this. That's what I wrote on my ema. Just one more day, in one of the most beautiful places in the world, where we don't have to worry about anything but each other."

"Only one more day?" he says, pulling a mock indignant face. "Oh, Kimi from America, what did I tell you: Don't forget that your imagination is boundless." His expression softens. "I wished that this would not be the end for us. That we would have *many* days like this."

"But how?" I whisper, the tears creeping into my eyes again. "How would that even happen?"

"I do not know yet—it is a wish," he says. "But who knows? Airplanes exist. You have family here. I have always wanted to visit the States." He grins at me and cocks a teasing eyebrow. "I could meet all the big movie stars, maybe one of those guys from an American detective show, ne? What do you say we keep talking and see where this takes us?"

I study his earnest, hopeful face. I have no idea where we'll end up—and there's definitely potential for heartbreak. But isn't it the same with my big decision to pursue what I actually want, to apply to fashion school? I keep saying there's no certain outcome there, either. And yet I can't imagine doing anything else.

If I stopped talking to Akira after today, it wouldn't make the wanting go away.

"Okay," I say. "*Yes*. Please. Let's keep talking. Keep wishing. For many more days like this."

He smiles and pulls me close again. We kiss for what seems like hours in one of the most beautiful places in the world and it's definitely not just another day.

It's one of the best days I've ever had.

When we finally manage to stop kissing, we hike the rest of the way up to the top of the mountain, where there's another shrine. Akira uses his phone flashlight to show me some of the tiny fox statues peppered throughout, we take in more incredible views, and then finally, reluctantly decide we should start our descent.

"Wow," I say as he leads me back to the torii gates. "You were right, this has such a different feel at night." The scarlet tunnel is lit by lanterns placed in various corners and there's no one walking through but us. The darkness and the sporadic illumination and the lack of tourists bustling about give it an eerie, secluded cast. The quiet is occasionally punctuated by sounds from the forest, the soft chitterings of bugs and the gentle rustle of leaves. It still feels magical, but in a whole different way.

My heart is full and I'm suddenly so glad I finally let

myself celebrate this as my last day. Because our walk back feels weighted with meaning—in a good way. I'm still sad to be leaving, but I'm also excited to go home and share all the memories I've made with my friends. And to face my future.

I think of my application piece: the garment I started with Grandma, the garment that gives me so much joy whenever I think about it. I can't wait to finish it and to show it off. I can't wait to show it to Mom.

That last thought trickles in unbidden and I frown a little—I mean, I need to really explain everything to Mom before I show her. But I *do* want to show her, I realize. I want her to finally see the passion I've been so afraid to show her in the past.

"What are you thinking about?" Akira says, jiggling my hand. He hasn't let go of my hand since Yotsu-tsuji. "You have the look you get when you are thinking very hard about something."

"Everything and nothing," I say. "Going home. Applying to fashion school. Dealing with my mom. And how glad I am to be here with you—whoa!" Something skitters across the path and I jump out of the way.

What in the world . . .

"Ah, I should have warned you," Akira says, laughing a little. He lets go of my hand and crouches down, motioning for me to do the same. I kneel next to him and he gestures to the side, where the torii touch the forest. "Look," he says softly.

I do. A small, inquisitive face with huge eyes and pointy little ears stares back at me.

"Is that a *cat*?" I exclaim.

"There are a bunch of them in this forest," Akira says. "Lurking around. But more bold at night, for some reason."

"I guess cats and foxes are sort of related, right?" I say, giggling as I stand back up. "Maybe the cats get the nighttime shift when it comes to watching over this place."

"Maybe," he says, grinning at me. "Shall we see how many we spot before we get to the bottom of the mountain?"

We continue our walk through the tunnel of torii, counting cats as we go, making up elaborate personalities and backstories for them. It feels easy and light and Akira keeps making me laugh with his increasingly ridiculous explanations of the various kitty characters. It keeps me from dwelling on the fact that even the best days have to come to an end.

As we reach the last section of torii gates, my heart drops a little. Yes, I'm totally celebrating my last day and yes, I know we're going to keep talking—but I still don't want to say good-bye to Akira.

"Here we are," he says as we reach the final torii gate. "At the end. Do you want your last mochi?"

I almost say no because the last mochi definitely means the day is over. But I make myself nod. He reaches into my bag, pulls the box out, and hands it to me. I pluck the last piece free and take a bite. I want to savor this one rather than cramming it all in my mouth in one go. It tastes sweet and fruity.

"Strawberry," Akira says. "Like the mochi I gave you on your first day here. Of course it is not a *real* strawberry because I did not think that would keep all day during our hike, so it is not *exactly* like the mochi I gave you your first day, but I thought this would be close enough."

"It's wonderful," I say, meaning it. Why is he acting so nervous all of a sudden? I scrutinize his face and realize that his eyes are shiny, that he's looking at me like he's trying to memorize every single thing.

He doesn't want to say good-bye, either.

I pop the last bite in my mouth, take the final slip of paper from the box, and turn it over. And my heart does a somersault. Because I know this kanji. This kanji is one of the few I learned from my mother. She showed it to me when I got that little watercolor set, holding my hand in hers to trace the gentle brush marks on scrap paper.

Akira runs a fingertip over the kanji. His voice is low and hesitant. "This one means—"

"—love." I meet his gaze. "It means love."

He laces his fingers through mine. The slip of paper is still nestled in my hand and I swear I can feel my heartbeat right at the point where our palms touch, pressing that last kanji between us.

He's looking at me with that tenderness that makes me melt. And he's not telling me not to cry now—because he's already crying.

I rest my head against his chest and pull him close. His arms go around me and we stand there in the beautiful, eerie light of the scarlet torii gates, holding each other one last time.

"Kimi," he says softly.

"I know," I whisper. "Me too."

CHAPTER TWENTY-FOUR

That night, I send my mother one more email. It's much shorter than anything I've written to her while I've been here.

Dear Mom,

Is that spot in the Voices of Asian America exhibit still available? Because I have something I'd like to show.

Love,
Kimi

She hasn't answered any of my other emails and it's very early morning back in the States, so I'm not expecting a response. But one comes just a few minutes later.

Yes, it is. I will let them know to hold it for you.

I smile, a bright spark of hope threading through me, and cuddle Meiko to my chest. I think about my grandparents holding on to things all these years—Meiko, the yukata on the dress form, Ojiichan's letters—hoping for Mom's return. And how it seems that maybe Mom held on to something for me, too.

"Kimiko-chan!" My grandmother is calling me from the living room. "You need to catch your train!"

"Coming, Grandma!" I yell, hauling my suitcase and my carry-on out of my bedroom. "Oh, hold on just one more sec . . ."

I leave the suitcase in the hall and dash into the sewing room to grab some scraps of fabric I forgot to pack the night before. I come to a screeching stop and look around for my fabric . . . and then I see something out of the corner of my eye and do a double take.

"Kimiko-chan." My grandmother bustles into the sewing room. "We do not want you to be late." Her gaze follows mine and she sees what I'm staring at.

"The yukata," I say. "You put it back on the dress form. And . . ." I move in closer to make sure I'm seeing things correctly. "You finished one of the sleeves."

"I have decided I am going to, eto . . . to finish it—the whole thing," she says. "I think . . ." She studies the yukata for a moment, like the last twenty years are flashing before her eyes. "I think it is time for me to give it to your mother."

I reach over and squeeze her hand. "I can't wait to see it when it's done. It's going to be so beautiful."

"Ah, there you two are," my grandfather says, coming

into the sewing room. "We should go, Kimi-chan, you need to catch your train."

"Yes, yes, let's go," I say, herding them back into the hall. "Oh, I meant to ask you . . ." I walk over to my suitcase and pick up Meiko, who I've perched on the handle. "Do you mind if I take Meiko back to Mom? I think she would like to see her again."

"Of course," Grandpa says. "Actually, Kimi-chan, I was wondering if you would take something else back to her—something from me."

He passes me a packet of yellowed, crumbly papers, neatly bundled together with a rubber band. I turn them over in my hands, studying the kanji I don't know how to read yet.

"Are these . . ."

"Hai." He gives me a slight smile. "The letters I wrote to her years ago. I removed some of the, hmm, eto . . . the more colorful ones. But I thought maybe she would finally like to read these."

"I think she would," I say softly. I tuck the letters and Meiko into my carry-on next to my sketchbook, my mother's sketchbook, the slips of paper with Akira's kanji, and my bag of limited-edition Snickers. These are things I definitely don't want to get lost on the return trip. "And Grandma," I continue. "Let me know when you finish the yukata. Maybe you can come visit us in the States. Or we'll come here."

"You will come back," Grandma says, in that way that is most definitely not a request. She twists her hands together and looks at the floor. "Kimiko-chan. I . . . When you first came here, I did not know what was going to happen. I was angry at your grandfather for inviting you without consulting me. But now . . ."

She meets my eyes and . . . oh god. Like Mom, I don't think of her as someone who cries. And that's going to make me cry even more.

She reaches over and takes my hand. "I cannot imagine you not being here," she says, her voice shaking a little. "I cannot imagine you not being in my life."

I step forward and throw my arms around both of my grandparents, drawing them into one big hug. And, to my surprise, they hug back.

"Obaachan, Ojiichan," I say, my eyes full of tears. "You're pretty much stuck with me now."

We stand there for a long time, until Grandpa pulls back, his eyes lighting up like he's just remembering something.

"Ah!" he says. "I almost forgot. I found limited-edition Kit Kats, Kimi-chan. Sweet potato flavor. I have purchased a bag for you to take on your flight."

"Hakaru," Grandma admonishes, chasing after him as he bustles into the kitchen. "She does not need·more candy!"

I smile and follow them, dragging my suitcase behind me.

It's true, I probably don't need more candy. But I'm leaving Japan with so many things I *do* need, it hardly seems to matter.

I should be a zombie when I arrive in LAX after such a long flight, but I'm totally keyed up, giddy adrenaline humming through my veins. It doesn't hurt that I've eaten four candy bars from Ojiichan's stash.

Dad is waiting at baggage claim—and he has two unexpected guests with him.

"Kimi!" Bex shrieks.

She and Atsuko jump up and down, waving around a sign they've made that says WELCOME HOME in big, glittery letters. I run toward them and crash through the sign, accidentally ripping it in half, and we all get tangled in a three-way hug.

"Argh, sorry about the sign," I say. "I'm so happy to see you guys."

"I thought you'd like an extra special welcome committee," Dad says.

I turn and throw myself into his arms. He hugs me back hard.

"Missed you, kid," he says. He pulls back and studies me. "Did you grow while you were gone? You seem taller."

"Of course not, Daddy, still as shrimpy as ever," I say, rolling my eyes. "Um . . ." I look around, the obvious question on the tip of my tongue.

"Your mother is in her studio," he says. "She only has a couple days left before she has to submit her piece for the big art show, so she's basically going to be working twenty-four-seven." His eyes shift to the side a bit. "You may not see her very much."

"I need to work on my piece, too," I say. "So you guys might not see me very much, either. But . . . I want to show her when I'm done."

"Of course," he says. "Let's get your suitcase and then . . ."

He twirls his car keys around his fingers. "Who wants ice cream?"

"Ugh, we're too old for that, Mr. N," Atsuko says, waving a hand. She links one of her arms through mine.

"Don't listen to her, *of course* we want ice cream," Bex says, rolling her eyes. She takes my other arm. "Right, Kimi?"

"I can't imagine a world where I'd say no to ice cream," I say.

My friends pull me ahead of my dad, dragging me toward the baggage carousel.

"Tell us everything," Atsuko says. "You went kind of radio silent the last couple days and we need *details*."

It's true. I've been cramming so much into my last days in Japan, I haven't been the best about responding to our text chain. I'd told them about the jacket I'd made for Akira and the printouts and Ebi Filet-O he'd left for me—but nothing after that. Not how I'd given it to him and he chased me through the park. And nothing about our last date at Fushimi Inari. I'd wanted to keep those precious details to myself for a little while.

But now I can't wait to share them, to squee with my friends and see their faces light up as they follow the twists and turns of my final moments in Japan. And I want to hear about everything that's been happening with them, too, during their spring break adventures. I remind myself to ask Atsuko about that Naz guy, since the very mention of his name seems to make her blush.

"Unless there's nothing to tell?" Bex says uncertainly.

I beam at my two best friends. I'm *so* happy to see them.

"Oh, there's *plenty* to tell," I say, a sly grin spreading over my face. "Just let me figure out where to start."

CHAPTER TWENTY-FIVE

"So, Mom, what do you think? I mean, it's just all of my hopes and dreams and, well, honestly my entire identity distilled into a single garment. And by the way, I also happen to think said garment is a pretty kickass piece of art. I know you might disagree, but let me explain to you how I had this big revelation about my artistic journey and my identity in Japan and it led me here, and now I'm just hoping you'll be able to see it, too. Kthanxbye."

I stare at my reflection in my mirror. Does my face look tough? Resolute? Do I look like someone who has, in fact, gone on a successful journey of self-discovery and is about to explain all of this to the mother who's barely spoken to her in weeks?

It's been two days since I returned from Japan. Mom's mostly been in her studio and I've mostly been either at school or in my room, both of us preparing for the big Voices of Asian America show. The actual show is in two weeks, but we have to submit our final pieces tomorrow. Mom popped out at one point and we exchanged a perfunctory sort of hug and then we both had to get back to work. She seems muted and distant, but I can't tell if that's because she's in deadline mode or if that's just how we are with each other now.

But I'm about to find out. I've finished my garment and asked both of my parents to wait for me in the living room, so I can do the big reveal.

I sit down on my bed carefully, not wanting to wrinkle my creation, and take a deep breath.

A text pops up on my phone.

Did you show her yet?

Akira. I smile and get that fluttery feeling around my heart.

Just about to, I text back. Wish me luck?

You don't need luck. The dress is amazing—and so are you.

The three bubbles appear, indicating he's typing something else. A picture appears—the stuffed tanuki from the park.

See? Akira adds. Even he thinks so.

I burst out laughing. We've been texting pretty much nonstop since I got back (using one of those international texting apps so as not to run up a gigantic bill). The time zone thing is definitely a challenge and we haven't been able to do much Skyping, but I love waking up and seeing a bunch of messages from him, telling me about his day.

I hold the phone out and snap a picture of myself, trying to get as much of the dress in as possible. I've sent him pictures of the garment as it's been in progress, but it's been on a dress form or spread out on my bed. He hasn't actually seen me *in* the dress yet.

What do you think? I type.

The three bubbles appear immediately. I watch the screen, expecting more commentary from the tanuki or maybe a funny photo in response. Instead, a single word appears.

Beautiful.

I blush—and the fluttery feeling around my heart morphs into a full-on flock of butterflies. I make myself set the phone down. If I keep texting him, I'll just stay in here forever.

I stand, smooth my skirt, and square my shoulders. It's time to show Mom the artist I've become.

I emerge from my room and stand in front of my parents. Mom studies me intently, but I can't tell what she's thinking. And Dad keeps sneaking looks at Mom. Probably also trying to figure out what's going through her head.

I decide to just start talking.

"So. This is the art piece I'll be showing. It's a dress. Um, I guess obviously. And it's made of a mix of materials: satin, organza, and paper that I figured out how to soak and treat and process so that it's fabric-like. The vision of this dress was inspired by my trip to Japan." Talking about the dress starts to get me excited, makes me a little giddy, even. I really do love it. The base of the dress is white and the shape of it is bold and exaggerated and there are lots of contrasting textures. The skirt is big and full, made up of several different panels of varying lengths. The bodice is fitted and swoops away from my body and juts above my shoulder on one side and flows into a long, billowing sleeve on the other.

"I wanted the overall look to be like an elaborate piece of sculpture, the various shapes inspired by things I was awed by during my trip," I continue. I'm kind of cribbing from the personal statement I wrote up for my Institute application, but I'm too nervous to do anything else. "You can see a bit of the graceful bamboo stalks from the grove in Arashiyama in the movement of the skirt. Or maybe pick up a hint of the torii gates of Fushimi Inari in the architectural swoop of the bodice. And my sleeve is modeled after a kimono sleeve: that beautiful, flowing shape. But you might see Japan the most in the bits of paper I've sewn in all over the garment." I gesture to various spots on the dress, where there are bright pops of color—they look especially bold against the white background. "These bits of paper are copies I made from my sketchbook, where I documented a lot of my trip through fashion design—oh, except this one is just the deer in Nara. I drew them because they were cute. And this one is this, um, guy wearing a mochi costume—I saw him the first day I was there. And tried to redesign his costume." I smile slightly, brushing my fingers over that bit of the dress. "And these other drawings . . ." I point out a few more pops of color. "Those are from . . ." I take a deep breath and meet my mother's eyes. She gazes back at me, still revealing nothing. "Those are copies I made from *your* sketchbook, Mom. The one you left in Japan. You can see a bit of your tanukis right here." I point to a section of the skirt. "This dress shows my artistic journey—and part of that journey was seeing your sketchbook. I think . . ."

I twist my hands together. That stupid lump is back in my throat again. I can't look at my mother anymore, so I look somewhere off to the side.

"I think it helped me understand you better. Before, I only saw all the sacrifices you'd made for me—what I thought you'd given up. And all the pressure I felt like you were putting on me to achieve a dream you didn't get to have. But now . . ." I pause and will my voice to remain steady. "Now I see your whole journey, too. How you discovered your love of art and found your voice. How you probably felt pressure from your family, too. How you're *still* on that journey, working to achieve that dream after all. And Obaachan helped me understand how a lot of the things I saw as sacrifices were actually choices you made to help you have the life you have now."

I force myself to meet her eyes again.

"I've found that artistic voice you're always talking about, Mom. I have that 'point of view' you've asked me about. I know what my passion is, what lights me up inside. It's *this*." I gesture to my dress. "I researched and applied to this really cool fashion design school. I sent in all my materials this morning. And . . ." Tears well in my eyes and the lump in my throat rises again. "It *is* important, Mom. It's as important as the fine art painting you always wanted me to do. It's important because it's important *to me*."

She's still staring at me, still silent. Like a statue. My dad looks from me to her and seems kind of afraid to say anything. I draw myself up tall. I'm proud of what I made, even if she isn't.

"And if you don't *see* that, Mom—"

"Kimi-chan." Her voice is shaking. I scrutinize her more closely—and realize that her eyes are full of tears, too. "Please. Come here."

I practically run to the couch. She pulls me into her arms and holds me tight and I bury my face in her shoulder and finally let out the long, heaving sob I feel like I've been trying to shove down forever.

"I got all of your emails," she says, through her own tears. "I . . . I have not been able to stop thinking about them. I did not know how to respond or talk to you about them, I felt so . . . so . . ." She pulls back and cups my face in her hands. "How could I not understand my own daughter for so long?"

"You do understand me," I say. "You understand me better than anyone."

It's something I always say, but I realize then, deep in my bones, that it's *true*. Even if my mother hasn't always gotten what I'm doing, she *knows* me at the deepest, most molecular level. That's why, as Obaachan observed, I've been so afraid to lose her. Maybe that's the ultimate equation in Asian Mom Math.

"I just . . . *I* didn't even know what my passion was—I didn't know it wasn't something I had to search for, it was already there. I had to figure all that out," I continue.

She shakes her head. "I should have given you more space to figure it out. I had too many of my own ideas about what you should be." She smiles. "But just as my old sketchbook helped you see me better—these emails helped me see you. And who you already are." She gestures to my dress. "This is incredible. A tour de force work of art."

"Thank you," I say, smoothing the skirt. "Do you think the people at the Eckford Gallery will like it?"

"Yes," she says, nodding emphatically. "But even if they do not, who cares? *You* love it. And so do I." She beams at me. "Perhaps you can make your mother something very— how do you say it? Very *cool* to wear. I do not think my inside clothes will cut it for a fancy opening." She gestures to her patterned leggings.

"You always look fantastic," my dad says to her, and we both whip around to face him. I think we kind of forgot he was there—he backed off and blended into the woodwork while Mom and I had our big moment. "Yes, I am still here," he says, as if reading my thoughts. "I'm glad you two are, well . . ." He grins and arches an eyebrow. "*You* again. And this is amazing, Kimi." He gestures to my dress. "I agree with your mom, a real tour de force."

"Yes," my mother says, her eyes wandering to a particular piece of the dress. She taps her finger on it. "Tell me about this, though, Kimi-chan—the boy in the mochi costume." Her eyes narrow shrewdly. "I feel there is much more to this story."

I flush.

Like I said, my mother understands me better than anyone.

CHAPTER TWENTY-SIX

Two Weeks Later

"Hurry up and take the photo," Mom urges.

We're standing in front of her painting at the Voices of Asian America opening and Dad is fussing with his phone camera, trying to get the perfect shot.

"Here, Mr. N, I can take it," Atsuko says, coming up behind him. "I have excellent framing skills. And anyway, don't you want to be in it?"

"We need a picture of just the artists first," Dad says, beaming at Mom and me. He's practically bursting with pride. "Kimi, the Institute will probably want a copy of this for their display of distinguished alums."

"Daaaaad, I'm not an alum yet, I don't even start until fall!" I say. "Give me some time to *become* an alum."

"You're already so accomplished, I can't imagine they won't want to show that off," he says, finally snapping the photo. "They gave you that big scholarship—obviously they're fans already."

I laugh and shake my head. My dad has a knack for catching people making the most awkward faces, so I'm sure this photo is going to be astounding levels of unflattering. At least our outfits are both *spectacular*—I'm in my gorgeous art piece of a dress and my mom is wearing the cool, slouchy white jumpsuit I designed for her. I sewed some of my special paper fabric into the pattern so there are little pops of color and we kind of coordinate.

"Ms. Nakamura?"

My mother and I both turn to see a tall Black lady with funky gold glasses and close-cropped red hair smiling at us—Janet, one of the owners of the Eckford Gallery.

"Ah, sorry, *this* Ms. Nakamura," Janet says, laughing and gesturing to my mother. "There are some people asking about your piece—a few buyers and a rep from a gallery in San Francisco that I'd love to introduce you to."

"Oh . . . oh, of course," my mother says, suddenly looking nervous. "Kimi-chan," she hisses, as Janet strides off and beckons for her to follow, "how is my hair?"

"It's perfect, Mom," I say, hugging her. "Go get 'em."

"I should get some more atmosphere shots, right?" Dad says, waving his phone around. "Your grandparents asked for pictures of *everything*. I want to give them the real scope of the event. I mean, they should see how many people are here!" He hurries off, still muttering to himself about the pictures he wants to get.

"Does he mean your grandparents as in his parents?" Atsuko asks. "Aren't they, uh, dead?"

"He means *Mom's* parents," I say, nudging her in the arm. "Can you believe that?"

Just thinking about it makes me smile. After I revealed my dress creation, Mom and I had a long, tearful catch-up (and she pried as many details about Akira out of me as she could), and then I presented her with Grandpa's letters and Meiko. I told her all about my time in Japan, how I'd connected with Grandma and Grandpa—with Obaachan and Ojiichan. How being there and talking to them and learning about her life made me feel like I was finding little bits of myself I didn't know were missing. I desperately want her to feel that way, too; she's denied what seems like an essential piece of herself for so long.

I mentioned I thought maybe they could leave all those things that were said in the past behind and move forward. And I told her about how Grandma had been so sure of the bond between Mom and me—that it wasn't something that could be easily broken. Hadn't she been right about that?

Mom didn't say much. Just took the letters from me and turned them over in her hands, considering. Then patted Meiko on the head, a slight smile playing over her lips.

A couple days later, I happened to be walking past the kitchen when I heard short bursts of Japanese being spoken on the other side of the door. I poked my head in, thinking maybe Mom was watching a show. She wasn't. Her laptop was propped up on the island in the center of the room and Mom was staring with laser-like focus at the screen—at my grandmother.

"Ahhhhhhh," Mom said, shaking her head in frustration. *"No."* She spat out another long stream of Japanese.

Obaachan frowned, looking off into the distance, and poked at something just offscreen—her keyboard, maybe?

Oh.

I realized then that Mom was trying to teach Obaachan *to use Skype.*

I ducked out of the kitchen quickly so they wouldn't hear me giggle.

After that, they started talking more regularly—and even my dad got in on it, emailing my grandparents various photos of our daily activities. Whatever's happening still feels new and awkward and delicate—but at least it's a start. Mom's even making noises about going to Japan next year.

"It inspired Kimi so much on her artist's journey," she mused the other day. "Perhaps returning would inspire me as well."

Maybe Obaachan will have the yukata done by then.

"Hey, guys!" I snap out of my reverie to see Bex running up to Atsuko and me, dragging Shelby behind her. "Oh my god, Kimi! This is amazing. And your dress . . ." She waves her hand around. "*Double* amazing!"

"It's cool," Shelby says, nodding. Shelby is a woman of few words.

"The guy at the front said this package came for you," Bex says, handing me a small box wrapped in delicate pink paper. My name is written in calligraphy on a card affixed to the top. "We said we would be more than happy to deliver it to the arrrr-*teest*."

"Thank you," I say, laughing.

I open the box first, carefully removing the wrapping

and popping the top off to reveal ... mochi. Six perfect pieces. I scrutinize it. Wait. I could swear this is from ...

"Open the card," Atsuko urges, taking the box from me.

I slit the envelope and pull the small card out.

So. This is from your dad's restaurant.

I laugh. That's what I thought.

I needed same-day service and no amount of international shipping could get Ojisan's mochi to you. But I figured your dad's is the best you can get in America.

Congratulations on your big night and on being accepted to fashion school. You are going to do great things.

I am *still* in awe of you.

Love,
Akira

"OoooOOOoooooooh!" Atsuko and Bex hoot over my shoulder.

"*Hey!*" I say, clutching the note to my chest. "That's private!"

"Go call your *boyfriend!*" Atsuko bellows. "And thank him for his adorable gift!"

I'm pretty sure my face is bright red, but I stick my tongue out at her and scurry outside to the little courtyard area. It's deserted and the night is bright and clear. I take a deep breath, enjoying the quiet away from the bustle of the party.

I pull my phone from the small, jeweled clutch I'm carrying and do the math in my head. Eight p.m. here means lunchtime in Kyoto? Not bad.

I pull up Skype and dial Akira. He answers immediately.

"Kimi!" he says, his face lighting up. "You got my present?"

"Yes—thank you, I love it," I say. I peer at his surroundings. "Are you . . . at the pug café?"

"I am," he says, laughing. He lowers his voice to a conspiratorial whisper. "There is no one here again, so I can talk on my computer." He reaches down to pick something up, then brings it into frame—the tiny pug. "Look how he misses you—so sad!" Akira pulls a face.

"I miss . . . him, too," I say. "Very much."

He grins at me. "You should go back and enjoy your party. I am sure it is very exciting, ne?"

"It is," I say. "And I will. But I can talk to you for a minute."

We talk about everything and nothing and even though we're an ocean away, I feel like I'm sitting right there with him, my heart lighting up whenever he flashes me that irresistible dimple.

I go back to the party and see Mom standing in front of her painting, gesturing expansively and talking very seriously to a cluster of enraptured people. Dad running around and snapping pictures, trying to capture everything. Atsuko and Bex goofing off while Shelby looks on, smiling indulgently.

My heart is so full.

In the past, I might have been scared to jump back into

the party fray—to make things real by actually living my life instead of just fantasizing about it. I was always so afraid I'd ruin everything.

Now, I don't hesitate.

I run back to Atsuko and Bex and twirl around in my beautiful dress and then Atsuko makes some dopey joke and we laugh until we can't breathe.

"Oh, look, your dad posted that picture of you and your mom," Atsuko says, waving her phone around. She frowns at the screen. "He really should have let me take it."

I take her phone and study the photo. My mouth is open and I'm laughing at my dad's dumb joke. Mom looks vaguely annoyed at how long he's taking. It is, as I predicted, astounding levels of unflattering. But that's not what stands out.

No, the thing that really sticks with me about this photo is how I feel seeing Mom and me standing next to each other, wearing our coordinating art piece outfits. Caught in a perfect, spontaneous moment of celebration, surrounded by so many people I love.

"Kimi-chan, what is this?" Mom says, coming up behind me. She peers at the photo, her nose wrinkling.

I watch her as she studies it. I think about how I don't know *exactly* what the future holds. I don't know if I'll always make the right choice or if Akira and I will experience more sadness than joy at being so far apart or if I'll become the greatest fashion designer who ever lived or something else entirely.

But I do know this: There are so many amazing experiences in my future. So many more moments like this. They extend in front of me like the beautiful scarlet tunnel of torii gates. Endless, boundless, unlimited. And I'm going to enjoy every single one of them.

"Ahhh, this photo," Mom says, shaking her head and tapping the phone screen. "Not very good, hmm?"

I rest my head on her shoulder. "I think it's perfect."

ACKNOWLEDGMENTS

Thank you to all my favorite superhero teams: my beautiful Girl Gangs, my brilliant Shamers, and my amazing Asian American LA arts community. You are all incredible, and I'm honored to be in your company.

Thank you to my editor, Jeffrey West, for your boundless enthusiasm and for loving tanukis, pugs, and Kimi as much as I do. Thank you to my agent, Diana Fox, for being your usual badass self, and to everyone at Scholastic for believing in this book.

Thank you to everyone who chatted with me for hours on end about everything from specific locations in Japan to nuance in familial relations and slang that somehow crosses language barriers: Keiko Agena, Shin Kawasaki, Ally Maki, Naomi Hirahara, Adam Douglas, Eri, and the Okamoto family—Scott, Geri, Ethan, Audrey, and Owen. You all provided invaluable conversation and support and helped me make this book the absolute best it could be. I would totally dress up in a mochi costume for you any day!

Thank you to Jenn Fujikawa and Mary Yogi (Food Librarian!) for their excellent documentation of all things mochi. Your work is both informative and delicious!

Thank you to Fern Choonet for all your beautiful, swoon-worthy artwork and to Shivana Sookdeo for making this book the cutest thing ever.

Thank you to Diya Mishra for being an awesome first reader, to Patrice Caldwell for playing matchmaker extraordinaire, and to Rebekah Weatherspoon for being the best deadline buddy ever.

Thank you to The Ripped Bodice and its proprietors—Bea and Leah Koch and Fitzwilliam Waffles—for creating the most wonderful space and letting me write there.

Thank you to Jenn Fujikawa (Again!), Tom Wong, Andrea Letamendi, Christine Dinh, Amy Ratcliffe, Christy Black, Mel Caylo, Amber Benson, and Jenny Yang for pep talks and support and basically being the best ever.

Thank you to my family for being my family: Kuhns, Yoneyamas, Chens, Coffeys, and everyone in between.

Thank you to Jeff Chen for absolutely everything.

And thank you, all these years later, to my mother for giving me a red kimono, an orange obi, and the heart of this book. I wish you could have read this one.

ABOUT THE AUTHOR

Sarah Kuhn is on a quest to eat every kind of mochi in the greater Los Angeles area. She is the author of the Heroine Complex series and has penned a variety of comics and short fiction about geeks, aliens, romance, and Barbie (yes, that Barbie). Additionally, Sarah is a finalist for the John W. Campbell Award for Best New Writer. In her spare time, she thinks way too much about one day adopting a pug and the lasting legacy of Claudia Kishi. A third-generation Japanese American, she lives in LA with her husband and an overflowing closet of vintage treasures. You can find her online at heroinecomplex.com.

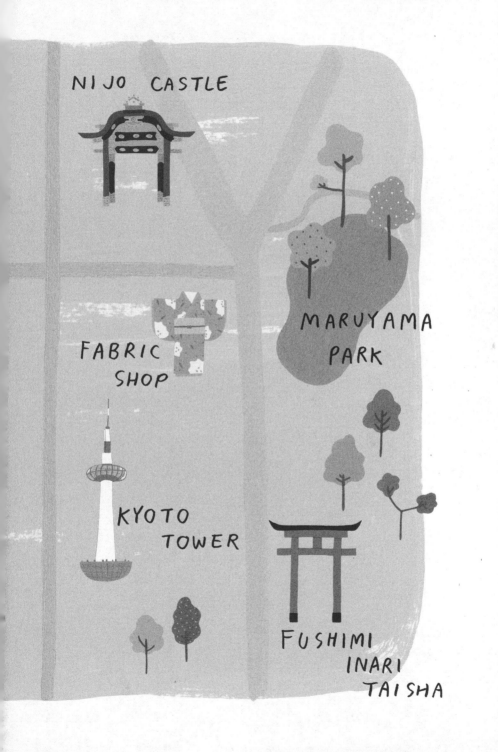